Mr BOOTS

To Timothy and the acme pension plan!

Although this book is set in and around the City of Edinburgh and the grand metropolis of Oban, both real places with actual live people and jolly good distilleries, all other characters and some of the locations are purely fictitious and any similarity to anybody living or indeed dead is simply coincidence and the product of my overworked imagination.

MR BOOTS

LINDA MANN

Priory Press

Published by Priory Press Ltd
The Priory, Abbots Way, Abbotswood,
Ballasalla, Isle of Man IM9 3EQ
www.priory-press.co.uk

ISBN 0-9551510-0-7

First published 2006

Typeset by
Frances Hackeson Freelance Publishing Services,
Brinscall, Lancs
Printed in Great Britain by
Biddles Ltd, King's Lynn

acknowledgements

With many thanks to Kevin, Kay and Ruth who read the unedited version and liked it!

To Gillian who chuckled and David who helped.

To Jill my Editor and Frances who produced the finished product.

To all at Mercat Tours.

To Mr Boots for being a really miserable old git with attitude.

And to everybody who bought my first two books and so gave me the confidence to write this one.

prologue

a scottish loch — the present day

Mist the colour and consistency of warm school milk, rose and fell in slow billowing folds across the vast expanse of grey water. A dispassionate silence reigned, broken only by the sibilant and strident coughs of a pair of flying swans, necks outstretched and legs dangling in a near perfect imitation of Max Wall.

Amid this amiable landscape sat two figures perched on an uprooted tree at the water's edge. Both were middle-aged men and both were soaking wet. Weed from the bottom of the loch glistened on their thinning pates and globules of mud caked their skin and sodden clothing.

"Well," the rather portly gentleman on the left exclaimed, "this is another fine mess you've gotten me into, Quentin." He sniffed loudly and pulled a small and still wriggling fish from his breast pocket. The fish was discarded by the simple expedient of a flick of thumb and forefinger; there was a soft splash, a ripple or two and a short silence broken by the second gentleman sneezing loudly.

"I knew it," the second gentleman muttered in a complaining tone. "I knew that somehow or other this would get blamed on me. It just isn't fair and more importantly it most definitely wasn't my fault."

"Oh really?" scoffed his companion. "Well all I know, Vernon dear, is that it wasn't me opening and closing my big mouth behind the bar."

"How was I to know who they were?" Vernon Flint mutinously muttered.

"I would have thought that the fact that they looked like a couple of hoods from a bad seventies James Bond movie would have told you something."

"They were a bit odd," Vernon admitted as he stared pensively at the distant mountains.

"Odd? They called themselves Mr Burke and Mr Hare and the emphasis was very much on the Mister! They couldn't have been more obvious if they'd come in with a submachine gun in one hand and a fluffy white cat in the other!" Quentin barked. "And what about my poor 'Arabella Butterworth'?"

"What about that floating travesty?"

"Where is it?"

"Who the hell cares? The only good thing anyone – and I mean anyone – could have possibly said in its favour, was that it floated, just."

"Your point being?"

"But then so do trees, although one really wouldn't want to set sail on one, obviously." Vernon paused in his heated diatribe to inspect pale and dirt-encrusted fingernails.

"I didn't leave the lights off." Quentin retorted.

"Neither did I," Vernon replied, whilst glaring at him through wire-rimmed spectacles.

"Oh." There was a short pause as memories were gently prodded. "Well if you didn't and I didn't, who did? Because I for one distinctly remember coming home, putting the box down from the cash and carry, opening the door, flicking the switch and – nothing."

"I vaguely remember a crunching sound and something heavy falling."

"That, I think, must have been me."

"Yes it was, wasn't it? You didn't scream though. Honestly Quentin you really are absolutely hopeless, I mean to say, the least you could have done was to scream."

"I didn't have any time! For goodness sake what did you expect them to do – hang around while I baked a cake?"

"I don't suppose you saw who they were?"

"No." There was a short pause until further reflection produced the correct recollection. "It was Mr Burke. I could, now I come to think of it, smell that ghastly stuff he used to slick down his hair. I can't remember Mr Hare but I could definitely hear someone clicking their knuckles."

"It's what comes of walking on them, I suppose," Quentin quipped before remembering another minor detail. "All I smelt was a very strong odour of exceptionally sweaty armpits, not at all nice really. You know I do feel most strongly that one's last breath should at least be free from somebody else's personal hygiene problems."

Vernon nodded in agreement and said. "After all, how much does soap cost!"

"That all depends on where you get it from."

Vernon inhaled noisily and half turning, fixed his companion with an icy stare. "If you are referring to that divine toiletry from that absolutely super little shop down the road from Harvey Nicks, I can only plead in my defence that it was for Christmas. Anyway, what was I supposed to do? Sit quietly in the lounge while you swanned off to some museum or other? There would have been absolutely no point in accompanying you to Edinburgh if I hadn't done something useful with my time and gone shopping."

"I suppose so. Was that where you bought the hand-painted glass candlesticks and the embarrassingly well-endowed reindeer?"

"Of course."

"Then in that case you have my sincere and abject apologies. When I think of the look on that frightfully vulgar and self-important Winifred Bowen's face I could kiss you all over again."

They sat together arms touching and grinned.

"Do you think someone will come soon?"

"I don't know."

"I'm so cold I can't feel my feet."

"Lucky you, I can't even see mine."

They both stared down at the place where feet should have been but evidently weren't.

"Bugger!" They both swore in perfect harmony.

Water lapped around their solitary tree and the surrounding mist slowly dissipated upwards in curling opaque strands. A large and evil-eyed fish jumped from the water, snapped at a surprised insect and then with a flick of its tail somersaulted back down into the depths.

"How come they never do that when I have a rod with me?" Quentin complained.

"Too busy laughing, probably," Vernon replied, watching the ripples fade and then added, "Oh Quentin, look at that, would you?" A soft rose pink glow suffused the surrounding area and spread along the rim of hills beyond the water's edge, before being overtaken by a burst of gold as the sun loomed large and majestic above the opposite shore.

"Now that's what I call a perfect sunrise."

"Absolutely perfect."

"Vernon."

"Umm."

"I really am most dreadfully sorry."

"I know."

"I really didn't think that my minor brush with the world of the private detective could ever have remotely led to this. It's not as if I ever got any clients."

"What about Mr McGregor?"

"Everybody knew about Mrs McGregor and the bank's five-a-side football team. All he wanted was a few pictures."

"What on earth for? He never even saw a lawyer."

"Actually I never asked." Quentin's mouth twitched and he made a soft snickering sound of amusement. "Dirty little beast."

"You know what really sticks in my throat?"

"No, what?"

"All the unfinished bits, for instance I shall never get to paint the lounge and I so wanted to see the new curtains up with those blinds we brought back from that awful little bazaar in Morocco."

"So tacky. Do you remember that wretched man in the fez?"

"The one that offered you his second cousin twice removed on his mother's side?"

"The one with adenoids, acne and a tendency to spit."

"Face like a camel."

"That was the camel."

"Oh."

"We shall miss out on our Wodehouse weekend too."

"Seven courses including coffee and hand-rolled chocolates."

"I saw the menu. I remember at the time thinking that the whole thing was worthy of the great Anatole himself."

"Guinea fowl boned and stuffed with herbs and fresh toasted pinhead oatmeal with …"

"A juniper and red wine jus …"

"And oven roasted vegetables with pureed butternut squash."

They sat in a moribund silence broken only by the hectoring of frogs under a nearby clump of sagging weeds.

Quentin sighed as another regret hit a startled synapse. "Do you know what's even worse?"

"No."

"We shan't be able to watch my new boxed set of 'Will and Grace' that Fiona sent me for my birthday."

"Good grief – I'd almost forgotten that. Now that really is beyond the pale; I'd bought in extra nachos and dips and invited Donald."

"Was he bringing the Budweiser?"

"Naturally."

"I'm gutted, I really am. Absolutely …"

"Gutted."

They both sighed in unison and disconsolately dripped.

"Do you think anyone will find out why?" Quentin asked his companion.

"Do you think anyone will care?"

They looked at each other and then solemnly clasped hands, which had begun to grow more and more transparent.

"I do."

"And I."

They sat in companionable silence, their shortened reflections mingling with the ripples of rising fish.

"Well, I'll be nibbled to death by ducks if I let them get away without a fight!" Quentin suddenly shouted, raising a semi-transparent fist to the sky.

"You tell them, Quentin old fruit."

Quentin drew himself up and straightened his shoulders and then as an afterthought, his tie.

"I call upon all who live here to witness that I Quentin Rowse and my lifelong companion, friend and love Vernon Flint have been most murderously disposed of and that I will be avenged."

"How?"

"Shh. I'm pausing for dramatic effect."

"Um, sorry, please do continue."

"Thank you. Ahem … I conjure and er, command that … Who was that old biddy that went around finding out deadly secrets and bringing the evil perpetrators to justice?"

"Er do you mean Miss Marple?"

"No, I'm absolutely positive that she was Greek or Roman or some other foreign female of Mediterranean extraction. I most distinctly remember seeing a statue at some dusty museum. Huge marble thing it was, all Amazonian curves and transparent drapes and she was carrying a scourge in one hand and a knife in the other. Or was it a pair of scales? No it was a knife, definitely a knife. Very sharp it looked with a knob on the end."

"Are you sure?"

"Definitely. In point of fact she looked exactly like Mother when she found out that I had no intention of asking Chloe Watts to marry me because I'd met you at that ballroom dancing class."

"Oh."

"Hang about – I'm absolutely certain the name sounds like a plant. It has sort of pinkish flowers. Fiona grew some at school in a bucket."

"Nasturtiums?"

"Aren't they orange?"

"Sometimes."

"Nemesia – that was it. Anyway this bird, goddess or whatever, went about spreading the old vengeance around like it was going out of fashion."

"Oh you mean Nemesis."

"That's the ticket. Good old Nemesis. Excuse me for a moment while I find my centre and start again."

"That's fine by me."

There was a short pause while a wandering lock of hair was slicked back down across the bald patch and the tie was re-straightened.

"I insist that Nemesis be awoken and that she will without prejudice or delay avenge our deaths and bring to justice all perpetrators of this most foul and dastardly act!"

As the last impassioned words were carried out across the loch the two lonely figures faded and merged. A solitary sheep browsing amongst the soft grasses at the water's edge thought it distinctly heard something.

"And what will that do?"

"Probably nothing, but I've always felt better after a good dramatic moan."

"Quentin?"

"Umm."

"Somebody somewhere just switched everything off."

"Everything, except that one pool of light over there."

"After you."

"No, after you."

"I insist."

"So do I."

The sheep lifted its head and stared out across the gently undulating expanse in front of him and then with a woolly shrug moved unhurriedly back towards his bleating siblings.

* * *

Nemesis flicked through the glossy pages of one of the more expensive celebrity magazines and extracted another cocoa-dusted chocolate from the gold-coloured box beside her, with a long, red and highly polished talon. She sniffed disdainfully as she read details of the latest famous coupling, whilst carefully filing away in her mind the details of where exactly she could purchase the latest thing in almost indecent evening wear. Something buzzed furiously as it tried to head-butt the faceted window behind her. Nemesis lifted a pale and languorous hand and the fly found itself suddenly pinned to the wall. There was a momentary bone-scrunching squelch followed by a short silence into which the words, 'Oh bugger,' could be very faintly heard. Nemesis smiled unpleasantly and turned the page.

A door in the opposite wall opened and a translucent bearded face with all the aesthetic appeal of a mummified scrotum glared at her.

"You're wanted," it barked before disappearing.

Startled, she sat up, dropping her magazine on the floor and dislodging on to the cat several of the large gold fringed cushions upon which she'd been lounging. The cat, who had up to that point been quietly dreaming of world domination and a large amount of fish, spat fiercely and flexed its claws.

"What?" she cried.

There was no answer from the blue-rimmed doorway, only the ghost of an expectant silence. Nemesis narrowed her eyes and then with exaggerated ill grace stood up.

The cat opened one onyx green eye and hissed venomously.

"Now, now, who's being a naughty little kitty? And you can take those claws out of the carpet or I shall cut them off."

The cat glared at her and then thinking quickly, as cats do who are downright lazy and don't possess thumbs, yawned and went back to its Machiavellian slumbers.

Nemesis regarded the animal for a brief and jealous moment, the words taxidermy and vets struggling for cranial supremacy before she dusted off the flakes of chocolate still valiantly clinging to the folds of silk almost covering her. After that she reluctantly picked up her trailing skirts in one hand and a small Louis Vuitton handbag in the other and left the room.

She stalked quickly down a long whitewashed stone corridor, the metal tips on her high heels extruding sparks as she went. The hallway was lit at intervals by large fiery sconces held up by hunched and scowling gargoyles, one of whom lit a cigarette with his torch as she passed.

"Is that you Crouch?" she asked, stopping abruptly.

"Yes, Mistruth."

"What on earth are you doing here?"

A gargoyle standing behind them sighed pointedly, stuck his still flaming torch in a bucket of sand and proceeded to unwrap a large brown square. He took a tentative bite.

"Sngood eggncresh." He rumbled happily.

Nemesis gave him a glacial look which he completely ignored and then, pointedly turning her back on him, continued her conversation with Crouch, who was now blowing perfect smoke rings towards the ceiling.

"Last time I saw you, you were holding up some obscure bishop and a bunch of grapes."

"Datsright – you was chasing dat mad axe murderer …"

"And you kindly dropped the bishop on his head."

"I likedde grapes."

"Quite."

"They pulled id doun, de cathedral."

"Oh."

"Sed it wos toospensive."

"Right."

"An de ertquake didot elp. Bits kept fallin on der confraglation. Sode bilt a curpark. Cart ave a gargoyle on a curpark itud luke thilly so ere I yam.

"And a jolly good job you're doing too, young Crouch."

"Fank yu Mistruth."

Nemesis smiled briefly and then she spotted the doors at the end of the hall and relapsed back to her usual dour and unamused self. The doors were set as a pair of folded wings to either side of a thin ruby red archway and they never, ever, stopped talking to each other.

Nemesis glared at them, strode forwards and, gritting her teeth, knocked three times with her fist on the feathers. The wings muttered more fiercely and with her hands firmly covering both ears, she waited. Diamanté glinted as her red and silver Gina sandals drummed a short tattoo against the stone. After some time the doors slowly opened, the wings folding up with each feather moving of its own accord.

Smoke filled the space immediately in front of her and arguing voices could be distinctly heard amongst dark shadows, which moved and glided about the huge amphitheatre. Blue sky gleamed above a multitude of marble pillars, which soared ever upwards, their height tapering gracefully into a nest of high cirrus.

"Well – what is it?" Nemesis snapped. The roar of sound continued unabated and with a shrug of annoyance Nemesis fished around inside the folds of cloth covering her ample bosom and found a large silver whistle. Standing up straight, she blew a fearsome blast which still echoed around the vaulted ceiling some considerable time after she'd gone, much to the annoyance of a pair of absconding cherubs who were having a quiet game of Monopoly in one of the upper balconies.

The heated debate stopped and semi-distinct figures moved slowly towards her, their faces veiled and their bodies draped in a variety of gauzy cloths.

"You are wanted," a voice growled from above the melee.

"Wanted?" she enquired a trifle petulantly. "By whom and for what?"

"For the avengement of an evil deed and for justice."

"What deed?"

"Murder most foul and unlawful."

"Murder usually is," she quipped.

"Don't get smart with me, madam," the voice barked. "Do you want the job or not?"

Nemesis looked around her at the everlasting sunshine and the never-ending faces of her peers and suddenly realised how very bored she actually was.

"Yes," she muttered under her breath.

"I'm sorry, I didn't quite catch that?"

"I said yes."

"And the magic word for today is?"

"Oh for goodness sake, this is ridiculous."

"I don't think I can hear you?"

"Please."

"Please what?"

"Yes please."

"You see, it didn't hurt a bit, did it?"

Nemesis bit back a tart reply and tried to think pink and fluffy thoughts, which in no way contained the words, 'patronising', 'old' or indeed 'git'.

"Robin here will give you all the relevant information," the voice continued.

A small wiry man with nervously darting eyes emerged from the smoke, he had an air of browbeaten subservience and was clutching a collection of brown box files.

"Will I have an agent?" she asked, remembering her last assignment with a frown.

"Naturally, there is always an earthly agent," the voice intoned magisterially and dismissively.

"Who?" she demanded, standing her ground and eyeing the shadowy figures with the eye of one used to handing out lines and homework marked in red ink.

The air changed, becoming a little foggier and there was a short embarrassed silence.

"Oh come on now, he – or indeed she – can't be that bad."

"He is, oh yes he is," Robin murmured, grabbing her arm and steering her back towards the corridor.

"My office is this way," he muttered, darting swift glances

up and down the narrow hallway. "We need to talk."

Some time later Nemesis sat and pondered, a cup of nectar in her hand and a frown of intelligent concentration on her once beautiful but still handsome face.

"This could be a tricky one," she finally stated.

"I know, I know," Robin agreed, pouring himself another drink and wiping his brow with a square of damp cloth.

"This William Reginald Winkie is, you say, of a noble and honest character?"

"Well not exactly …"

"Not exactly?"

"He's … well … he was a whisky-still maker and wine … er … merchant. But he does know about the kind of people we are dealing with, having had personal experience."

"He was himself a victim of the 'Resurrection Men' and of their employers?"

"Yes."

"The thing is, as I see it," Nemesis stated, tapping the pages in front of her, "that William died in 1821 and is to be the instrument of justice a mere two hundred years later."

"Give or take a decade or so."

"Don't quibble!"

"Quite. Anyway he's the best we have and hopefully when all this is finished, he'll finally step over and join our higher plane."

"Do you mean to tell me that he's still down there?"

"Well, yes."

"Didn't you call him?"

"Several times, but he refuses point-blank to come."

"Why?"

"Who knows? He seemed at first to have some strange

14

desire to make sure that his family was all right after his demise and not to put too fine a point on it, refused to leave the mortal plane until he did. Now – who knows – he's been down there so long. I tell you he's not a popular man in records."

"Umm ..."

"We even sent his daughter Rosie down to try and talk him into relinquishing the ectoplasm and all he did was play hide and seek with her and endless games of checkers."

"But what can he possibly find to do all day? Isn't he bored?"

"Apparently not. He likes being a ghost. And since his haunt under Edinburgh's South Bridge has been open to the public he's actually taken on a new lease of life – or rather death."

"Oh?"

"He's become part of the tourist trade, invisible earnings or some such fiscal description. After all, you can't have a ghost tour without a ghost."

"Oh I don't know, how about those ghastly funfair rides?"

"Not the same thing at all."

"No, I suppose not."

"I expect if he actually went, we'd receive no end of complaints from the Scottish Tourist Board, to say nothing of being inundated by the badly spelt gripes of several tour companies. To be perfectly frank he likes haunting and most people who go down there want to be haunted. In fact they expect it."

"But surely there must be somebody he's upset?"

"Well, there was an incident involving a large and very old potato, a portaloo, a missing drain cover and a valve mechanism which blew instead of sucked."

"Sounds nasty."

"It was. We did consider sending someone else down, until it was pointed out that aiding and abetting reality television wasn't something we actually wanted to condone. Besides which they had evidently outstayed their welcome if the catcalls, jeers and delighted clapping which followed their departure was anything to go by. In fact I believe that the security firm and several administrative staff and tour guides sang three full verses of 'For he's a jolly good fellow', before finally locking up and going home."

"Oh well, I can see your point."

"Anyway that's partly why we've given up for the time being, and frankly as a non-corporeal agent he has managed to acquire the ectoplasmic and spiritual equivalent of enough muscle to turn himself into a kind of ghostly Mr T, or even, Gods help us, that ghastly Terminator. Of course that and his historical experience may be exactly what we're looking for."

"You said 'partly'?"

"Well, it's a bit embarrassing really."

"Go on."

"The thing is, if he really doesn't want to leave, we can't actually think of any way we can possibly force him to go. Not now that he's been down there so long."

There was another brief silence broken by Nemesis returning a few brown curling pages to the box file in front of her, before she closed it with a snap. "I see. And has he been notified?"

"Actually we thought it might be better if he didn't know that we're in the driving seat, so to speak."

"Anti-authoritarian?"

16

"Anti-religious, anti-establishment and a downright pain in the a ..."

"Attitude problem?"

"Quite."

"And my mortal agent? My avenging angel?"

"A woman. Niece to the deceased."

"Good. There's always been a blood link, it's traditional and as you know, I am nothing if not a traditionalist.'

"As always, Your Vengefulness."

"And this girl, how exactly will she communicate with William Reginald Winkie?"

"She is a necromancer and so can see and commune with the dead."

"A useful trait in a bank clerk."

They gave vent to a chuckle of mirth.

"It may work but they'll need friends, although hopefully we should be able to sort that out as we go along." Nemesis set down her goblet and with the air of one beginning to really enjoy herself, rolled up her sleeves.

"Well then Robin, we'd better make a start. Open the chess board and let the games begin." Robin gave her a tentative grin and began to place a collection of carved figures on the corresponding black and gold squares.

"Robin, Robin ..." Nemesis mused, "an odd and unusual surname."

"Um ... actually Your Vengefulness, it's my Christian name."

"I was under the impression that it's normal protocol to use one's family name?"

"I had special dispensation."

"Well I'm sorry, Robin," Nemesis stated, sounding anything but. "I do prefer to keep to the traditions – after all it surely can't be that bad."

"It's Bastard, ma'am."

"Oh I see, Robin Bastard."

"Yes."

"Parents can be very cruel."

"My father was an antique dealer and he thought it would be a good name in the trade, get you used to things from day one, so to speak."

"And did you follow in his footsteps?"

"Not exactly – I ended up working for the Inland Revenue."

"Well they do say names maketh the man. On balance I think we'll just stick to Robin, it might cause confusion otherwise."

"I do so agree, Your Vengefulness. Which piece shall we put out first?"

❉ ❉ ❉

"I can see them, I can see them! One – no two hooded figures, and they appear to be pulling – no, no – dragging something across the floor. Right here, right here."

William had had rather more than enough of the shifty weasel-like face in front of him and said so with various expletives. The feral eyes which were now glowing red coals glared right through him and the voice of one of television's foremost authorities droned on.

"I'm getting something here, right here; oh it's nasty, really nasty. Shh."

Grey hands fluttered aimlessly as the sound man hastened to move the mike into a new position. A cameraman lay on the ground aiming a small digital camera at a spot in the corner and William rolled his eyes in exasperation.

"Will nothing shift you buggers?" he muttered.

The diminutive blonde in a smart purple velvet suit looked anxiously behind her.

"What was that?" she asked.

Everyone stopped and listened. From the shadowed walls surrounding them a distinct rumbling sound was clearly heard.

The woman screamed and jumped backwards.

"Who did that?" She squawked, rubbing her backside. "Somebody pinched my ..."

The soundman shook his head and tapped the small hand-held sound meter; the red dial wobbled and then spun wildly.

"Is it my imagination or is it a bit cold, just here?" asked the perfectly groomed youth at the back of the group.

"My temperature gauge is going nuts," muttered the assistant director with unrestrained excitement – this was after all what good ratings were made of.

"Someone just brushed their hands against my face!" the assistant to the assistant whimpered in dramatic tones.

"What's that?" the blonde screamed, pointing to the furthest corner of the brick-lined vault.

Slowly and glowing an eerie shade of gangrenous green, a pair of brown leather boots emerged from the dust-covered bricks and shuffled towards them. A bloodcurdling groan emanated from behind the wall. And then all the lights went out, including all the carefully lit candles.

William grinned into the darkness and juggled an elderly and offensively putrid potato from one ectoplasmic hand to the other. If they wanted authentic ghastly ghostliness that's exactly what they'd get, together with a side

19

helping of noxious smells and anatomical imprecations in fluent Gaelic and if all that failed he had a very old Dolcelatte sandwich he'd been assiduously saving for just such an occasion.

After they had gone amidst a flurry of fear, sweat and agonized screams, William sat down on an upturned packing case, relit the large squat candle at his elbow, turned the page of his favourite book and settled down for a quiet and undisturbed read. He had by now got to his favourite bit in the book and as he read the hysterical account again, wondered if it might actually work.

chapter one

Fiona Harris shuffled her feet and shivered. All around her the stagnant air of centuries oozed through the gaps between the people avidly drinking in the words of their guide, whilst at the same time preparing themselves mentally for being scared witless. They were in the vaults of the city of Edinburgh, directly under the South Bridge and the teaming streams of traffic and people. Beside her someone coughed and somebody else sneezed. A man, his thickened neck covered in what looked like half a snake, and with the kind of voice which could have sold china in an East End market, had a state-of-the-art digital camera, which at regular intervals would bleep, whirr, click and then be pointed in the direction of their guide and anyone else who happened to glare at him. The guide, a tall educated lady with iron-grey hair and the air of one used to dealing with a class of educationally challenged seven-year-olds, took a deep breath and consulted a thick wad of papers on a clipboard before beginning to describe the terrible fate of cadavers dug up and allegedly stored within the arched and vaulted room in which they were currently standing, by the 'Resurrection Men'.

Darkness reached out and hovered just beyond the billowing candle on Fiona's right. 'Was this it?' She mused 'Were they about to be visited by the pale wraiths entombed within these very walls? Would the vengeful spirit of city clerk William Mowatt, skewered into the big sleep by tavern temptress Mary McKinnon in 1822 rise up and groan in dreadful protest? Was she about to be scared senseless by Mr Boots, the resident ghostly equivalent of Ronnie Kray or Arthur Bell, depending on which storyteller you had been listening to?'

A tall figure behind her muttered "Mr Boots; I'll give her boots" and then noisily broke wind.

"Do you mind?" she asked frostily, half turning towards him.

"Not if you don't, love," he replied, grinning with bad teeth and a third world country's national debt in glittering metal deposits.

Fiona moved further to her right, rigidly folded her arms and exuded ice.

The man, noting the rapidly heaving woollen-covered breasts, grinned wickedly and moved closer. "Scary, huh?" he whispered, almost in her ear.

"Go away," she hissed, unfolding her arms as she realised what he was now leering at.

"So can you smell it?" he asked.

"Smell what?"

"That whiff of group fear, the heady aroma of tourist willies."

"Listen Mr whatever your name is – and no I don't want to know – all I can smell is dry rot with the possible addition of rising damp."

"You a builder?"

"No."

"You left out the interesting pong produced by decaying rodents."

"Really?"

"Yes."

"Look I'm sure you really are an expert on all things anal – sorry – slip of the tongue there, I meant to say nasal but ..."

"I could tell you some really good stories about this place. Turn that pretty head of yours white in minutes," he remarked in sepulchral tones, whilst mentally noting that under the shorn remains of a highland sheep was a figure that would have had Reubens reaching for a paintbrush. He moved a little closer.

"Listen mate, why don't you just push off and find somebody else to annoy?" Fiona hissed.

"Temper, temper. Did you know that your eyes go all green and sparkly when you're angry?"

"Will you go away?"

"If I go then you'll be all alone with the big scary ghoulies and ghosties."

"I'll take my chances."

"Fangs dripping with green gory gunge, entrails trailing ..."

Fiona took a long breath and then stared him straight in the eyes. "The only truly frightening thing in here is you," she snapped.

"Too bloody right," he retorted and with a broad wink, vanished.

She shivered furiously, not from fright but with a certain amount of deep-seated anger. "Why me?" she asked herself. "Why the hell do they always pick on me?"

Somebody at the back screamed.

Somebody else shouted that she could feel a cold spot behind her and then the candle and all the torches went out.

There was a moment of silence, followed by mad panic and the room emptied as the serried ranks scattered. All except Fiona and the man with the camera, who between expletives was trying to get the battery to recharge, in order that he could record for posterity whatever it was that was about to manifest itself.

What happened next was almost funny. It certainly made two shadowy figures lurking in the dim doorway laugh in ghostly unison.

A pair of brown leather boots marched across the floor towards them after first detaching themselves from the bricks in the furthest darkest corner of the room. Walford Man groaned, the camcorder hit the floor at the same time as he did and Mr Boots, aka the irritating clown with the teeth, materialised in front of Fiona with outstretched arms and a badly sung rendition of 'My Bonny lies over the ocean', only with the word 'bonny' supplanted by the word 'body'.

"Oh very funny, very mature," Fiona spat, before kneeing him in the groin.

Squealing in pain and clutching testicles he'd forgotten that he had, Mr Boots glowered up at her.

"How the f***ing Norah did you do that?" he groaned.

"I have no idea, but my grandmother always said it would come in useful and now it has. So if you don't want to acquire a black eye and a twisted ear as well, I'd bugger off so I can get the prat in the corner back to our illustrious group leader."

Mr Boots vanished with consummate ease and dark mutterings, mostly anatomical and decidedly sexist and Fiona tipped half a bottle of Highland Spring over the recumbent figure of Mr Video Ham.

It took some time to get him a) coherent and b) upright but she managed it at roughly the same time as their guide dashed back in, gasping apologies and helpful hints regarding fainting fits and nosebleeds. Fiona wondered briefly why she was wittering on about stemming nasal blood flow right up to the point when she rejoined the now totally subdued group and discovered that three of them were sitting on the floor with heads raised and scarlet-coloured reams of toilet tissue protruding from their flared and bloody nostrils.

A large security guard in a thick padded jacket clunked towards them out of the gloom and sniggered.

"Looks like the Battle of Culloden before the crows turned up," he stated, looking around.

"Oh, very funny Michael. Just help me with Mr Takimoto here and open the doors at the top," their guide hissed at him.

"Old Bootsie been at it again?" he asked conversationally, as he hoisted the limp body of a diminutive Japanese over his shoulder. Mrs Takimoto and several smaller Takimotos watched him with worried faces.

"It's alright Hen, I used to be a fireman," Michael announced before stomping back up the stairs to the relative warmth of an Edinburgh night.

Everyone else hurriedly followed in his wake furtively looking to left and right and starting at every sudden noise. Everyone, that is, except Fiona. Halfway up the wooden steps Fiona spotted something glittering in the dust, and thinking that it was some trinket that one of the group had lost in the stampede towards freedom popped it in her back pocket for safe keeping. Up in the fresh air and the white frosted light of a street-lamp, she realised that it was just an irregular nugget of some silver-coloured metal and dropped it back into her pocket without a second glance.

After a brief but animated chat with a middle-aged couple from the Isle of Man and an elderly lady from Hamburg, she straightened her back, clutched her handbag protectively and trudged back down the Royal Mile towards the steps leading down to Princes Street and eventually to her hotel and hot food.

Fiona loved Edinburgh and always would, with the possible exception of certain Saturday nights. Saturday nights saw the return of the old dark Edinburgh. A city walled in ancient stone and grim histories, the mental birthplace of Dr Jekyll and Mr Hyde, of Sherlock Holmes and the fleeting cloaked figure of Professor Moriarty. An Edinburgh steeped in mystery and pickled in alcohol and definitely not the place to be walking on your own if you were of the female gender and the entire indigenous male population had just started leaving a variety of hostelries, after spending most of the day watching Celtic lose to Rangers after extra time.

She would normally have hailed a taxi, only she couldn't find one that would stop and as she'd inadvertently left her mobile phone behind in her hotel bedroom, couldn't call one up either. She stood undecidedly at the bottom of Waverley Bridge and with a heartfelt prayer of thanks spotted a lone button-nosed cab waiting outside the entrance to the railway station. At almost a sprint she hurled herself the last hundred yards and grabbed the doorhandle at almost exactly the same time as a couple of women with loud Birmingham accents approached the cab from the other side.

They stared at each other in growing dismay and the cabbie who had been reading a copy of *The Scotsman* looked up and watched them from the warm safety of his vehicle. It had been a slow night and the scene before him was ripe with the promise of verbal female mudwrestling.

Fiona sighed: there were two of them and only one of her.

"Go on, take it," she muttered a trifle gracelessly as she stood aside.

The largest lady, who sported a bleached spiked haircut and an orange and silver velour jumpsuit with a long zip and no obvious underwear, stared at her for a moment before saying, "I know you, don't I love?"

Fiona backed away a few steps and then, puckering her brow, had to agree.

"I think so." Fiona racked her brain and then grinned back at her. "Porridge!" she announced emphatically.

"That's right, I remember you dear, Gloria here dropped a load of spoons and you helped that lovely girl from Belfast pick them up."

"Oh, I remember," her companion, a thin woman in a grey parka with a long, verdantly green, striped scarf announced, "she's staying in the same hotel as us."

"You going back?" the blonde asked.

"Yes. I thought I'd eat there as it's a bit ... er ..." Fiona stopped and waved her hand in the direction of a gaggle of semi-vertical men, who were clutching each others appendages and singing a version of 'Scotland the Brave' that would have been banned by both Channels Four and Five after only one stanza.

"You can eat with us then, love. In you get, Gloria old thing. My name's Violet, by the way," the blonde informed her as she hustled everyone into the cab and barked "Channings Hotel please, and don't spare the hamsters."

The cabdriver winked broadly at her in the driver's mirror and they were off.

After breaking the ice with her tale of the recently supernatural, coloured by reminiscences from their driver whom they discovered was called Bob, Fiona arrived back at her hotel, happy, hungry and ready for a very large drink. They emerged from their taxi just as the remnants of Gloria and Violet's party arrived back from the theatre.

Introductions were made and they all trooped arm in arm down to the basement bistro for wine and sustenance. They dined on lamb shanks with a rich and creamy tranche of mashed potato, washed down with Rioja and told each other rude tales and tall stories. All in all it was a splendid evening, right up to the point when Fiona staggered up to her room, drunkenly opened her door after the fourth attempt and discovered the body of a man fully dressed and stretched out on top of her bed.

✻ ✻ ✻

In the room next door Nemesis put her ear to the glass that she had wedged up against the wall and listened.

"Tell me again why we can't just drift through the wall and eavesdrop in comfort?" Robin asked as he sat on the bed surveying a pair of lily-white, sockless feet.

"Because we don't want them to know that we're here," Nemesis answered, putting down the glass and surveying her companion with a mildly curious frown.

"What are you doing?" she asked.

"I have blisters. I knew I would, it's all this walking on the surface. Why can't we just use the odd breeze and float? I hate wearing shoes, it's so constricting."

Nemesis cast him a look of unadulterated scorn and moved towards the window.

"We have to blend in until we're needed, which may not be for some time," she stated, folding her arms and looking down into the moonlit garden below. A cat swore and hissed amongst the shrubbery, as another bigger feline defended his territory with a paw full of steel-tipped claws.

"Now that's what I like to see – justice red in tooth and claw," Nemesis grinned.

"Er, shouldn't that be nature …" Robin's voice tailed off as he was rooted to the spot by a gimlet stare. "I thought it went well though. The meeting, that is," Robin added, pulling on two pale grey socks and rolling down his trousers to cover long, spindly and almost hairless legs.

"So what do we do now?" he asked.

"We catch up on a bit of light reading, I have a well-earned bath and then tomorrow I'm going shopping."

"Would you mind if I watched a little television, as it's here?" Robin asked, a trifle nervously.

"Oh, I don't see why not," Nemesis replied, moving towards the bathroom in a gentle glide.

"Robin?"

"Yes."

"I feel that now that we are, as it were, sharing the immediate amenities that we ought possibly to be on a first-name basis. By the way, did those jocular parents of yours give you a second name?"

"Er yes, it's … um … Henry."

"Henry – a good strong name and one which I'm sure you'll grow into," Nemesis observed, her hand on the bathroom door knob. "Mine's Janet."

"Oh." Robin, nonplussed, looked at her with ever-widening eyes.

"Well then Robin, be a good boy and separate the beds would you, before you switch the evil box on?"

"Erm … well yes, quite … I mean certainly."

"After all, we wouldn't like to give rise to any rumours of inappropriate behaviour while we're here. Now would we?"

"Certainly not." Robin Henry Bastard shot up from his lolling position and hurriedly began to push the two single beds as far apart as they could go, his mind alive with the sort of thoughts he'd never entertained even when, a very long time before, he had rushed through puberty with both eyes firmly closed.

Nemesis smiled to herself as she closed the door and surveyed the large and welcoming bath before her. Tomorrow she would visit the department store that she had overheard an elderly couple from Perth discussing. It had, she speculated, everything that she might need and a few things that she probably wouldn't but she'd have fun buying anyway.

Head Office had that day dictated that Fiona and William Winkie were to be allowed to bond in their own way without any intervention from her and that suited her just fine. All she had been instructed to do was to ensure that the Pratchett book had been left where William could have seen it and that Fiona had been persuaded to purchase a ticket for the correct history tour. Both had been achieved quite satisfactorily and were worth at least one new outfit and a pair of matching shoes, with the possible addition of a handbag: small, leather and with a discreetly brazen logo.

✳ ✳ ✳

Two dark-suited figures garbed in a shade of black mostly worn by undertakers, senior civil servants and the common or garden crow raised brimming glasses to their lips and drank in noiseless unison. The seedy backroom in which they sat was empty except for a fat grey brindled cat, which was snoring loudly upon a dirty hearth. Occasionally a gaunt face would appear at the open hatch leading to a well-stocked bar, glare at them both and then disappear to serve other less parsimonious drinkers.

"Well, Mr Hare?"

"I have received further instructions, Mr Burke."

"Which have, I take it, been accompanied by the usual largesse?"

"But of course, Mr Burke."

"I believe that our previous task was completed with the necessary tidiness."

"Indubitably Mr Burke."

"And yet the job appears to be unfinished. Our tasks like Hercules grow with every succeeding day, which makes me wonder ..."

"What, Mr Burke?"

"If perhaps our employer is not after all as levelheaded and as logical as we were at first led to believe."

"My thoughts exactly, Mr Burke."

"In which case contingencies must be made, Mr Hare, contingencies must be made."

"And in the meantime?"

"Our employer has paid in cash and is deserving of our toil."

"I will in that case purchase the necessary incendiary liquids and some more nylon rope."

"I do hope that Mr Rowse and Mr Flint were not perspicacious enough to leave any information concerning ourselves and our current employer."

"That would indeed set the cat amongst the pigeons, Mr Burke."

"It would indeed, Mr Hare."

"Indeed it would, Mr Burke, indeed it would."

chapter two

Fiona took a deep breath and leant drunkenly against the door. 'I am going ever so slightly insane due to an overdose of alcohol and unlimited carbohydrates. Dear God, make it go away.' Fiona thought, closing her eyes, but the room spun violently so she opened them again. He was still there.

"Go away," she groaned. "Please," she added as an after-thought, just in case politeness would work where demands wouldn't.

The body on the bed sat up, turned itself on its side and grinned broadly at her.

"Hi honey, you home?" it said. blowing her a kiss.

"Oh God in heaven, it talks," Fiona moaned, sliding down the wall. She met the ground coming up with a soft thump and then tried closing her eyes again. The room still spun but on a gentler orbit.

"Dear God, I promise never to drink again and I'll go back on the diet first thing tomorrow … er … today," she fervently prayed.

"Want a coffee?" the voice enquired. "I can put the kettle

on, I got the cups ready earlier on, had a little trouble with the milk thingies though."

"Everyone has trouble with the milk thingies," Fiona muttered, looking up. The complimentary basket of pre-packed dehydrated beverages was somewhat depleted as most of the contents appeared to be decorating the wallpaper behind the kettle. A lone cup sat proudly beside the kettle which was now gently puffing steam in all directions.

"I don't think the lid is down properly." Fiona observed in carefully neutral tones.

"Oh, right," Mr Boots said, and wafted over to the kettle and gave the lid a thump with the flat of one semi-transparent hand.

"Bloody marvellous this electricity stuff, used to take me ages to get the fire hot enough, grind the beans ..."

"Milk the cow ..."

"Knock off the odd sugar seller ..."

"Really?"

"No, I got the milk from one of the local milkmaids and the sugar we bought in sacks off a merchant down on the docks. Well I say merchant – he was more sort of unofficial."

"Unofficial."

"He did the books when they unloaded the boats, stuff gets spilt, bags split, you know the sort of thing."

"Had difficulty counting once he'd run out of fingers?"

"You catch on quick. Here's your coffee such as it is, although to be brutally honest it smelt a lot better in my day."

Fiona gratefully took the gently floating cup and saucer and took a hesitant sip.

"Probably tasted better too," she agreed.

"Anything wrong?"

"No. Unfortunately it always ends up as bad as this."

"Oh."

"I think I may just have a nice long bath and finish this while I soak," Fiona grimaced, trying to stand.

"Want any help?"

"No thank you, I shall be ... er ... vertical in a minute."

"I meant with the bath."

"No!" Fiona snapped.

"Right."

"I didn't mean to be rude especially after you made me a hot beverage but I'm quite capable of washing myself. If on the other hand I drown, I'm sure my departing spirit will let you know."

"Then in that case I'll just hang around for a bit until we can have a proper chat."

"Can't you just go?"

"Disappear sort of thing?"

"Yes."

"All right then, how's this?" Mr Boots suddenly vanished. Fiona stood up and peered around the semi-lit room and then moved as quickly as she could, without throwing up, to the bathroom.

When she finally emerged half an hour later the room was still devoid of any ghostly shades; tentatively she looked around. Nothing happened. Fiona moved as quickly as she could to the bed and crawled thankfully under the duvet. After a few minutes snores reverberated around the room and Mr Boots emerged from the wardrobe and moved cautiously towards the gently vibrating heap on the bed. He tucked in a stray appendage and then with a decidedly thoughtful expression went back to his chair overlooking

35

the moonlit garden.

* * *

Morning slithered reluctantly into the room some time later, complete with bird ensemble and a vague aroma of smoked fish.

As the first beams of brilliant sunshine hit the outskirts of her beaten pillows, Fiona awoke and opened her eyes.

"Ow," she moaned.

"You look awful," a voice remarked from the chair in front of the window.

"Oh no," Fiona groaned, "I thought you'd gone."

"The thing is I can go, but I can't actually – you know – *go*."

"You mean you can disappear but you can't actually leave?"

"That's it."

"Oh God."

"I have a feeling that appealing to a higher authority won't actually work at this juncture."

"And that makes me feel so much better."

"Ah sarcasm, you must be on the bump strewn and rocky road to recovery. Just think how much livelier you'll be after a good breakfast, you may even manage gentle irony."

"I feel like I've been nibbling hamsters wearing fluffy angora twin sets." Fiona swallowed and then ran a furred tongue around her mouth. "Or possibly bats."

"Next time stop before you reach the brandy."

"I'll try and remember that gem of worldly wisdom the next time I want to commit death by drinking, shall I?"

"Good idea," Mr Boots agreed, throwing a commodious

hotel bathrobe at her. "Another good idea would be to have a shower and then a really good breakfast with lots of lovely hot coffee and litres of orange juice."

"Why?"

"Because we need to talk. Or at least I need to talk and you need to be able to listen. An impossible mission for the few meagre grey cells currently working in that befuddled brain of yours."

"Oh goody, a ghost that can be witty in the mornings, my cup runneth over."

"Shower, breakfast, now!"

"Or what?"

"Or I'll remove your covers, drag you into the bathroom and help scrub your back."

"You wouldn't dare!"

"What have I got to lose?"

Fiona gulped and then grabbing the proffered robe, hastily wrapped herself in its soft towelling folds and raced to the bathroom, slamming the door behind her.

Mr Boots smirked briefly and then went back to his chair by the window and his interrupted perusal of the hotel's information pack.

He was still reading it when Fiona returned, scrubbed, dressed and just about awake.

"Breakfast," she muttered, moving slowly towards the door as if she had a large earthenware jar on her head.

Mr Boots allowed himself a small snigger as she fumbled with the lock, whilst trying not to move her neck or look down.

"Want any help?" he asked.

"No thank you, I can manage."

"Is there something wrong in the area of the upper torso,

a crick perhaps? I do a great massage."

"I am perfectly all right. Nor do I need a massage. It's just that if I move too quickly my head may fall off or ..."

"Or?"

"Explode."

"That will be the tumour caused by a surfeit of Lampreys or in your case ..."

"Calvados."

"Ye Gods girl! You really know how to die, don't you?"

"I am now going and when I get back you had better have a really good reason to still be here."

"Or what?"

"Or I shall see if room service can rustle up a vicar."

Fiona opened the door and closed it behind her as gently as she could and tottered off to the restaurant. Mr Boots waited a few minutes until he was quite sure that she had actually gone and then began to read the collection of papers she kept locked in a small plastic briefcase at the bottom of the built-in wardrobe.

❋ ❋ ❋

Fiona returned after indulging herself in a huge three-course breakfast and enough coffee to keep a small Columbian coffee grower in credit for several months. At first her heart rolled over in relief as she failed to see her companion of the night before and then she heard the snores.

"Wake up!" she barked, kicking the side of the noisiest chair with her foot.

"Wha ... t?" Mr Boots grumbled, materialising slowly from the head down.

"You were snoring," she stated accusingly.

"Are you sure that you're not married?"

"Yes."

"Ever been in the marital frying pan then?"

"No."

"Bet you ..."

"I might have done, not that it's any of your business."

"Oh?"

"Why?"

"Just wondered." Mr Boots rubbed a stubbly chin and looked around. "I'm still here."

"Don't rub it in."

"You know that Terry Pratchett really does know his quantum from a hole in the ground."

"If this is some variation of toilet humour I'm ringing room service."

"You know atoms and er stuff."

"Look I know that after a night on the ..."

"Demon drink."

"I was going to say tiles."

"Really? Are you sure? I mean, for a start you didn't sleep on the bathroom floor but ..."

"Town, a night on the town ..."

"Strictly speaking you did most of your quaffing here in the hotel which I suppose is on the outskirts of ..."

"Do you have any idea how annoying you are?"

"Am I?"

"Yes."

"Oh."

"Just please tell me before my head melts what exactly it is that you want and what the hell it has to do with me?"

"It all started with a book."

"It usually does."

"One of the guards or guides, I can't remember which ..."

"Does it matter?"

"Do you want to know or don't you?"

"Yes."

"Good, then shut up for a few seconds so I can tell you." Mr Boots took a deep breath and glared at her. "Anyway, somebody left a book on one of the wine shelves by this bloke called Pratchett. So I read it. I read anything, me. Stops the boredom and I can imprecate in modern and easily understood terminology."

"Which book?"

"The one with the three witches, the fool, the ghost and more insults to lawyers than you can shake a tort at."

"Wyrd Sisters."

"Did I mention that tit Shakespeare?"

"No." Fiona stared at him in a vague unseeing way before the full and awful truth revealed itself. "That bit of silver."

"Left molar as was." Mr Boots smiled at her, displaying a set of fillings with which you could have opened a small account at any high street bank. There was a gap at the back on the left-hand side.

"So let's see if I have understood this correctly? You couldn't leave your old haunt."

"Right."

"But if somebody picked up something which belonged or had been a part of you, you could escape as long as you stuck with them?"

"Correct on all counts, give the monkey a banana."

"But ..."

"It didn't work with bits of brick and the odd stone

40

because I tried that. I spent nearly a month dropping them in pockets, handbags, and any other open orifice."

"For goodness sake, just stop with the information overload."

"And then I found my old filling behind the brick at the back of the fireplace and knew that if anything would work, that would and I waited."

"For what?"

"Someone who could see me who didn't have four legs and a tail."

"Animals can see you?"

"Some of them, cats mostly and the more intelligent dogs. Babies too but they lose the ability when they learn to talk, so pretty useless as far as companionship goes."

"So you waited."

"Yes, I waited. I'm dead good at waiting – been doing it for decades now. Mind you, I was really disappointed by that last load of television twits. Thinks he can see ghosts eh? Not even if they got up and bit him on the buttocks, and don't think I didn't try."

"And then …"

"I stood next to this really attractive little redhead and she kicks me in the balls."

"Ah."

"And voila here I am."

"Here you are."

"And it's all thanks to Morag's toffee." Mr Boots rubbed his hands together and looked to Fiona's jaundiced eye like the fat cat in a cream factory after it's been locked up and everyone's gone home.

"Who the hell is Morag?"

"The wife. Normally she could cook anything. I still

41

remember the rat haggis with extra onion and a Clootie dumpling that would fill the stomach for days. Unfortunately like most great cooks she had an Achilles heel."

"Toffee?"

"It either went all runny and ended up as fudge sauce or hard as Edinburgh granite. That time we actually thought she had beaten her own personal jinx so I ate some and it set in my mouth. My filling broke, the root became infected and they were buying coffin nails a week later."

"What happened?"

"We called it the green, odorous and lingering death. You call it septicaemia. You have antibiotics, we had French brandy."

"At least yours tasted better."

"Didn't do a lot mind except help you hallucinate in colour."

"But if you died and they bought the coffin nails I really don't see how you ended up under the South Bridge?"

"Ah well, that's where it starts to get complicated on account of the insurance."

"Insurance?"

"We didn't have any."

"Oh."

"So Morag was left with a still she couldn't fix, that was my job see being a trained engineer and only slightly mad inventor."

"Inventor?"

"Meet the original Mr Gadget." Mr Boots smirked. "Where was I? Ah yes, and five bairns including the wee one."

"So what did she do?"

"The only thing she could have done. She sold my body

to old Doctor Williams."

"What!"

"Clever eh? And she got a good price to, seven pounds two shillings and threepence halfpenny."

"That was good, was it?"

"In 1821 it was a bloody fortune."

"From the thoughtful expression on your face I gather that there was a slight snag to this financial masterplan."

"Well yes. And don't think for one moment that it was in anyway Morag's fault because it wasn't."

"Right."

"The thing is I wasn't exactly dead."

"Oh."

"I was nearly dead, comatose to be precise. There was death on one side of me sharpening the scythe and my old man grinning on the other and some angel with a stop-watch and a clipboard waiting to see which way I would go. So you see it was almost impossible for Morag to have known."

"But what about the doctor surely?"

"A medic know his cadavers from his corpses? Give me a break – that's on par with getting two lawyers to give you the same opinion on anything!"

"Right. I still don't …"

"It was when one of his assistants was cleaning me up."

"Cleaning?"

"The good Doctor was giving a lecture on the lower intestine and other wobbly bits so he needed a clean not too odorous corpse. The assistant was the miserable little sod that had sold all the tickets and pocketed some of the cash."

"Tickets?"

"People liked to watch a good post-mortem, much more

interesting than a hanging and probably warmer, some even took along a packed lunch."

"The mind boggles."

"I reckon it was the cold water, must have triggered something. I remember opening my eyes and before I could get up he had a hand over my mouth and nose and was pressing down for all he was worth."

"So you were murdered."

"Well it wasn't assisted suicide." Mr Boots snorted derisively before taking a deep breath and continuing. "After that I just sort of stuck around. 'Resurrection Men' came and went. Morag packed up, sold the still and the stock such as it was and moved to the country and that was that."

"Until the vaults got opened up and the tourists came to stand and stare."

"Something like that."

"And now I'm stuck with you."

"Well ..."

"What?"

"There is a way of freeing this spiritual shell ..."

"How?"

"You really sound like you want to get rid of me."

"Yes."

"I'm hurt but not, alas, surprised. All you have to do is allow me to atone for past sins and – did you have the porridge by the way?"

"Yes."

"With cream and brown sugar. I used to dream of proper porridge. Thick and creamy with chewy lumps made from real oats."

"I really don't see how I can possibly find something you can help me with."

"I'm a ghost."

"And ..."

"A real one."

"So?"

"Look, little Miss Thicky, do I have to draw you a picture?"

"It would help, possibly."

"Well I can get in and out of buildings and rooms and observe without of course being seen and ..."

Fiona started, and then pushing back her chair, stood up. "Have you been reading my papers?"

"What papers? You don't mean the ones informing you about the sad demise of your Uncle and the small bequest?"

"The ones carefully locked up ..."

"Small black plastic briefcase."

"And they're still in there?"

"Yes."

"You are good aren't you?"

"Yes."

Fiona sat back down and regarded Mr Boots in a thoughtful fashion.

"And you think that you could help me run a small detective agency in Oban?"

"Why not? I could follow suspects, sneakily read documents, track down fraudsters, chase criminals ..."

"Standard James Bond cloak and dagger stuff."

"Exactly."

"In Oban?"

"Yes."

"You've not, I take it, ever been there?"

"No, but it's a big place isn't it? So it's bound to be positively teeming with people needing our kind of help."

"Right."

"Well, what else can I do?"

"There is the other part of the bequest."

"Yeah, a flophouse." Mr Boots waved a dismissive hand.

"Small select and homely guesthouse with …"

"Hot and cold water in every room, yeah I read the pamphlet – flophouse."

"I admit it wasn't doing too well."

"It had a three-week summer season."

"So?"

"In November?"

"I could bring it back into credit."

"How?"

"I have a few savings and I thought I could do a sort of themed weekend."

"What sort of theme?"

"Murder, mystery … er … ghost …"

"Me, Mr Boots, haunt for monetary gain! Do you think for one moment that I have no pride?"

"Well?"

"Do I get my own room and a widescreen television with at least five speakers?"

"Maybe."

"All right, I'll do it. There's just one thing, however, that I'd like you to try and do in return."

"What?"

"I'd like you to try and track down Morag. I waited, you see. I thought that when they grew up they would at least come to see where their old dad died or even if they couldn't make it that they'd send their children or their children's children."

"Oh."

"Then I thought, what if Morag was set upon and murdered? There was that whole family who hid in the hills and ate people. It was in all the papers. And then of course there was the plaque and other assorted diseases."

"I'll try. So do we have a deal?"

"You find my family and I help you out in the noble art of detecting and scaring the paying guests witless."

"Yes. Only I can't keep calling you Mr Boots."

"Why not?"

"Because you sound like the male lead in a Christmas pantomime, the hairy male lead with pointy ears and a good line in rodent munching."

"Oh."

"Come on, it can't be that bad – besides which I'm going to have to know to hunt Morag and your family down."

"It's … its William, William Winkie. But I prefer to be called Bill."

Fiona, noticing the hesitation in Bill's voice, stared at him until comprehension dawned.

"So when you were a small boy they called you …"

"Wee Willie Winkie."

"Parents can be so cruel."

Bill smiled and then frowned.

"Did you hear that?" he asked.

"Hear what?"

"A sort of echo?"

"No."

"Oh right, must have been my overworked imagination but I could have sworn that …"

Fiona watched him float over to the far wall and then stop.

"Are you all right?" she asked.

47

"Umm." Bill turned and floated back. "So do we have a deal?"

Fiona grinned at him and held out her hand.

She smiled, "Welcome to the family firm, Bill Boots."

❋ ❋ ❋

Neville Albert Foolscap tore open the envelope with trembling fingers, read the contents, groaned dramatically and then tottered to the sideboard. He filled a murky tumbler with about an inch of gin and a splash of tonic and downed the lot without the need to take a breath between gulps.

Before he had finished the first drink he felt the weight of the literary world heavy upon his stooped and bony shoulders. By the second he was feeling tearful and by the third had managed to bypass self-pity for the more rewarding emotion of righteous wrath.

"How dare they say those vile and filthy things about my work, the sweat of my brow ... the ..." Neville took another gulp and realised that the glass was empty. He looked down myopically at the solitary slice of lemon clinging to the side of the glass and reached for the gin bottle.

"And not a drop to drink?" he muttered, trying to tip the last few dregs into his glass. He turned the bottle upside down and tried to suck the last atom of alcohol out with his tongue.

"Do you hear that Gravel old thing?" he shouted at a black hunched shape perched upon the curtain rod on one gnarled leg. "Nothing left to drink and my opus nothing more than a febrile attempt at self-delusion. No foreseeable market, 'niche market' is what they said. The bastards. You know what, Gravel old chap? I'm too good for them.

Too erudite by half. You know what they want don't you. Eh, Eh? Well I'll tell you shall I? They want pap! That's what they want. Pap. And jeno what they got, eh? They got culture. That's what they got, bloody marvellous culture and they don't know what to do with it."

Gravel the mynah bird changed legs and regarded his master with a jaundiced eye.

"They're all the same, yer know, all the same; parasitic Neanderthals with brains the size of peas."

"Brains the size of peas," Gravel echoed back, trying out the words for future reference.

"Or is that teenagers?"

"Teenagers?"

"Gravel old bird, you may be right – it's teenagers. Something to do with growing too fast and hormones. Filthy things, hormones. You mark my words nothing good ever came from filling teenagers up with hormones, what they need is a good dose of ... of ... need another drink."

Neville sank down into a nearby chair, his limbs folding up around him.

There was another bottle in a safe place – all he had to do was remember where it was.

"What's the point, eh? All that work, all those hours all for nothing," he railed.

"All for nothing," Gravel squawked, picking at a guano-covered curtain ring with his beak. 'Bet the silly old fool forgot the nuts again,' he thought to himself, moodily hunching further into his own feathers.

"It's because those bean counters, those illiterate thugs who call themselves accountants won't print anything from anyone if they don't have a name to go on the front. I bet you anything you like that if I'd shagged the Archbishop of sodding Canterbury or attempted to throw paint at the Prime Minister or paid for some minor royal's golfing ambitions I'd have been published then. Oh yes, play football on the international stage and then have it off with some plush bit of totty with a higher bra size than her IQ and they'll all be queuing up with a cheque in one hand and a bottle of Bollinger in the other."

"Nuts."

"What?" Neville shot up out of his chair and staggered to the small kitchen. On the table was a plastic bag and in the bag was a large packet of mixed nuts and ... "Gin!" Neville yelled, holding up the bottle.

The discarded bag of nuts and a soggy packet of economy fish fingers from a non-named source of fish fell to the floor. Gravel swooped down and began to tear at the packets with his beak and a talon or two.

Neville extracted a cold bottle of tonic from the fridge and looked around for a glass. Finally his eyes settled upon a solitary upturned coffee mug and with a shrug he began to mix himself yet another drink.

He would get his own back, he fumed inwardly. They would all be sorry – the whole parasitic bunch. From that evil twisted bastard of a bank manager who wouldn't even lend him the money to self-publish to that last bunch of timid sheepshaggers who'd sent his manuscript back – and they'd made him pay for the postage. Cowardly worms – he'd make them suffer. Decomposing rodents in a box on a spring was too good for the likes of them. Death was the only thing that would make them sit up and take notice. They were all vampires, draining their victims dry and then throwing them on the scrap heap of humanity. May they rot in hell and may carrion fly down and peck out their eyes as they burn in the everlasting flame of avarice. Actually that last bit wasn't at all bad, Neville mused, reaching for a stray notebook as tears coursed down his face.

He downed the entire contents of the garishly decorated mug and wobbled.

"Wash I need is a nuzzer dwink," he mumbled, as his lips grew numb.

"A pox on all their houses!" he shouted, before falling over.

Gravel looked up at him from the detritus of crushed nuts and soggy day-glo orange breadcrumbs.

"Silly bugger," he squawked, his mouth full of grey flaked fish.

Neville dribbled drunkenly over the tacky kitchen vinyl and fell into a merciful sleep as two figures emerged from the wallpaper. One regarded him in a thoughtful fashion, the other glared with barely concealed contempt from the rancid collection of scum-coated crockery in the sink to a pair of faded tartan jockey shorts drying on the radiator.

"Is this really the best you can do?"

"Actually, I rather think he is," Janet Nemesis replied.

"He's a drunken hack with all the imaginative thinking power of a jellyfish!"

"All he needs is a little gentle push in the right direction."

"What he needs is a bloody good bath and an economy bottle of Kaolin and morphine."

"Oh, don't exaggerate. I'll just leave him with a divine and inspirational nightmare while you amend pages 16 to 120. He can easily work the rest of it out without any need for us to actually be here."

"What?"

"Come along Robin, we don't have all day and there's a darling little bag in Jenners with my name on it." Nemesis turned and with an imperious glance beckoned the minor bird towards her with one long, newly polished, sapphire-coloured index fingernail.

Gravel regarded the mutilated debris in which he was standing and then her silk-clad and clean shoulder. He was no slouch in the grey cell department and jumped with alacrity and a satisfied squawk just as the two bickering figures faded back into the wall.

Neville Foolscap twitched and shuddered as he dreamt a long and very strange dream. He'd written a book. There was a ghost and a girl with long red hair and green eyes the shade of marrowfat peas. There was also a queue of hooded robed figures and they were carrying large bottles of single malt and very sharp knives. The knives flashed as they passed him, cowering amongst rows and rows of mortuary slabs. He ran and ran; he had a feeling that one of the figures was Alistair Campbell but he had no idea why.

chapter three

Fiona eventually checked out with the minimum of fuss and a good-looking young man with one of the nicest bodies she'd seen for a long time hauled her case out of the hotel and down the steps to her small Nissan Micra. She closed the driver's door, started the engine and drove slowly out of her cramped parking space. Mr Boots, as she still thought of him, sat in the passenger seat with a map on his knees, and looked, with avid interest, at every button and knob he could possibly press, tweak or click.

"Will you stop that?" Fiona shrieked, as his hand slid towards the handbrake.

"Why?"

"Because if I do a handbrake turn here and now, I'll be in hospital if not dead and you'll be wherever it is ghosts go to when they don't have some idiot about who has stupidly agreed to carry ex-body parts around with them."

"It's only a bit of silver."

"That was once part of your dental features."

"I've never been in one of these before, fascinating – no

horse and it smells good."

"That will be the froggy air freshener and no, you can't eat it, so leave it alone!"

"Um, do you really have to go this fast?"

"What? Oh come on, you have got to be joking, we're currently only doing about ten miles an hour. Not exactly fast or even reckless."

"It's still a bit too quick for my liking, makes me feel a bit sick."

"Well get used to it, buster, because I normally do at least fifty."

Fiona had never seen a ghost go pale before, in fact she hadn't known that ectoplasm could change colour, but it could and it did.

"Fifty!"

"And that's slow for me, unless of course we get stuck behind a caravan all the way along the bonny banks of Loch Lomond."

"What happens then?"

"I get very cross and apoplectic, and you nip out and scare the stuffing out of them until they have a heart attack and pull over."

"That's not very nice."

"Listen mate, when I'm in the driving position the last thing I do is nice. Anyway you've not got stuck behind one of those scary white biscuit tins. Just you wait until you do, that's all I'm saying."

Mr Boots sat and scowled at the speedometer as she turned left and made her shaky unsure way out of Edinburgh. They did take a few minor detours, mainly the fault of unmarked roundabouts, but eventually made it onto the M8 to Glasgow.

After Glasgow had been thankfully skirted with only a minor loss of temper on the part of Fiona, they stopped at Dumbarton for a late lunch at a Little Chef. Fiona read the paper over a plate of steak and chips whilst Mr Boots wandered around outside being nosy and upsetting a pair of small yappy Yorkshire terriers. The bored animals were temporarily incarcerated in a battered blue Ford Mondeo. Occasionally their elderly lady owner would shoot from her seat, totter outside, open the passenger door and shout at both quivering canines until they shut up. Mr Boots would then gurn through the window at Fiona until the dog's owner had gone back inside, and then go off and annoy them again. Fiona actually found it quite amusing the first couple of times. Eventually the dogs collapsed exhausted and could only stare helplessly at their tormentor with panting tongues and white flecked drool, which now covered most of the back seats.

Bill Boots wafted through the window and with a bored sigh sat in the seat opposite Fiona.

"Didn't the ickle doggies want to play anymore?" she asked, spearing the last chip with her fork. "And leave the cruets alone," she hissed, as he upended the pepper pot.

"Honestly, anyone would think you were eight the way you have to fiddle with everything."

"You're still cross with me, aren't you?" Mr Boots muttered, picking up the vinegar.

"What – me – annoyed with the spiritual answer to the newest line in in-car satellite navigation? Yes, I'm still cross. Put the condiment down now," Fiona whispered, as she folded up her newspaper and stood up.

"Don't you want another coffee?" Mr Boots asked.

"I did, but somehow the thought of levitating sugar

doesn't exactly fill me with relaxed and happy thoughts."

Mr Boots looked down at his hands and then hastily replaced the small packet of granulated sugar in the appropriate bowl.

"Sorry about that. It's a sort of habit, used to drive Morag mad."

"Really? Now there's a surprise."

Fiona extracted a plastic card from her handbag and hastily paid the gum-chewing trainee at the till. Mr Boots watched in abject fascination as the transaction was enacted, a small slip of paper was signed, something bleeped and they then had to wait patiently for the manager to turn up and sort out the rogue till.

"So," Mr Boots observed, as they finally left, the plate glass door shutting behind them with a muted clank. "You pay for a meal by handing over a slip of shiny plastic, which may or may not work depending on whether their till will speak to another one over a telephone line, several thousand miles away. Then you spend another ten minutes trying to fit in a roll of paper in order that you can tell that you've done it?"

"Yes."

"Despite the fact that all I used to have to do was to take some coins out of my pocket, hand them to someone who put them in their pocket and that was that, apart from possibly the transfer of a few smaller coins back to me?"

"Yes."

"And this is still called progress?"

"Bill."

"Yes."

"Just get in the damned car!"

It was while they were meandering along the invisible

banks of Loch Lomond, which lay mouldering under a thick blanket of dank mist, that Fiona asked the question that had been bothering her since they'd departed from Edinburgh's sun-washed streets.

"So you didn't run a brothel then?"

"Pardon?"

"A brothel that sold children?"

"What!" Bill Boots spluttered, as he turned his head to glare at her.

"And you didn't knife someone in the back and sell his body to one or other of the Resurrection Men whilst dressed as a badly deranged monk?"

"No I bloody well didn't!"

"And you weren't a slum landlord?"

"No."

"Nor did you go around knocking off prostitutes?"

"If you'd ever seen my Morag cutting carrots with a cleaver you wouldn't dare ask."

"Right."

"Prostitutes? I tell you if she had even caught me looking at anything passably female I'd have been scouring pots with sand for a fortnight."

"So what did you do? I mean the accent is hard to place and that chap on 'Totally Terrified' said …"

"Oh, I know what that charlatan said all right, I was there, wasn't I? Pulled my character to shreds, and what he said about poor old Morag and some of her girls, well it's just a good thing that they locked the knives away and there wasn't a handy sized bottle about or he'd still be walking in an interesting and unusual way even now."

Mr Boots spat and then just as suddenly relaxed with a chuckle.

"What?" Fiona asked, noting the look of self-satisfied merriment.

"He'll not be using the toilet in the dark ever again."

"Is this something I should know about?"

"Probably not"

"Good."

Fiona put her foot firmly down on the accelerator, sped up and passed, with only a few inches to spare, a minibus complete with a clutch of muddy bikes and a trailer harbouring a metal racked marmalade of kayaks.

"Do you really have to go this fast?" Bill asked, as he clung to the strap suspended above the passenger door.

"We are not going that fast," Fiona shouted back between gritted teeth.

Fiona screwed her eyes up in a frown of concentration. There had been a brief glimpse of a small, white, unidentified fleeing object in front of her and her heart sank into her boots as she realised that it was indeed the dreaded mobile lunch box. Then the road in front widened, taunting her with its open and friendly face, a road that would shortly dwindle to nothing more than a RAC rally assault course with steep wooded sides and cunningly concealed parking places.

Fiona scowled horribly as she gripped the steering wheel and coaxed every ounce of speed out of her straining gearbox. Mr Boots closed his eyes and prayed for the first time in centuries. With a rush of acceleration and a cacophony of irate horn-blowing they overtook miraculously and the Nissan slowed to a more respectable and appropriate speed of 50 miles an hour.

Mr Boots slowly opened his eyes and in front of them was a large ungainly bus and four other vehicles, including a dark blue people-carrier with several sticky kids glued to the back windows.

"And we are now better off are we?" Mr Boots warily enquired, as one of the urchins in front stuck its tongue out and appeared to lick the glass.

"Well, put it this way, they won't have a Bontempi organ on board."

"I wouldn't bet on it," Mr Boots replied, as they slowed to a crawl and then stopped.

"Now what?" he asked, folding his arms in resignation.

"Traffic lights, roadworks or an accident."

"And this is progress?"

Fiona turned her head and glared at him.

"Look, if you don't like it get out and walk."

"Fine – I might just do that and I bet it'll be quicker."

Mr Boots promptly slid sideways and a few seconds later Fiona could clearly see him stomping along the narrow path bordering the sparkling loch. Minutes later he was back.

"Well, you were sort of right," he muttered.

"Oh?"

"Traffic lights and an accident, and don't ask me which came first because we'd be here all day."

"So no chance of reaching Oban before tea then?"

"Not unless this thing has the optional extra of sprouting wings and a propeller," he replied, studiously studying the map.

"Rats."

Fiona turned off the engine and sat in thought-laden silence. Somewhere there would be a place open on a Sunday, which did reasonable food at affordable prices and that wasn't full to the gunnels with tired hikers or holidaymakers.

Four hours later she stopped outside another Little Chef.

"Well," she muttered, as she carefully parked in the already overcrowded car park. "Two out of three isn't bad."

She sauntered in and was eventually guided to a plastic-covered seat, still warm from the previous occupant. A glossy ketchup-smeared menu was passed silently to her by a pimply youth in an ill-fitting uniform sporting a haircut that required only three things; a plastic pudding basin, a pair of scissors and a blind chimp.

Fiona hastily requested a coke and studied the menu.

"We've had a bit of a rush on today," the youth volunteered, his voice ranging horribly between octaves.

"Oh."

"Half the world has turned up today, except for the delivery truck."

"Right ..." Fiona paused before finally deciding. "I'll have the pie and chips."

"You've only just had steak and chips," Bill snorted, as he settled in opposite her. "What's happened to this so-called diet of yours?"

"The thing is ..." the youth muttered.

"Yes."

"We don't have any."

"What?"

"Like I said, we've been a bit rushed and what with the delivery truck not delivering, well ..." His voice tailed off unhappily.

"Chicken?"

"Er, no."

"Steak?"

"I'll check."

He was back before she'd taken a second sip of cola and,

looking at her sideways, after consulting a list scribbled on his notepad, he sadly shook his head.

"No steak, no chicken, no pie, come on tell me what else you don't have," Fiona asked.

'Can this day get any worse?' she silently pondered as the youth squirmed in front of her.

"No chips."

Fiona sat with her face the classic example of the stunned mullet. A Little Chef with no chips. The world was obviously heading pell-mell towards an early and unannounced Armageddon. The sort that had the four horsemen of the Apocalypse stuck in the pub while death was still trying to sort out the paperwork.

At that moment a short bespectacled man with an unamused portly wife and three pot-bellied children silenced the room with the clarion shout of the alpha male not being able to bring home the bacon.

"What do you mean – no chips, no baps and no burgers? What in God's name do you have?"

Silence fell in a steady cloud of volcanic ash and pumice as the red-faced waitress was glared at by the hungry hordes seated in all directions.

"Beans, eggs, bread and mashed potato," she muttered into her chin.

Fiona looked up at the youth and smiled.

"Beans on toast and a pot of tea," she ordered and then added, "please."

It has obviously been one of those days and the sooner it is over the better, she thought, sipping the remaining blood-temperature cola.

The day was definitely at the state described by many a pontificating poet as 'gloaming', as Fiona finally approached the outskirts of that grand Highland metropolis called Oban.

Mr Boots, now wide awake and beady eyed, scanned the horizon enthusiastically.

"So," he asked, "where is this new home of ours?"

"Somewhere near the last large hotel on the front!" Fiona answered, negotiating a cunningly disguised roundabout and its accompanying traffic cones.

"It isn't anywhere near the blue flashing lights over there is it?" Mr Boots asked.

"What!" she shrieked, almost ramming the car in front and inflicting minor whiplash on the driver behind.

She drove in an ever-increasing state of dread as far as she could towards the lights and, when it became patently obvious that she could go no farther, hastily parked at the side of the road. A quickly increasing throng of people was clustered behind an abandoned police car and makeshift barrier, and looked uniformly set on having a grand and dramatic night out.

In front of them two fire engines were engulfed in billowing clouds of smoke and steam. Helmeted and neon bright figures scuttled to and fro with lengths of plastic hose and high powered torches. Other official figures spoke rapidly into mobile phones or stood quietly conversing in uniformed huddled groups. Thrusting her way to the front, Fiona finally managed to attract the attention of one of the police constables manning the barricade, and beckoned him to her side.

"I'm terribly sorry to bother you, but is the Mellrose Guesthouse anywhere up here?" she shouted.

He gave her a thoughtful look and then spoke quietly into his own radio. A few minutes later an older bulkier policeman joined them.

"You told young Constable Devine here that you are looking for the Mellrose?" he enquired politely.

"Yes."

"Mind if I ask why?"

A cold feeling of inevitability began to creep into Fiona's stomach.

"Because I own it," Fiona replied.

The policemen exchanged a look and then the older of the two beckoned her to follow him. They walked in silence to stand at the side of the blazing building, its blackening carcass now clearly visible as the flaming inferno within took a greater hold. There was a sudden ear-splitting roar and then the entire chimney collapsed inwards, dragging part of the roof with it. Orange flames and glittering white and yellow sparks hissed and spiralled upwards. Jets of water tore through the broken and hollow window-frames, steaming and twisting in the intense heat.

Fiona stood and stared in total disbelief as the Mellrose spectacularly burned to the ground before her eyes.

"I don't suppose you know if anyone could have been in there?" the policeman shouted.

"Not as far as I know," Fiona shouted back.

"Oh."

"You see the lawyer only sent me the keys last week and as far as I know it's been unoccupied since my uncle died."

"Your uncle?"

"Quentin Rowse, he drowned in a boating accident."

"Ah."

"I don't suppose that there's any possibility that there is another Mellrose Guesthouse around, maybe smaller with a roof?"

"Er, sorry, no," the policeman chuckled.

"Didn't think so," she groaned. "Not the way my luck's been running recently."

"Would you like a cup of tea?"

"Pardon?"

"A cup of tea and a bun. Only I think you could do with one and I'd like a quiet word with you about your uncle."

"What?" Fiona spluttered, before being gently turned around and escorted firmly back towards the high street.

Bill Boots, who had been enjoying his front-row seat, reluctantly followed in their wake occasionally turning back whenever a new explosion rent the smoky air.

The small café that Fiona found herself hustled into was warm and fuggy, and smelled of fried fish and curry sauce. The Formica-topped tables were, however, spotless and the mug of tea and large glistening currant bun that was cheerfully placed in front of her were, she realised with a start, exactly what she needed.

"Right then, young lady, drink up. And don't look like that! I'm not going to eat you, just ask you a few questions, totally painless."

"Right."

"Especially as the thumbscrews are still down at the station."

"A plod with a sense of humour, now that's definitely a new one on me," Bill Boots whispered in Fiona's ear, as he sat down beside her.

Fiona made a choking sound and glared at him.

"Is it too hot?" the policeman solicitously enquired.

"No, no, it's fine; went down the wrong way," Fiona assured him.

"So you're Quentin's niece."

"Yes."

"Were you particularly close then?"

"Why?"

"Well I just wondered why he left the Mellrose to you."

"It was me or the cat's home I guess – I mean, Vernon had shares in it, but he had no immediate family as far as I know and Quentin only had the one sibling, my mum. To be perfectly frank neither of them could stand the sight of each other."

"Happy families."

"Tell me about it."

"I don't suppose your uncle contacted you at any point? For instance, around about the time that he had his ... er ... accident?"

"No. Why, should he have?"

"No, not particularly."

"Then why is Mr Flatfoot asking?"

"Shut up."

"Sorry."

"No, not you. Look, this is all a bit upsetting really."

"Yes, of course."

"I suppose I'll have to sleep at the agency now. Good thing I packed a sleeping bag ..."

"Agency?"

"Uncle Quentin ran a small detective agency somewhere near the ferry terminal."

"Do you have the keys?"

"Yes."

"Where?"

"In the car with the ones from the Mellrose. Mr Finlayson sent them to me."

"The advocate?"

"Yes. Mind you, I haven't a clue which is which and to be honest I had no idea Uncle Quentin even ran a detective agency, I mean neither he nor Vernon ever mentioned it."

"You know maybe it would be a good idea to just check that everything is all right. I don't suppose anybody other than Mr Finlayson was expecting you?"

"Well, a girl called Katya rang me last week and said that she did a bit of cleaning up at the Mellrose and that she'd be happy to stock up the fridge for me."

"Nobody else?"

"No one I can think of."

"Finished your tea?"

"Yes."

"Good, then in that case we might just as well go and take a look at this office."

They hurried out of the café and scurried back to Fiona's car, which was then carefully turned around and hurriedly driven off to the address Fiona had been given.

Fiona, who had been tersely told to sit in the passenger seat, hung on to the overhead strap for grim life, whilst Bill sat in the back and biliously complained about the entire constabulary's total lack of driving skills and absolute disregard for speed limits and other road users. He was still belligerently muttering when they slewed to a rapid halt outside a run-down block of Victorian warehouses and cramped offices.

The office door of Rowse Investigations Ltd had been at some time a rich deep red, evident by flakes of the peeling paint still attached to the cracked wood. When opened it led directly to a dank and dismal narrow staircase that smelled strongly of mice. At the top was a thin white door with the word 'toilet' written on it in black marker pen.

Opposite a threadbare landing, another door stood ajar, the empty blackness beyond anything but inviting. Fiona's living companion pushed her gently to one side and carefully climbed the stairs, Fiona following tentatively in his wake. At the top he stopped and switched on a powerfully bright torch, which he carefully played over and around the quietly gaping opening leading in towards the gloomy, ill-lit office.

"Police. Is anybody in there?" he shouted into the void.

If anything, the silence deepened. Suddenly there was the sound of a muffled crash, followed by the eruption of a black-clad figure who pushed past them both and then raced down the stairs trailing a very strong smell of petrol behind it.

A pinprick of bright orange glowed briefly and then Fiona and her companion fled as fast as they could, back down the stairs. The blast caught them as they reached the outer door at the bottom and they were blown clear. Glass and timber shattered behind them and Bill Boots, who had helped them both leave the ground before the first of the flames could reach them, sat on the ground and laughed.

The policeman wiped black smuts across his face and groped for his radio.

"It's McKinnon here, I'm at ten Ferry Wynde and I need another fire engine now."

"Why me?" Fiona spluttered.

"My thoughts exactly," Bill agreed. "I mean to lose one property could be considered unfortunate, but to lose two looks like sheer bloody arson."

"If it's any consolation I don't think that this was aimed at you specifically," McKinnon advised, helping Fiona to her feet.

"Like that will help," Bill sneered.

"You think."

Fiona groaned, trying to wipe the worst of the debris from her previously clean and expensive designer jeans.

"It's odds on that it was done to prevent you finding out what it was that was important enough to get your uncle and his partner murdered."

"Murdered!"

Fiona and Bill both stared at him with their mouths wide open.

"Aye – you know I was never happy about that so-called boating accident, nobody was, but without some sort of concrete evidence ..." He shrugged and turned to look at the burning building behind them. "I guess that this and the Mellrose is proof enough that something is most definitely going on."

Fiona and Bill looked up at the flames flickering around the corners of the upstairs windows and had to concede that he had a point. At that moment the fire engine arrived together with a police van and an assortment of grime encrusted officers from the fire service, the police force and a couple of heavies from the council clutching a tower of parking cones. Fiona and Bill hastily moved away to the other side of the road where Fiona squatted morosely and dwelled on the unpleasant and novel idea that a member of her immediate family, other than her mother, had managed to annoy someone badly enough to get themselves permanently removed.

As if reading her thoughts, Bill sat down beside her and draped a ghostly arm comfortingly over one shoulder.

"This sort of thing happen often in your family?" he asked, watching the mayhem across the street.

"No."

"Did in mine."

"Oh."

Fiona sighed and wiped a solitary self-pitying tear from her eye.

"You all right down there?" McKinnon asked, bending over her.

"No, she's not bloody all right you gormless tit! She's lost her home and her livelihood, and now you go and tell her that her uncle's been topped by felon or felons unknown! Talk about the sympathetic approach!" Bill shouted. "And I bet you anything you like he's been on some course, costing an arm and a leg, so that the silly sod can do it properly."

"Shh." Fiona sighed, trying gamely to stand. "I'm fine. Just point me in the direction of a good B&B and half a quart of vodka with very little tonic and I'll be feeling no pain in no time."

McKinnon laughed out loud and then smiled a genuine smile that reached far into his eyes and made the crinkles at the corner of his lashes curl. Bill watched the smile grow and then become reflected in Fiona's green orbs.

"Oh God, here we go again," Bill remarked, rolling his eyes. "I may just find a place of solitude and vomit."

"You're a game little lass for a southerner."

"Thanks, I think."

"You just wait there and I'll escort you around to my sister Heather. She runs a very small and exclusive guesthouse with hot and cold running room service and a breakfast to please the gods themselves."

"Oh."

"So don't you go away and I'll be back just as soon as I

can get this shower organised." With that he was gone.

Fiona sank back down onto the ground and patiently waited. She had nowhere else to go and her options were becoming smaller with every breaking window and broken beam.

"You do know what you have to do now don't you?" Bill asked, sitting back down beside her.

"Catch pneumonia and die?"

"No."

"What then?"

"You get mad and then …"

"Then?"

"You get even."

❋ ❋ ❋

A solitary figure sat hunched up in the driver's seat of a dark blue hire car and watched the arrival of firefighters and policemen with resigned interest. A dark shadow detached itself from a larger one at the base of a nearby wall and sidled into the passenger seat. After a minute or so he broke the interior silence by blowing his nose hard into a black silk handkerchief.

"Well, Mr Hare."

"It wasn't there, Mr Burke."

"Ah, that is not good news at all, Mr Hare, not good news at all."

"No, indeed not, Mr Burke."

"Our principal will not be at all pleased."

"I looked everywhere, even inside the toilet cistern."

"And you destroyed everything?"

"Yes, Mr Burke."

"I see."

They sat perfectly still as an ambulance raced past, lights flashing and sirens blaring.

"Who was the girl, Mr Burke?"

"I don't know, Mr Hare. The man was undoubtedly a senior policeman and I at first presumed that she was an assistant."

"She had the keys with her."

"So, not an assistant."

"I think not."

"So we may, on reflection, have lit the fuse a trifle early?"

"I think that it would be safe to assume that, yes, unfortunately."

"That doesn't sound good, Mr Hare."

"No it doesn't, Mr Burke."

"In fact the young lady who we thought was newly arrived from Edinburgh may not have been the right young lady at all."

"Then who was she?"

"I have no idea, Mr Hare, no idea at all and that does not please me. No, not at all."

"So what do we do now, Mr Burke?"

"We retreat and we watch, retreat and watch."

"And then?"

"We await an opportunity and then like the clever cobra we strike. Quickly and without, as our American cousins would say, prejudice."

"And the policeman?"

"Will be dealt with as and when our employer deems fit. As for the girl, however, well there it begins to look more than a little messy and I really do abhor messiness, Mr Hare."

"I really, really don't like where this is going, Mr Burke."

"No more do I, Mr Hare."

"But we have contingencies, do we not, Mr Burke?"

"Yes, we most fortunately do, Mr Hare."

"Good. Then in that case I will continue to watch the girl."

"And I will contact our employer and give him the bad news. Perhaps this time he will be more generous with the truth. In which case the outcome may be altered to our considerable advantage."

"Considerable advantage. Oh, I do like the sound of that, Mr Burke."

"So do I, Mr Hare, so do I."

✹ ✹ ✹

Amongst the crowd still standing in desultory groups around the smoking embers of the guesthouse stood a smartly dressed man and woman. Both stared at the tired and dishevelled firemen as they poked the smouldering remains with long metallic rods and rolled the remaining blackened hoses onto their respective drums.

"She was very young," Robin mused.

"Yes."

"And according to the files she was the one who opened this particular can of worms."

"She was seventeen, old enough to give birth, old enough to die."

"But she shouldn't have, should she?"

"We couldn't let them kill Fiona."

"And the numbers have to tally."

"Exactly."

"And she would have been dead hereafter," Robin whispered, his voice bordering on the verge of nastiness.

Janet Nemesis glared at him.

"Cynicism does not become you, Robin, however well quoted."

"This job sucks."

"Welcome to my world."

"I thought it would be different, but it's not. It's just numbers played on a board. For heaven's sake, Janet, she was only seventeen!"

"Don't you think I don't know that?" Janet hissed back at him. "This isn't just a game, Robin, this is vengeance, justice and vindication, and unless we can stop the ones at the top, Katya, Katya's brother and all the others will have died for nothing and ..."

"What?"

"They will continue to die."

Robin stood and stared at her. She was right, horribly, logically right.

"So what do we do now?" he asked.

"We go back to our hotel and wait for Neville to arrive. William can continue to watch over Fiona and I may just nip back upstairs and have a quiet word with that snotty little busybody cupid. I got the distinct sniff of that ghastly aftershave he insists on wearing when we were down near Fiona's car."

"So you don't actually need me for a bit?" Robin asked, a part of his mind spinning the possibility of an idea.

"No, why?"

"Thought I might just go for a walk, clear the head, erase a few memories."

Janet gave him a mildly worried look and then shrugged.

"That's fine by me. Don't be too long though."

"No, I won't," Robin replied and then, turning on his heel, he walked quickly off in the direction of the town centre.

In the distance a clock chimed the hour and the distant tangerine glow of another conflagration ebbed and then suddenly ceased. The rich tang of smoke remained for some time afterwards in the ash-clogged air.

Thoughtfully, Robin Henry Bastard walked the length of the promenade with measured strides. He had no faith in Neville Foolscap and he had absolutely no confidence in his being able to successfully commit suicide, in which case he would have to take control and do something himself.

At that point he found himself staring up at the offices of McKenzie, Devine and Finlayson, Advocates and Estate Agents. Robin fumbled briefly in his pocket before finally unearthing a long silver wire that he'd borrowed from a friend in records. He quietly applied the wire to the Yale lock beside the brass plate and gently opened the door. The alarm was silenced with a small plastic gizmo he had also cautiously acquired from the same source and he then, almost cheerfully, added breaking and entering to his own lengthening personal list of crimes.

"And in a few moments I shall add forgery to it as well," he mused aloud. "That is, if I can find the right envelope and something to write with."

chapter four

Mr Hercule McFee stalked into his office and regarded the matronly proportions of his personal secretary, Miss McMillan, with a decided twinkle in his eyes.

"Well, Miss McMillan, it's a nice sunny day," he chortled, rubbing his hands together in delight.

"Aye well, it is that Mr McFee."

"The sort of day that makes scraping the barnacles off the odd bottom, a perfect occupation."

"But what about your ten o'clock, Mr McFee?"

"Can't they come back tomorrow?"

"It's Maggie Muir, Mr McFee, and she has to catch the bus all the way in from Port Appin."

"Oh well, Maggie is it? I'll see her, but I want you to cancel everything else."

"And the post, Mr McFee?"

"Anything from head office?"

"Only a request that the staff cut down on the number of toilet rolls they use."

"Tell them to bring their own."

"But how will they know which one is which, Mr McFee?"

"Aye well, that's a tricky one. Let me see, I'll have the wife buy in some extra quilted whites for me, you can have pink."

"Aye well, that will be nice."

"Martin can have blue, Mary Jane yellow, Sally orange and young Simon can have green."

"But what about Mr Fitzherbert?"

"Ah well now, Miss McMillan, there's a conundrum. Really he ought to have pink, all things considered, but then if I give him that colour he'll say I'm being sexist and pandering to a stereotypical image - it will be the staff party all over again. I still have nightmares over that ghastly confrontation with the restaurant manager."

"Aye, the poor wee girl, I felt that sorry for her."

"And all because of a pink party hat with tassels."

"It was the tassels that did it, especially as young Simon had the Napoleon Bonaparte and you got the pirate hat with a skull and crossbones."

"I've not been back since and I used to enjoy a small snifter after a leisurely round. Still that doesn't solve our current administrative crisis. Ah, got it! Tell him he can have battle grey or purple, on the grounds that, unlike Mr Ford, Kleenex doesn't do black. Now he can't possibly take exception to that, can he? Right then, if there are no more executive decisions to be made I'll just ring for the weather forecast."

"Well there are one or two little things, Mr McFee."

"Oh bother, are there really? Can't you just slide them onto my in tray and say the post was late? At this rate I'm going to miss the tide again."

"No, I can't, Mr McFee."

"Well, go on then."

"Mr Dedbroke wants to increase his overdraft."

"What – again?"

"Yes, Mr McFee, he says that in the current economic crisis he finds that by the end of the month he's living on beans, and apart from that he needs a new gearbox."

"Tell him to sell that wretched car for scrap and take the bus."

"He won't like it."

"He never does. Last month he wanted money for a new exhaust system and the time before that it was to fix a dodgy carburettor. For the amount of money he's had over the past few years, he could have bought a brand new Jaguar and still had some left over for a three-bedroom house."

"But it's a vintage car, Mr McFee, they always go wrong."

"Then tell him to go to a vintage bank. Is there anything else other than begging letters?"

"There are two invitations to lunch. One from a new fish smokery on Seil and the other from Mr Heckett currently employed by Messrs Sprockett, Hittet and Thump, engineers and suppliers of exhaust attachments."

"Have a look in my diary and if it's somewhere decent say yes to both. Except for next Thursday. It's the wife's birthday and I promised her we'd go to some new exhibition down in Glasgow and have lunch afterwards."

"Aye, well now, that'll be nice."

"No it won't. If I know my wife it'll be some semi-illiterate offspring of one of her old schoolfriends and the only way you'll ever make sense of the pathetic daub is to stand on your head or else be as high as the proverbial kite on wacky backy or booze, or possibly both."

"Oh!"

"Right then, is that it?"

"Well yes, except for a note from Mr Neville Foolscap."

"Oh God, what does he want now? Please tell me it's not more money?"

"Well, apart from something to do with frying your liver and having worms – no, sorry – birds pecking out your … I hope it's eyes, he says he's going to turn on the gas and that you'll be sorry."

"Good God. Give me that."

Mr McFee gradually changed colour from white to green to puce as he read the blotched and grimy note, and then picked up the telephone. After punching a few numbers he barked:

"Martin Pendlebury and tell him it's Hercule and it's urgent."

After a matter of mere moments the phone crackled into life.

"Martin, Hercule. I have a note from that idiot Foolscap threatening to commit hara-kiri and fall onto his oven. You're the nearest, so get around there pronto, turn the gas off at the mains and throw a bucket of cold water over him."

There was a burst of angry chittering until Mr McFee lost his temper completely, which made his skin glow an angry shade of rich claret.

"Because when he asked me to lend him money, to pub-lish his own attempt at the Booker, you told me that it was a load of old horse whatsits. Therefore, I told him it was too much of a risk and he'd be better off sticking to doing what he knows best, which is the shipping reports and the obituaries. If this gets into the papers, the ones you *don't* own, it won't just be *my* position in jeopardy – besides which, I would have given him the money ... Why? Because I give it to everyone until they can't afford it and then I take the house ... It's called 'common bank policy'. How else do you think I can possibly run this place, since those tits in Edinburgh introduced free banking? Exactly, now bugger off and sort the silly sod out before he expires. Right then, I'll expect to hear from you later, and ring me on my mobile if you can't get me here because I will leave it on this time. Bye."

The phone was banged back down and Mr McFee stood and quietly stared at Miss McMillan in a ruminative fashion. Miss McMillan stared back and then, with a sigh, handed him the rest of the post.

✻ ✻ ✻

Neville Foolscap opened a bleary eye and looked upwards. An immense head hung over him, lit from behind with a brilliant light. This is it then, he mused, this is Nirvana.

"Can I go back and take my just revenge now?" he asked in quavering accents of abject humility. "Please, your great and overwhelmingly wondrous godliness," he added as an afterthought.

"No you bloody well can't. Get up and clean yourself off man."

Neville blinked. "Why, you sound just like my dear old editor," he exclaimed.

"That's because I am, you silly tit," Martin Pendlebury barked, moving away from the light.

The policeman beside him raised his notebook and thoughtfully licked the end of an HB pencil.

"But I'm dead," Neville pleaded, loath to give up.

"No you're bloody well not."

"But I should be."

"Ruddy lunatics who wish to gas themselves should remember to stick enough money in the meter first before passing out due to an overindulgence of gin."

Martin Pendlebury surveyed the wreckage of Neville Foolscap's kitchen and noisily exhaled. Bottles of various sizes and shapes, and all of them empty, littered every flat and listing surface.

"Did you drink all these?"

"No, not all of them."

Neville sat up and rubbed his head with a shaking hand.

"Where's Gravel?" he asked, realising that the place was uncharacteristically silent.

"Gravel?"

"My mynah bird, he always makes a hell of a row in the mornings."

"I'm not surprised. I'd make a bloody row if I had to live in this tip!" Martin Pendlebury roundly observed before lumbering to the back door and kicking it open.

"Didn't I lock that?" Neville asked.

"No you didn't."

"I could have been robbed!" Neville shrieked.

Martin and the policeman looked at each other sadly.

"How would you possibly be able to tell?" Martin asked, helping Neville to stagger to a standing position.

"Perhaps Gravel just wanted to go for a bit of a walk. You did leave the lounge window open," the policeman stated in carefully neutral tones.

"I didn't want to gas him," Neville explained.

"Right."

Neville rubbed his forehead.

"There was something I had to remember," he muttered. "I had this really vivid dream. Actually it was more like a vision."

The policeman brightened. Attempted suicide was one thing, but attempted suicide *and* drug abuse that was quite another, and it had been a very slow morning.

"I have to go to Edinburgh," Neville said.

"Why?"

"To right a wrong to … Only I have to be dead to do it."

Martin Pendlebury and the policeman exchanged looks and while Martin steered Neville towards the lounge the policeman requested the services of a local doctor and then, as an afterthought, a local cleaner who specialised in as they advertised it, 'grime busting'.

As the policeman put his mobile back in his pocket he sighed a sigh of deep and unmitigated gloom. Visions of the piles of paperwork that Mr Foolscap was going to cause floated in front of him including, he realised with a sense of impending dread, a missing person chit for Gravel the absconding mynah bird.

❋ ❋ ❋

The next morning Fiona awoke and for a moment, as she gazed at the bright yellow wallpaper and ruched curtains, wondered where the hell she was. Slowly, as her eyes settled on her hastily abandoned suitcase and scattered clothing she remembered there had been a fire and a nice police-man with grey eyes, and then another fire. Actually he had really long black lashes too. She was just trying to remember what the rest of him looked like when there was a knock on the door.

"Enter," she croaked.

A friendly pert face framed with soft blonde curls peered at her from around the doorframe.

"I'm Heather," the face announced. "We passed briefly on the staircase last night."

Fiona must have looked a bit blank because Heather then added, "I'm Fergus's sister."

"The nice policeman?"

"That's him."

"Oh, Sergeant McKinnon."

"Actually it's *Detective Inspector*."

Fiona groaned. She'd assumed he was a sergeant and the toad hadn't put her right; no wonder everyone scurried around after him.

"It's all right, he's used to all sorts of titles around here and at least yours was polite," Heather informed her with a friendly grin. "Do you want breakfast?" she added, drawing the curtains.

The light of a bright summer's morning swamped the room and finally settled on a glass vase of yellow roses, placed carefully between a china dog and a squat brass candlestick.

"Yes please." Fiona smiled back at her as she stuck a tentative pyjama-clad leg onto the thickly carpeted floor.

"No, no, you stay there; you must still be exhausted after last night. I'll bring it up and then when you've finished you can have a nice bath and get dressed. You'll need to be bright-eyed and bushy-tailed for later."

"Oh, why?" Fiona asked, wrinkling her nose.

"Because Fergus wants a word with you about the statement you made last night and when my brother wants a word, it's as well to be fully alert and firing on all cylinders."

A little while later Heather returned bearing a large tray on which sat a plate brimming with the complete ingredients of a cholesterol addict's wet dream, a glass of orange juice and a small plate of buttered toast.

"Tea or coffee?" Heather asked, carefully placing the tray on Fiona's lap.

"Oh, coffee please. This looks really good," Fiona added, picking up her knife and fork with gusto.

"Well, tuck in before it gets cold and eat it all as I have a feeling that today may be a long one," Heather observed with a departing smile.

Fiona was just finishing off the last slice of sausage and golden egg yolk, when the door burst open and Fergus McKinnon entered bearing a tray containing a cafetiere of coffee and two cups. Heather was still berating him from the corridor as he bounced in, grinning.

"Will you no leave the poor thing to have her breakfast in peace, Fergus?" Heather shouted.

"I need to ask her a few questions and I need to do it *now*," he bellowed back.

The door closed with a snap and after unceremoniously dumping the tray on the windowsill and drawing a wicker chair up to it, Fergus McKinnon sat and proceeded to pour out two cups of aromatic dark coffee.

"How do you like it?" he asked, waving the cafetiere around.

"Milk and one sugar," Fiona replied, pushing the empty plate to one side.

"Good, was it?" Fergus asked, a little enviously.

"Haven't you eaten?"

"I grabbed a bacon bap earlier this morning," he rumbled, hungrily eyeing the toast and the accompanying pot of marmalade.

"Here, you had better have the rest then," Fiona advised, pushing the tray towards him.

"Thanks," he replied with a brief smile, as he passed her a brimming cup.

"OK, so what do you want to talk to me about?" Fiona asked, taking a sip. There was a short silence. "Come on, it can't be that bad."

"We found a body under what was left of the staircase at the Mellrose, or rather the firemen did."

Fiona sat in a stunned heap. A body. Someone had died in her guest house.

"I didn't do it!" Fiona squeaked, her mouth suddenly and unaccountably dry.

"They all say that."

Fergus grinned, only this time he accompanied the smile with a Roger Moore tweak of the eyebrows and she could have sworn that he'd done an almost perfect impersonation of Sean Connery.

"Stop that."

"Made you laugh though."

"But …"

"We've checked your story and at about the time that you were tucking into baked beans someone was starting a fire and either getting themselves killed in the process, or killing someone who had either disturbed them, or was helping and had outlived his or her usefulness."

"Oh!"

"Unless of course you can teleport or have an invisible Harrier Jump Jet?"

"Not yet, but I'm seriously considering learning how to teleport in the not too distant future."

"If you succeed let me know as I have a feeling that it might come in useful especially with this particular case. Anyway, the staff at the Little Chef remembered you. A day when you run out of chips is fairly unforgettable."

"I was late, got stuck behind a caravan and then just as I got into Crianlarich a lorry had jackknifed and hit a coach coming out of a car park on the corner near the railway bridge and …"

Fiona knew she was babbling.

"You would have arrived at the Mellrose before the fire had started if it hadn't have been for that?"

"Yes."

"We won't know for certain yet, but I wonder if the body we found was someone who was mistaken for you?"

"Me! But why would anyone want to kill *me*?"

"Why would anyone want to drown your uncle, torch your guesthouse and barbecue your office? To say nothing of crushing in the skull of your uncle's partner, Vernon Flint, with what we believe to be something not unlike the end of a rounders bat."

"Or a priest, a small implement used for delivering the last rights to floundering fish."

"Good grief, girl, you may be right."

"Uncle Quentin always had a couple on the boat just in case he ever caught anything bigger than a minnow."

"I'll get on to the diving team."

"How did –"

"Quentin die?"

"Yes."

"He drowned, but we believe that he was knocked unconscious first as there was a bruise on the back of his head, behind the left ear."

"It was quick then?"

"I doubt that either of them felt a thing or had much time to think about it if they did, although I could be wrong."

"A professional job?"

"At a rough guess, yes. Somebody brought up from Glasgow or Edinburgh, although my colleagues in Aberdeen tell me that they have a couple of colourful characters based in their area."

"Oh! So much for a quiet life in the highlands and islands."

"I blame too much television."

"Trust that Homer Simpson to start something." Fiona stared blankly at the wall. "So what do I do now?"

"Well, I suggest that you get dressed and we go and see old Finlayson and ask him."

"Right, yes, of course, he might know something."

Fiona was given a thoughtful look and then, after stretching tired limbs, Fergus levered his bulk out of the chair, stuffed the last slice of toast into his mouth and quietly left. A few seconds later Bill appeared sitting in the vacated item of furniture with a big evil grin on his face.

"This is great. I've been dead 270-odd years and there's still arson, murder and breaking into other people's property. I love this country."

"Didn't you hear him? That charred cadaver could have been me!"

"What?" Bill scoffed. "With me around to protect you."

"Protect?" Fiona gaped at him.

"Yes, lass, who do you think pushed you out of the doorway before the fireball hit?"

"Oh!"

"You are my ticket home, the means of finding my family if I can and of atoning for past misdeeds, and I'm not letting anyone hurt a hair of your shiny little head. Of course I may not be able to save you from a broken heart."

"Sorry?"

"The copper. PC plod, rozzer, bluebottle, peeler, flatfoot, pig …!"

"Fergus."

"Ah, first name terms already. I'm impressed."

"Don't be. Anyway, he wouldn't be interested."

"Oh?"

"Look at me – I'm a thirty-something, not exactly slim, almost destitute, former bank clerk."

"You have nice eyes and the sort of curves that keep a man warm on a cold night. As far as I'm concerned that makes you more than attractive," Bill assured her before adding, "Can you cook?"

"A bit. Anyway, he may be married."

"He *was*, divorced three years ago and nobody serious since or at least no one that lasted more than a week or two."

"How on earth do you know that?"

"I'm terminally nosy and in case you haven't noticed, completely invisible to the ordinary person."

"Oh."

"Anyway a man doesn't go out of his way to bring a girl coffee the way he did, if he's not interested."

"He just wanted to ask me a few questions."

"Somebody else could have done it, some underling. He's the boss around here you know."

"No, I didn't know," Fiona retaliated sarcastically.

"Aye, well now you do, so make a bit of an effort with the

brush and comb, and who knows?"

Bill the matchmaker chortled happily and turned in his chair to stare out of the window.

"You know this place is very, very pretty, all this sun and sea and stuff. I mean it's not the same as Edinburgh of course, but it's not bad, not bad at all."

"I suppose I could do a lot worse."

"Aye, you could. He's got a sense of humour, always useful when the passion of lust runs slow."

"Bill."

"Yes?"

"Shut up!"

❋ ❋ ❋

Mr Duncan Finlayson, advocate and notary public, was a tall, sparse man with the Duke of Wellington's nose and a florid taste in bow ties. Gold-rimmed spectacles caught the sunlight, which had managed to filter through the starched nets marching around the bow window framing his office, and spun shafts of light on to the papers he was studiously reading.

"Burnt down, you say?" he asked, pursing his paper thin lips together in obvious disapproval, before sitting back and steepling long thin fingers.

"Yes," Fergus replied.

"Arson?"

"Not proven, but I'd say it would be a fair bet."

"Ah."

Fiona and Fergus waited in silence as Mr Finlayson sorted out whichever knotty problem had managed to gain his full attention. After a few minutes he sighed and reaching for the phone barked a command into it and then, after replacing the receiver, sat back with a look of sad expectancy on his face.

They waited. Cars shuffled up and down the main road below them, interspersed with the odd articulated lorry and loudly grinding bus. Somebody shouted at somebody else in what sounded suspiciously like Italian and the door opened. A perspiring middle-aged lady with an immense, purple tweed-clad bosom deposited a small blue envelope on Mr Finlayson's desk and then withdrew, muttering something about biscuits.

"Well, here it is then; the envelope," Mr Finlayson stated, weighing it in his hand as if reluctant to hand it over.

"Envelope?" Fergus asked, giving Fiona a questioning glance.

Fiona shrugged despondently. She was still reeling from the news that the guesthouse may not have been fully insured and that the office most definitely wasn't.

"Mr Rowse, your late uncle, left an envelope that was to be given to his niece, Fiona Christiana Harris, only if three separate conditions had been met."

"Conditions?" Fiona asked.

"The first was that Mr Rowse was dead and that his body had been found, clearly identified and buried."

"Bit morbid, wasn't it?"

"Quite. The second was that either or both of Mr Rowse's properties had become uninhabitable for some reason, and the third ..." Mr Finlayson leaned forward and jabbed a bony finger in Fergus's direction. "The third was that for whatever reason the local police had become involved."

Fergus and Fiona exchanged the look of the sane suddenly finding themselves in a lunatic asylum by accident.

"I am currently following up certain enquiries, yes," Fergus agreed with a marked degree of frostiness.

"And these enquiries will ensure that Miss Fiona will be ... er ... protected in some way?" Mr Finlayson continued, his gaze becoming almost steely.

"I will be ensuring that she is looked after, yes."

"I have your word on that?"

"Aye, you have."

"Good. Miss Fiona, your envelope. I have no idea what it contains, but your uncle was most insistent that you should have it in the event of ..."

"The conditions having been met," Fiona replied, taking the envelope and with fingers that were only slightly trembling, ripped it open.

Inside lay a small silver key and a postage-sized slip of paper with the words, 'COLD HOUSE' written on it in bright red block capitals. Fiona shuddered. There was something oddly menacing about those two ordinary words, but for the life of her, she couldn't think what.

Fergus reached over and read the slip of paper with a frown and then carefully inspected the key.

"Safety deposit box?" he enquired, after looking at it for some time.

"I have no idea," Mr Finlayson stated. "I only wish I did."

They sat in contemplative silence. A horn blared below them and the smell of malted barley drifted in through the open window.

"Ah." Mr Finlayson sighed and almost smiled as he reached down into a drawer and produced a small bottle of gold-coloured liquid. "How about a coffee and a small libation?"

"I came off duty three minutes ago," Fergus stated, looking at his watch. "So why not?"

"Well, Fiona, will you have a wee drop of the angels' breath produced by our very own distillery?"

So that had been the odd smell she had kept inhaling; there was a distillery nearby.

The coffee arrived a few seconds later in delicate white porcelain cups, and after the secretary had withdrawn was liberally laced with Oban whisky. After the first cup, Fiona felt a bit more relaxed and after the second more than a little hungry. In the meantime, Fergus and Mr Finlayson had discussed the local football teams, the rising cost of petrol and the alarming lack of copulating shellfish, which they vociferously blamed on a local salmon farm and a cash-strapped government. Fergus, finally catching Fiona's eye as she finished her second cup, smiled briefly at her and then stood up. After expressing their genuine thanks for his help Fergus and Fiona left a gently beaming Mr Finlayson to his deeds and covenants, and headed off to find something to eat.

Lunch was slow and surprisingly, considering the circumstances, convivial. Fiona later remembered having eaten something that was very definitely of the finned variety and there may have been chips and a salad too. Afterwards they drifted off towards the smell and sound of the sea, and watched the ferries chugging in and out of the harbour, surrounded by small yachts and blue-blotched fishing vessels.

They must have sat watching the glinting water for some time before either of them spoke.

"I have a key," Fiona stated.

"I know."

"It's a nice colour for a key."

"Aye."

"Why me?"

"Hard to know. Sometimes it just happens."

"Stuff happens. I had a T-shirt once with 'stuff happens' on it."

"That's nice."

"It also had a picture of a large cowpat."

"Oh!"

"On the back."

"Nice."

"I thought so."

A figure sitting on the bench beside them snorted in barely controlled mirth.

"Why don't you two drunks go home and stick your heads under the shower?" Bill enquired, shaking his head in jovial disbelief. "Either that or go to bed."

"Bill!"

"What did you say?" Fergus asked. "Who's Bill?"

"Bill – I forgot the bill," Fiona quavered.

"Oh, don't worry about that, I paid."

Fergus grinned at her, before patting her on the shoulder and standing up.

"Come on, let's walk back to Heather's before I'm tempted to behave inappropriately."

"Inappropriately?" Fiona stammered.

"Aye, and that would never do," he answered, helping her to stand.

"I don't see why not," Bill hissed in an undertone. "The poor lad's paid more than enough to get you in the mood."

Fiona giggled, and linking arms with Fergus, walked unsteadily back to Heather's guesthouse where she promptly collapsed in a bedraggled but happy heap on her own newly made up single bed. Fergus, after briefly kissing her on the top of her head, departed for the warm and welcoming arms of the large old-fashioned settee in the lounge.

Bill sat in the chair next to the open window and sniffed with heavy disapproval.

"That was a complete waste of decent grog if you ask me," he barked.

"Bill?"

"Yes."

"Go away."

"And where would you suggest I went, oh pickled one?"

"Anywhere – I know, go and find Cold House, wherever that, is and the door or whatever that fits the silver key in the blue envelope in my pocket – and Bill?"

"What?"

"Do it ever so quietly, I think that brain tumour of mine is coming back."

chapter five

The moonlight scampered across the water like a school-boy on 'e' numbers, as the happy sound of drunken Scots wafted up from the harbour. Fiona's head felt as if a team of Morris dancers were practising 'Stripping the Willow' inside her skull and she groaned loudly.

"This brain tumour of yours, is it feeling any better?" a voice asked.

She opened her eyes to find Bill leaning over her. His voice had sounded sympathetic, disproved by eyes that were twinkling with malicious intent.

"I know that this is a novel idea," he added, sitting on the end of her bed and crushing her feet. "But have you ever thought of giving booze the elbow? I mean it doesn't appear to make you feel any better, you passed up a golden opportunity of waking up beside the hunk of your dreams and you look like death on holiday."

"Death has holidays?"

"Sometimes, but doesn't like them much."

"Why?"

"Nothing to do or so he says. Mind you, the old bastard's a complete workaholic, he even makes lists of the lists he's made and they go back to the year dot."

"So death is actually of the male gender?"

"Sort of, I guess."

"Sort of?"

"Well, he's whatever you want him to be."

"Right."

Fiona was wondering where the hell the rather surreal conversation was going, and if indeed Bill was in any way serious, when there was a soft tap on the door. She groaned even louder and pulled the covers over her head. She then wondered briefly how she'd managed to get into bed in the first place, but decided that in her current befuddled state she really didn't want to know.

The door opened slowly and Heather tiptoed in and stood in the doorway looking at her.

"Do you want anything?" she asked. "Tea, coffee, raw egg in some noxious liquid?"

"No, nothing," Fiona replied from the depths of the duvet.

"That must have been some lunch you two had. I've never seen Fergus so relaxed."

"Relaxed?" Fiona queried, risking a squint over the coverlet.

"Aye. He came in sat on the sofa and then very gently slid onto the floor in an untidy heap. He's been there ever since. I'm surprised you can't hear the snoring from up here."

"He snores, hah!" Bill crowed from the comfort of the window-seat.

"Anyway, I thought I'd leave him be. He's been working

almost non-stop since old Quentin drowned. Drowned, I'll believe *that* when it's proved."

Fiona sat up and focused.

"Do you mean Quentin Rowse?"

"Aye."

"My uncle?"

"Well, unless there were two Quentins both living at Mellrose Villa and both happily gay as the proverbial Gordon ..."

"Gay? What? I'd hit her! She's just inferred that your uncle was a shirt-lifter!"

Shocked to the core, Bill stood up, clenching his fists.

That's all I need on top of everything else, Fiona thought. Of all the ghosts in all the world, I get lumbered with one that's 300 years old and homophobic to boot.

"Why don't you think he drowned?" Fiona asked, ignoring Bill who was going the ectoplasmic equivalent of puce.

"Well," Heather muttered conspiratorially "wouldn't you like to know?" Then she got up and with a cheery wink left the room.

Suddenly sobered, or at least enough to make walking upright and forwards a viable option, Fiona staggered to the shower. After a long, hot wash and an extensive gargle and toothbrushing exercise, she emerged dripping wet, but feeling much better. She then dressed very carefully so as not to move her head too much, in a pair of her oldest most comfortable jeans and her baggiest Shetland jumper, completely oblivious to Bill who was sitting on the bed with his mouth open and his eyes standing out on stalks. Underwear had changed an awful lot from his day, firstly it was coloured and secondly there seemed to be very little of it.

Fiona, finally feeling that she could face the world or at the very least Fergus's sister, left the newly cluttered confines of her room and slowly made her way downstairs.

She found Heather sitting at a large scrubbed pine table reading the local paper and drinking tea. Heather looked up as Fiona entered, as did a large chocolate and cream tabby stretched out at the base of a dark green Rayburn. The tabby stretched and yawned extending long, steel-hooked claws and treated Bill, who had been following in Fiona's wake, to the sight of a large pink mouth full to the brim with pointed yellow teeth.

"Would you like a cup?" Heather asked, looking up.

"Er, yes please," Fiona replied, still staring at the cat, which was now eyeing up Mr Boots with large luminous orange eyes.

"Oh, don't mind our Mr Tibbs, he's just an old softy really." Heather grinned at her before placing another mug on the table.

"Er, nice pussy," Fiona muttered, edging past.

Mr Tibbs hissed at her as she pulled up a chair, and then stalked towards Bill, tail held high, the end flicking quickly from side to side. Bill stood his ground as the feline equivalent of Vinnie Jones glared straight at him.

"Now what's up with that animal?" Heather asked. "Tibbs, go back to sleep or it's a night out on the tiles for you!"

"And my boot up your backside as ye go," Mr Boots whispered, bending down and scratching the cat behind its ears.

Mr Tibbs closed his eyes and, purring like an old London bus, rubbed a sleek furry head up and down the side of Mr Boots' legs.

Luckily, Heather was searching in the cupboards alongside the fridge while all this was going on and so missed the sight of a semi-levitated cat having its neck massaged.

When she eventually deposited the tin of shortbread she'd been looking for on the table, Mr Boots was sitting on the floor beside the Rayburn with Mr Tibbs kneading his lap.

"So," Fiona said, risking the tea and breaking the silence. "What did you mean earlier about my uncle?"

"What? Oh, yes that. Well the truth is, I never really knew him that well; we'd meet at dinners and such and sometimes at meetings of the local hoteliers' association and he and Vernon were always very pleasant, but there was one thing Quentin never did."

"And what was that?"

"He never took risks. I mean he was one of the most naturally cautious people I've ever met, well except when it came to food and very odd colour combinations."

"Lime and pink."

"With a hint of magenta!"

"Oh dear, yes I remember, and that was just the fairy cakes!"

"He produced a green pudding once for a community supper. It looked very, very, strange, but turned out to be a kiwi and ginger roulade and it tasted divine."

"He made me a great cake for my seventeenth birthday; it was black and had a disembodied hand clutching a red candle on the top. I thought it was absolutely brilliant, but Mum had a fit."

"I expect Vernon made the hand, he was so good at that sort of thing."

Fiona was about to wax lyrical about the culinary

triumphs of her uncle and his friend when she received a hard kick in the shins and a hissed reminder to get on with it.

"Um, why did you think the drowning was odd then?"

"Well, for a start it wasn't that good weatherwise and Quentin never went out if there was a possibility of wind anything over a force three. I remember old Carruthers asking him where he'd be if the wind got up to a four and Quentin said 'In the pub'."

"Fair comment."

"I thought so. The other thing was they were found without their lifejackets and they always wore them. Vernon couldn't swim and was terrified of water. I swear that I saw him walking alongside the harbour in one once even though the tide was out."

"Anything else?"

"They were drunk, or so the autopsy said."

"*Drunk!*"

"I know, I know, we all thought it was odd, but the coroner couldn't find any other reason for the boat to sink as it was nae damaged when they brought it up."

"I remember now; the coroner said that they'd obviously had a bit too much, had gone out in the boat that had been swamped by a large wave and had then unfortunately drowned - death by misadventure."

"Fergus reckoned that it should have been an open verdict. It was all very difficult, there were no witnesses or anything and that in itself was odd."

"Why?"

"Have you never seen your uncle getting into a boat?"

"No."

"Well, he always went from outside 'The Wide Mouthed Frog' and people would book tables just to watch. It was

like something out of 'Will and Grace' with the more farci-
cal elements of 'Dad's Army' and 'The Navy Lark'."

"Oh dear."

"Exactly."

"And nobody saw them get into their boat and nobody
saw them out in the loch, they just found the bodies early
one Sunday morning tangled up in the oyster nets."

"Oyster nets?"

"There's an oyster farm up at the end of Loch Etive,
they grow the oysters and mussels on long ropes and bas-
kets."

"Oh."

"Before that no one had realised they'd even gone out in
the boat. The car was still in the garage and the only thing
missing was a picnic hamper and a pushbike."

"Just one bike?"

"Aye."

"Odd."

"Very."

"I can see why Fergus didn't like it."

"There was something else, but no one would talk about
it, even the coroner was uneasy."

"So they just waited to see what would happen next."

"Two fires and another body."

"So what will happen now?"

"I expect it will all get opened up like the proverbial can
of worms."

They sat in a contemplative silence.

"Heather?"

"Umm."

"Are you? I mean does anybody else live here apart from
Fergus?"

"What? Oh no, Fergus has his own place out at Connell Bridge. He just likes to keep me company sometimes when David is away with the children."

"David?"

"My husband, he works at the marine biological station down at Dunstffnage."

"How many children do you have?"

"Two: Kate, she's nearly thirteen and Alex, he's ten. Do you have any?"

"Never met anyone I fancied having kids with, well, apart from Tony."

"Tony?"

"He told me he had a low well, you know, and couldn't have children."

"Oh."

"He'd actually had four, a vasectomy and a wife in Yorkshire."

"What did you do?"

"I came here. Actually it's the reason – well, one of them – that I ditched the job at the bank, sold the flat, packed the car and accepted my uncle's bequest."

"Would you have come up if this Tony had been legit?"

"Probably not. I mean it was really one of those quick decisions."

"So you would have got Mr Finlayson to settle the estate and never seen the Mellrose at all?"

"Or that grotty little office."

"Fate, that's what it is."

"Bugger fate, this is feeling more and more like the greasy cold hand of that little shite, Nemesis," Bill barked at her, standing up and dislodging the cat, which spat malevolently.

"Nemesis?" she queried, staring blankly at him, unaware

of Heather's puzzled frown.

"Always poking her bony little fingers into somebody else's pie and then leaving everybody else to sort it out. Typical bloody woman."

"You mean?"

"We didn't meet by accident and you losing that two-timing bastard of a boyfriend was probably part of the plan."

"But Nemesis is some defunct Greek goddess?"

"A means of deserved and unavoidable punishment or downfall from the Greek retribution," Fergus stated from the doorway, which he was propping up with his not in-substantial bulk.

"Fiona love, who exactly are you talking to?" Heather asked, her face a study in nervousness.

"Er ..."

"I'd like to know that too," Fergus added, staring at her and then at the Rayburn.

"The cat."

"The cat!" Heather and Fergus scoffed.

Mr Tibbs, who was standing on one of Bill's feet and purring slavishly, turned and looked at them all, which was not a good idea as it meant that he could clearly be seen standing at least a couple of inches above the ground.

"Heather, I think your cat is levitating," observed Fergus.

"How did you do that?" Heather asked.

"Um ..."

Fiona stared helplessly at Bill who shrugged, and picking Mr Tibbs up walked with him to the back door and pushed him bodily through the plastic cat flap. There was a sharp silence broken by Fergus walking to the sink with the kettle and filling it up.

"So when were you going to tell us?" he asked in a

friendly fashion.

"Tell you what?"

"That ..." he stopped, leaving her to fill in the blanks.

Bill nodded at her and muttered, "So tell him the truth. It can't be any worse than what he and his sister are thinking."

"I can see ghosts," Fiona whispered, sitting back down at the table.

"And which ghost are you seeing now?" Fergus asked in a frighteningly reasonable tone, the tone he in all likelihood used to criminal lunatics just before the little men in white coats turned up to take them away.

"William ... but I call him Bill, Bill Boots."

"And where does this Mr Boots come from?"

"The South Bridge in Edinburgh, well, sort of under Edinburgh really," Fiona added.

"Mr Boots, not that Mr Boots, the one on 'Fabulously Frightened'?" Heather asked excitedly.

"Actually it was 'Totally Terrified', but really he didn't do what they said he did," Fiona hastily added whilst warily keeping an eye on Bill who had picked up a plate and was just waiting, she suspected, for any excuse to hurl it at something.

"I don't expect he did," Heather agreed, getting out some more mugs.

The plate was deposited back down on the kitchen units and Fergus refilled the teapot and took a fresh carton of milk from the fridge.

"This friend of yours wouldn't be the reason that we survived the explosion at Vernon Rowse's office?" Fergus asked.

"Um, yes," Fiona admitted, closing her eyes and mentally

crossing all ten fingers.

"Well, in that case he may be verra useful, verra useful indeed," Fergus remarked, rubbing his hands together in the time-honoured tradition of theatrical Fagins everywhere.

✳ ✳ ✳

Neville Foolscap tightened the rope around his middle and prayed that it would be quick. The cement block at his feet stared blankly and he was inclined to believe, somewhat smugly, up at him. Neville gave it a brief kick and then wished he hadn't.

Mr Burke, who was sitting in his darkened car under a tree, watched Neville's progress towards the sea wall with interest.

Neville pulled and pushed the great lump of concrete towards the edge and then, taking a deep breath, rolled it off the end where it fell with an almighty splash into the water quickly followed by Neville, who had temporarily forgotten that he was still attached to it.

Mr Burke, who had indeed been hopeful that this was what Neville was going to do, left the safe confines of his car and sauntered towards the shore.

Neville thrashed wildly as the waves swept over him. It was very cold, very salty and his eyes stung. He also realised, as another crest of water approached carrying on its back the entire ingredients of an obscure Japanese soup he'd once eaten in Bournemouth, that he wasn't drowning. He was, he admitted, chilled to the marrow, but unfortunately he wasn't dead.

"Do you need any assistance?" enquired a disembodied

voice from above him.

"No, I bloody well don't," Neville replied.

"Are you sure?"

"Yes, I am."

Neville turned his head towards the speaker and saw a black-clad shape sitting on the edge of the sea wall from which a few minutes before he had thrown himself.

"Are you Death?" he asked, in an effort to make conversation.

"For some people," Mr Burke replied, carefully lighting a cigarette.

"Oh! The thing is if you've come for me couldn't you just speed things up a bit? Only it's cold and my feet are going numb."

"Do you have any money?" Mr Burke asked hopefully, fondling the small economy sized cosh he always kept in his jacket.

"I'm afraid not," Neville said, and sadly shook his head.

"Well, I'm sorry too. Truly I am." Mr Burke took a long hard drag of nicotine and blew a perfect smoke ring into the night sky. "Your problem, as I see it, is that you have tried to throw yourself into the depths of the briny deep and the tide is actually going out."

"I fear that you may be right," Neville muttered.

The water was now up to his shoulders and, although the ebb tide was trying to drag him out to sea, the concrete block to which he was attached steadfastly refused to allow it.

"Is this the first time that you have tried to end it all?" Mr Burke asked conversationally.

"Well, no."

"Ah."

"I did try to gas myself first."

"And?"

"I forgot to put enough money in the meter."

"I see."

"It was all a bit embarrassing, what with my editor about to give me the kiss of life and that policeman trying not to giggle. Under normal circumstances I might have enjoyed it, but Martin! He makes a sumo wrestler look emaciated."

"Never mind, perhaps it will be third time lucky."

"I don't suppose you have any tips, being as it were, in the trade?"

"Pills and booze?"

"Tried that once; couldn't get the quota of pills to booze right and threw up all over the next door neighbour's cat. I think it was just after I saw a six foot seven, bright blue rabbit walk through the wall with a wad of timesheets."

"You could walk in front of a bus?"

"Messy – that's always provided that you can find one in the first place."

"Are you sure you don't have any money? I could arrange something short and painless."

"I spent my last fiver on the rope."

"Pity."

Neville, finally managing to undo the knot that bound him to his oddly shaped and weighted lifesaver, turned his face away from the receding water and trudged disconsolately back towards the sea wall and the road. Gravel was still missing and he had nowhere to go, having posted the key to his flat back to his landlady the previous afternoon.

Mr Burke watched him approach and thoughtfully extracted a miniature bottle of brandy from one of the pockets imaginatively hidden with many others in the seams of his suit.

Neville eventually stood on the sea wall and gently dripped. There was now nobody else there, however, some-one had carefully placed a half-smoked packet of cigarettes, a plastic lighter and a small bottle of brandy on the ground. There was also a handwritten note that said in perfect black gothic script:

Better luck next time.

chapter six

Fergus, Fiona and Heather sat huddled up in the kitchen with yet more steaming mugs in front of them and Fiona's almost new laptop switched on, booted up and ready to surf the virtual waves. All that they were waiting for was someone at the help desk to sort out one teeny-weeny technical difficulty and call them back.

"This could be a long night."

Fergus yawned, cradling the telephone receiver in his hands.

"Well, at least that last one spoke English," Heather observed, soothingly.

"You call that English?" Bill snorted from the cat's basket.

Fiona studiously ignored him and poured herself another shot of coffee. The phone rang and Fergus answered it, motioning them all to be quiet and carefully tapping various instructions into Fiona's computer. Finally, after a certain amount of discussion with the disembodied and, according to him, shortly to be disembowelled person on the other end of the line, he disconnected and gave them the thumbs up.

"We are ready to rock and roll," he quipped, sounding not unlike a slightly thinner Robbie Coltrane. Fiona raised a quizzical eyebrow and Heather shook her head in mock sorrow.

"Is there no end to this man's talents?" Fiona asked of the room in general.

"He also does Elvis impersonations for charity," Heather informed her in sepulchral tones.

"Does he raise much?" Fiona asked. "Apart from laughs?"

"Oh yes, loads."

"Now that does surprise me," Fiona scoffed.

"They pay him to stop," Heather added, grinning broadly.

"Will you two stop with your wittering and pay attention?" Fergus barked, glaring at them. "Now what was the clue you found?"

"Cold House," Fiona answered.

They waited while Fergus punched in the words and switched the printer on.

Eventually he sat in front of the screen, frowning.

"Well?" Heather and Fiona asked in unison.

"Not much, but I'll print it all out anyway, see what you make of it."

Paper shuffled up through the printer and as it lolled out of the machine they took a copy each and inwardly digested the contents.

"Anybody want to go on a three-day course to learn how to build and maintain interactive web applications, using a web database connectivity tool?" Heather asked.

"Do what?" Fiona replied.

"Sounds bloody rude to me," Bill remarked, reading over Heather's shoulder.

"Only cost you £411.25 for the three days," she added, looking up and shivering.

"Sorry, *my* mistake, it's outright larceny," Bill growled.

"Shut up," Fiona hissed at him.

"What did you say?"

"Nothing, and will you stop looking down her blouse?"

Bill cast Fiona a look of pure malice and moved back to stroke the cat. Heather stared thoughtfully at Mr Tibbs, who was now purring in deep and abject contentment as bony hands expertly found old flea bites he'd forgotten about.

"Remind me to wear a polo neck Shetland tomorrow, a big baggy one," Heather grumbled, picking up another sheet of paper.

"Will you two please concentrate. I have lowly constables with higher boredom thresholds," Fergus complained.

"It was … Never mind, we won't do it again." Fiona glared pointedly at Bill before adding, "I have a feeling that Heather's course in earth-shattering knowledge wasn't the clue and neither is this review for Hood's new album – unless Uncle Quentin was into some seriously weird stuff. Listen to this … Vocals from depressed students, mournful strings and sombre, subtle guitar lines, and then it goes on about embracing the rap culture and electronica."

"Wow."

"Sounds like that ponce, Vivaldi," Bill grumbled.

"I've got one on sheds and coldframes," Fergus stated. "Hey, Heather, didn't you say you wanted a hot tub? They do them as well and log cabins, but who the hell would want a Finnish log cabin?"

"The Scottish tourist board?" Fiona quipped, as she dreamily remembered one memorable student holiday and grinned lasciviously.

"I really, really don't want to know," Bill whispered in her ear and then added, "but Lancelot there might."

Fiona stopped smiling and picked up the last few sheets of A4 paper.

"Erm, Fergus, did you really want to vote Ulster Unionist?" she asked.

"What!"

"Well the voting box is outlined and it says, 'Thank you for voting Billy Armstrong'. In really big letters."

"Oops." Fergus winced. "Hang on a minute, what on earth has this to do with 'Cold House'?" Fergus went back to the screen, tapped in some more letters and sat back, a thoughtful look on his face. "Yep, he's actually under a cold house, something to do with the state of the Ulster Unionists' Charter."

"I can't see *that* having anything to do with Uncle Quentin's death though. Which makes me beg the question, what exactly are we looking for?"

"I suppose it's a bit like finding a new outfit," Heather replied. "You'll know it when you see it."

"I just buy it if it fits," Fiona growled, eyeing Heather's slim form with a certain amount of envy, especially as Heather was now on her fourth chocolate digestive.

"I'll do a check on this one anyway and see if he has any connections to this area – after all, you never know," Fergus rumbled, and carefully folding the pages, stuffed them into his pocket.

"Cold House, Cold House, why on earth is the name so familiar?" Bill muttered to himself.

"It will probably come if you don't think about it," Fiona advised, reaching across the table for a biscuit.

"Want to say that again and in context, as I'm going to have to wash my mind out with soap otherwise?" Fergus muttered.

"And me," Heather added.

"You two are so sad and twisted. Bill thinks he may remember something that happened, or is, or was, connected to our mystery words. Only he's temporarily mislaid the information, which by the way appears to be somewhat typical."

"Charming."

"Well, Fiona, when he remembers give me a call, only I'm going out for a walk to clear the cobwebs." Fergus yawned, stretching both legs in front of him and exposing a whole plethora of teeth and tonsils. "Coming?" he asked her.

"All right, Heather?"

"No thanks, I had enough exercise today getting the husband and children ready to go to Grandma's in the wee small hours of this morning. All I'm going to do now is to go upstairs and have a long, hot aromatic bath and then you two can rustle me up a nice supper of bacon and eggs."

Bill stood up and was about to follow Heather when Fiona beckoned him to her side with a well-aimed glare and an imperious raised finger.

"Don't even think about it," she hissed.

"Spoilsport," he grumbled, and went back to sitting in the cat's basket with Mr Tibbs who had returned from his early evening constitutional with fresh blood on his claws and a new nick on his right ear.

Fergus exchanged a blank look with his sister before staring down at the corner where the now squashed cat basket was situated.

"What did he say?" Fergus asked.

"Nothing much," Fiona replied.

"Now, listen you," Heather stated, staring at the same spot. "If I feel so much as a cold dribble that doesn't come out of the tap, I'm calling in the vicar and don't think that I won't."

Bill stared up at her, admiration written large upon his creased features.

"Now that's a superb specimen of Scottish womanhood – or rather," he added, running his tongue around his lips, "two superb specimens."

"Bill," Fiona hissed, holding out a small silver object that suddenly caught the full glare of the overhead light and gleamed. "What would happen if this went in there?" She nodded towards the Rayburn.

"Nothing much, it's oil-fired," he growled back at her. "But I get the point."

"Good."

Heather looked from Fiona to the silver lump in her hand and back to the cat's basket.

"So that's settled, is it?" she asked.

"Yes," Fiona replied, at the same time as Bill muttered an answering 'Aye'.

Fergus and Fiona grabbed their coats from the coat rack tacked to the back of the kitchen door and departed for the fresher air beyond. However, just as the door closed behind them Fiona could still distinctly hear the sepulchral tones of Mr Boots discussing her complete lack of understanding with a loudly purring Mr Tibbs.

"Perhaps it's an anagram?" Fergus mused, as they ambled along the promenade towards the ferry terminal.

"Possibly."

Fiona dug her hands further into the warm, fluff-lined pockets of her coat and thought about it.

"Cold House, Cool Shed?"

"You missed out the 'u'. How about 'loose chud'?" Fergus mused.

"What's a chud?" she asked.

"A chud is a small cylindrical device for measuring large-bellied river fish."

"You're having me on, aren't you?" she asked, a little uncertainly.

"Afraid so," Fergus replied, grinning down at her.

He had a really nice grin, a bit lopsided, but cute none-theless. 'Stop it, kid,' Fiona whispered to her newly awak-ened libido. 'The guy's a cop. OK, so he's a cute cop, but the bottom line is that he's a member of the establishment, a dyed-in-the-wool fascist and ...' Her subconscious sniggered back derisively and went back to watching the shadows that his long black eyelashes threw against the tanned skin of his rather handsome cheekbones.

"Perhaps it's another word for the same thing?" Fiona mused, leaning upon the railings that stopped the general populace from falling into the harbour. The tide was ebb-ing gently into the inky black murkiness of the night, mak-ing a gentle slurping sound as it hit the harbour wall below. Somewhere in the distance seabirds called rude and possi-bly derogatory things to each other, the overriding syllables being 'pee', 'wee' and 'it'.

"Cold House – another word for cold?"

He was still playing word games, so much for romance.

"Brr," she quipped.

"I don't think that anyone would kill someone else just because they said 'Brr'." Fergus shook his head in mock sorrow and returned to the inner thesaurus of his brain.

"Cold as …" he prompted hopefully.

"Ice."

"Ice House," they both said in unison.

"Come on, Watson," Fergus called, turning swiftly on his heel and heading back in the direction from which they had come. "Let's get back to the Net and see if they have anything on Ice House or Ice Houses."

Fiona watched as the new Sherlock disappeared rapidly into the shadow between two street-lamps, and then hurried after him. A car swerved from between a pair of parked vans on the other side of the road and roared towards her. There was a flash of light, she screamed, something hit the side of her body and she shot up and over the railings and into the water below. It was very cold. What was infinitely worse though was that someone, or something, was holding her head under and shouting the words, 'don't breathe' into her left ear.

After what seemed like hours she was shoved, coughing and spluttering, onto a flight of glistening concrete steps. Her ears buzzed and white dots of light were floating around inside her head and around her field of vision. She also had an overwhelming desire to be sick.

She didn't know how long it was before Fergus arrived, swearing incoherently under his breath, but by then she had stopped vomiting into the void below and the acute shivering had lessened to gentle shudders. Bill was crouched down next to her, stroking her hair and she realised with the clarity of the nearly killed, that he was the one who had somehow saved her from becoming one of the latest roadkill statistics.

Fergus, grasping the unbelievable fact that she was still

alive, stopped swearing and sank down beside her.

"I thought you were dead," he whispered hoarsely.

"I've been sick," she whimpered.

"Shock," Fergus stated, taking her in his arms and gently kissing the top of her head.

"More like the amount of drink she had at lunchtime," Bill scoffed.

"Just think," he hissed at Fiona, "you could have saved yourselves a fortune; all you two needed for that quiet romantic moment was a near-death experience!"

"Go away," Fiona snapped, glaring at him.

Fergus stopped stroking her hair and looked around.

"Ungrateful cow," Bill chuckled, floating off to hover a few feet away from them.

"Is *he* here?" Fergus asked.

"Who?"

"The ethereal, Mr Boots – Bill."

"Yes," Fiona grunted, and tried to bury her head in his arms.

"Thanks, Bill," Fergus whispered, and held out his hand.

To Fiona's surprise, Bill solemnly shook it and then, after giving her a broad wink, disappeared.

Somehow Fergus and Fiona staggered back up the steps and, wet and dripping, crawled into the fetid warmth of a waiting vehicle, which turned out to be Heather's old Skoda. Heather crouched anxiously over the steering wheel, her eyes constantly scanning the promenade for any signs of movement. Fiona was, she realised, at least a thousand or so yards farther down the promenade from where she had been thrown in. No wonder Fergus had been worried and her attackers quietly confident that she had died, otherwise why weren't they still around checking up on her watery demise?

"Did you see anything?" Fiona asked Fergus between rapidly chattering teeth.

"Not much. I heard a car mounting the pavement, saw you leaping over the railings, heard the splash, turned and saw two figures leaning over the rails searching the water with a torch. Naturally I ran towards them shouting, 'What happened?'"

"Naturally," Fiona sniffled before sneezing violently all over her already waterlogged sleeve.

"Do you know they actually had the gall to scan the water with a torch and told me to call the police? Then when we couldn't even see bubbles they got back in the car and drove off."

"Did you get the number?"

"Part of it. It's being checked now, thank God for mobile phones. Then I called Heather and swore a bit and then ..."

"You ..." Fiona prompted.

"Stood about like a pork pie at a Jewish wedding until something made me walk up here and look down at the steps, where a bundle of clothes was being ill."

"Something made you come up here, what sort of something?"

Fergus looked a bit shifty and a voice whispered in her left ear.

"Kicking people in the unmentionables works both ways, ye ken?"

"That was way too much information," she whispered back.

"What did you say?" Fergus asked, as Heather drove carefully into her driveway.

"Nothing, nothing at all, just glad you had the gumption to take the hint."

"Hint!"

Fiona could actually feel Bill smirking as they tottered into the front porch where she stood and dripped. Heather opened the hall door, shook her head and bundled Fiona out of her coat, up the stairs and into the bathroom, where she was presented with a huge fluffy bath towel and a vast array of bottled luxury.

After about an hour of perfumed steam and iridescent bubbles Fiona finally felt fully thawed and relaxed. The shivering fear had been replaced with a healthy dose of riotous anger and she was ready and willing to solve the mystery, avenge her uncle and kick a certain amount of butt. Unfortunately, as she was not in possession of demonic strength or any form of magical powers she would have to resort to aiding the police and surfing the Net. If all else failed, that morning in one of the local travel agents she'd seen a really good deal on a two-week holiday in Mexico.

Fiona was still musing on the rival merits of taco versus tortilla when the unmistakable aroma of bacon and eggs wafted along the corridor and attacked the olfactory buds in her nose. She was suddenly and overwhelmingly hungry. Mexico could wait, as could universal puzzles and the meaning of life.

Tomorrow after all was yet another day and as she sat with her new-found friends in Heather's warm and cosy kitchen she realised that they had one thing her would-be assassins didn't have. She had not only the full and awful power of the police, even if it did appear to be coming down with a cold, but she also had Mr Boots, the scourge of 'Totally Terrified', the wild card in the pack, and that whatever

118

happened it couldn't possibly get any worse.

It really was amazing what falling in love could do.

❈ ❈ ❈

"Crude, Mr Hare."

"I thought so, Mr Burke."

"It had no merit and was, I am sad to say, the work of a complete amateur."

"My thoughts exactly, Mr Burke. It lacked a certain …"

"Finesse."

"I think that this may be a case of too many cooks."

"And the wrong kitchen."

"I do so hate the unruly masses walking roughshod over our carefully and exactly arranged plans."

"You have a suggestion, Mr Hare?"

"I was wondering if this might be the time to change our perspective."

"I have already considered that aspect and I must unfortunately concur."

"All that effort wasted."

"Not entirely, Mr Hare, not entirely."

"Oh?"

"We still have our contingencies."

"Ah, yes."

"And a numbered Swiss account is always a comforting thought."

"Oh yes, indeed it is, Mr Burke, indeed it is."

They sat in a contemplative silence for a few long thought-filled minutes, their minds working like a pair of recently set abacuses.

"I made a new acquaintance tonight, Mr Hare."

"A paying acquaintance?"

"Unfortunately not, but an interesting one nonetheless."

"Oh?"

"He tried to commit the last sin by jumping into the sea with a lump of concrete ballast around his feet."

"Ah, a traditionalist."

"Unfortunately, the tide was on the turn and going in the wrong direction."

"Ah."

"The previous attempt was not without problems either."

"How so, Mr Burke?"

"He tried to gas himself with an unfortunate lack of the same."

"Ah."

"Through the thoughtless inadvertence of not having primed the meter first."

"Sloppy work, Mr Burke, sloppy work."

"I did consider, however, that he might offer us a pro bono case?"

"Interesting, but not, however, lucrative, after all we have overheads, we have out-of-pocket expenses to consider."

"Umm."

"What does this interesting incompetent do?"

"I believe that he is some sort of journalist and writer, Mr Hare."

"A journalist – ah, at last I see a certain logic to your interest, Mr Burke."

"I thought you might, Mr Hare."

"And where do you think that our serial suicider will strike next?"

"I have it on his own authority that he is interested in travelling to a certain address in Edinburgh. He has, he believes, received divine and supernatural instructions to that effect."

"He is in fact completely deranged?"

"Indubitably, Mr Hare."

"Is this a chemically induced state do you think?"

"No, not unless, that is, you count a surfeit of gin on a regular basis."

"Perhaps we ought to assist him in his quest?"

"But only after we have used his particular area of expertise …"

"An area to which our principal has a long and well-founded antipathy …"

"We could offer him a quick and painless release, on the house so to speak."

"For services rendered, Mr Burke, for services rendered."

They sat and smiled in the darkness. There are times, Mr Burke thought in happy unison with Mr Hare, that our job is thoroughly enjoyable.

✳ ✳ ✳

Nemesis angrily stalked up and down her hotel room and with a surge of rage threw the remains of her supper at the wall, under which dripping spot, a quivering and sadly chastened Robin huddled. Fat chips settled on his nose and then plunged to the floor, in a grey and glistening heap, together with a solitary, wilted lettuce leaf.

"You did *what*?" she raged.

"I was only trying to help."

"*Help!*"

Nemesis took a deep breath and stared down her not inconsiderable nose at him.

Robin, looking up, was treated to the sight of two firm pink globes heaving up and down in a rhythm, which certain forgotten and largely neglected parts of his anatomy found oddly fascinating.

"Not only did you add breaking and entering to your lengthy list of crimes, but forgery as well. And why on earth did you use red ink?" Janet asked, pausing for breath.

"It was the only pen I could find, besides which, I thought that if all they had was a key they'd never in a month of Sundays work out where it fitted. Especially as all the information went up in flames with the office."

Robin cowered and waited for the inevitable tirade. Nothing happened, so he looked up and spotted the fact that his lady boss didn't, as the Greeks were wont to do, wear any underwear.

"We will have to do something about Neville. Honestly, this case is acquiring more protagonists than an Oscar Wilde script."

Robin sat up and watched her pace up and down; he was particularly interested when she appeared briefly silhouetted against the moon-bathed window. Nemesis slowed her balletic stalking and gave the now gently panting Robin her full and undivided attention. Something was most definitely up.

"What," she barked at him, "are you staring at?"

"You, you're ..." Robin answered, wetting his suddenly dry lips with the edge of his tongue. "God, you're beautiful when you're angry."

Nemesis stared back at him temporarily bereft of speech. Robin, sensing that a tactical advantage was now miraculously within his grasp, stood up.

"I don't suppose you fancy moving the beds back?" he

asked, aware of the sudden and unexpected bulge at the front of his now very much tighter trousers. "Janet," he added in a somewhat softer tone.

"What? How dare you even think that I would even for one moment consider ..." Her voice tailed off as the bulge grew even larger and quivered.

"Oh well, all right then," she muttered, switching off the solitary wall-light. "But it had better be quick. We've got work to do."

Robin lunged towards her, inadvertently grabbing the tasselled belt of her flimsy gown and more by beginner's luck than judgement had her completely naked in seconds. Janet, realising that he was actually now at the point where previous experience was of the no digit variety, decided to lend a hand by quickly divesting him of his trousers and pinning him to the bed.

Some time later they lay side by side and Robin, who after the third attempt was beginning to get the hang of his new-found sexual prowess, murmured into his companion's ear.

"I found this illustrated book once in records, and I've always wondered how on earth they managed page one hundred and fifty six."

"A large yellow volume with an appendix by Mata Hari?"

"The one from the original Aramaic translation with diagrams."

"Oh, *that* page, one hundred and fifty six."

"Of course I don't expect to get it right the first time, but ..."

"Practice makes perfect?"

Janet Nemesis giggled in a way she'd not done in many a long and celibate year.

"I couldn't have said it better myself," Robin agreed,

nibbling her right nipple in an experimental manner. "I don't suppose ..." he mumbled between mouthfuls, "that the expenses would run to a bottle of wine and some frozen strawberries."

"Oh, sod the expenses."

Janet squirmed upright and, grabbing the phone on the bedside table, hurriedly dialled room service. On ascertaining that there was actually a member of the human race on the other end of the phone, albeit from Dundee, she announced their order.

"I'll have a bottle of Bollinger champagne, some frozen strawberries if you have them, a bowl of whipped cream, lots of ice and ... a bag of jelly babies," she added as an afterthought, remembering an article in a lonc copy of *Cosmopolitan* she had once perused in shocked silence whilst waiting for Hera to join her for lunch.

"Oh, and you can leave it outside the door as I may be taking a bath."

Robin looked up at her in an attitude of puppy-like devotion as she carefully replaced the receiver.

"After all," she added, "I'm sure there's enough room in the shower for two."

chapter seven

It was two in the morning and even the cat had given up and gone to sleep. However, Fergus was determined to find out who had tried to run Fiona down and after supper had looked up the two simple words, 'Ice House' on the Net. A plethora of information was run off on the printer, shared out between the three of them and perused with varying degrees of tiredness. Heather had taken herself off to the lounge with a double gin, Bill lay in front of the fire and snored gently and Fergus, after handing Fiona a large mug of freshly brewed coffee, went off to join his sister with a determined look on his face. Fiona sat at the kitchen table and tried to keep her eyes open.

"Hey, Heather, listen to this: 'win £10. All users who either survey a pub or send us a photo of a pub will be entered into our monthly prize draw'. I could get a picture of the 'Jolly Acorn' sent in ..."

Fiona could almost see Heather sadly shaking her head before replying, her tone of voice the sort used for calming lunatics before inserting the hypodermic, applying the straitjacket and carting them off down the road in a white van with very small windows.

"That shed where you and Finn sit amongst the homebrews and berate the chief constable ..."

"And all his little wizards ..."

"And all his little wizards, is not a pub. It's a garden shed with two grotty old armchairs and a plastic fold-up table!"

"We have optics and bar snacks."

"Speaking of which, you still owe me for that box of cheese and onion crisps."

"Ah ..."

"Anyway, what the hell does your shed have to do with ice houses?"

"The 'Ice House' is a pub in Southampton."

"Right."

"Mind you, no one has reviewed it and there's no map, so perhaps it doesn't really exist and is in actual fact a blind for some Glaswegian drug baron with Croatian Mafia connections."

"Either that or it's just too bloody grim and nobody goes in, except locals who fancy a pint and a quiet smoke away from the wife. Anyway, I'm not going all the way down south just to find out, so put that in your pipe and smoke it, Sherlock."

"All right then, what do you have?"

At that point Fiona hit dreamsville and it was while she was surfing a huge wave covered in beer bottles and miniature wizards, wearing purple and orange tartan board shorts, that Bill roughly shook her awake by the simple expedient of removing her chair.

"What, what ..." she croaked blearily from the floor.

"It's me, Bill."

"Go way, must sleep," she dribbled, closing her eyes and drifting off.

"This is important. Wake up."

Bill then proceeded to shake her, until her teeth felt numb and she was cross enough to focus.

"If it isn't, first thing tomorrow I'm seeing a priest."

"This is first thing in the morning and you have visitors."

"What!"

"Shh."

Fiona was now fully conscious and aware of the first glow of dawn edging around the window-frames. She crawled on hands and knees in the semi-darkness to the other side of the kitchen and clicked the light switch. Nothing happened.

"Bill, someone's cut the electricity and ..."

Fiona sniffed and then sniffed again just to make sure; there was a distinct aroma of petrol. To hell with it. They, whoever they were, knew that the gang was all there and Fiona knew they were there so she threw caution to whichever wind was currently on duty and raced into the lounge and shook, kicked and shouted until she had both McKinnons awake and fully functional.

"Fire, fire, get up now!" she shrieked hysterically.

"Where?" Fergus grunted, lifting his bulk from the sofa.

"Petrol – can't you smell it? The whole house reeks of the stuff."

Heather and Fiona had almost reached the door when Fergus shoved them back into the gloomy archway of the hall.

"But it isn't lit, and it only really smells here where they managed to pour it through the letterbox, so if we go out the back door?" Fergus suggested.

"And what happens if that's exactly what they want us to do?" Fiona hissed.

They looked at each other in mounting horror. Fergus, breaking the silence, whispered to the cold spot of air beside him, "Bill, if you're here can you go outside and see what they're up to? I'll phone the station and get a squad car and fire engine."

Bill wafted past Fiona grinning and Fergus dug his mobile out of his jeans. After punching in a few numbers he slowly spoke quiet terse instructions to whoever had picked up the receiver at the other end.

They waited. Bill returned, looking somewhat smug.

"What have you done?" Fiona asked

"Nothing much," he replied, with a shrug.

"Liar," she countered.

"What did he say?" Fergus asked.

"There are two guys all in black hiding behind the hydrangea next to the gate and a third man in a car with no tyres parked across the street, and they all have guns and what looks like a large drainpipe with a knob on the end into which one of them is trying to stuff a large firework."

"Guns!" Fiona squeaked, before repeating to Heather and Fergus what Bill had said.

Fergus swore loudly and used his mobile again. Heather and Fiona huddled miserably together and sat on the bottom step of the stairs.

"So they smoke us out with the petrol and then shoot us with a missile launcher. Well, I guess they've tried everything else," Fergus mused.

At that point the fire engine arrived, sirens wailing and blue lights flashing. There was a loud bang and the front and back doors shattered almost simultaneously, glass flying in all directions. After that came muffled shouting, the crash of metal scrunching into metal and an uneasy silence. A foot kicked at the door frame and a round ruddy face with a large pencil moustache, grinned broadly at them from the tattered shreds of a once beautifully glossed front door.

"You all right, Heather?" it asked. "Only there's a very strong smell of petrol in here."

"I'm fine thank you, Finn," Heather replied, easing herself upright.

"Did you get them?" Fergus barked from his semi-recumbent position on the floor.

"Aye."

"Good, help me up and I'll come down the station and interrogate them."

"You mean, ask them to help us with our enquiries?" Sergeant Finn queried, carefully removing a small, fringed rug from Fergus's head.

"No, I mean interrogate, water hoses, red-hot pokers, hungry rodents in upturned pudding basins, ants, honey …"

"Might have a wee bit of a problem there, Fergus."

Finn shuffled uneasily and looked at the floor. Fergus, who was by now fully extracted from the debris that had entangled itself around his person, stood a matter of inches away from him and glared.

"Problem?" Fergus hissed, his temper now way past the red part of any pressure dial.

"Erm weel, young Binthar says they may be from some Eastern Bloc country. Wherever they come from they don't speak English, although they say the F-word a lot in between all the other foreign sounding stuff. They may also kill each other before we manage to find an interpreter."

"Why?"

"Because some clown had punctured all four tyres and rammed something soft and sqelchy up the exhaust pipe of their getaway car and, before you ask, I have a good idea that you'll need rubber gloves and a clothes peg on the nose to get it out."

Fiona exchanged a knowing look with Heather and at the same time heard a faint snicker from somewhere above her head. Fergus allowed himself a brief grin before realising what else Finn had said.

"Don't speak English at all?"

"Not as far as we can tell. If they are shamming it's pretty good as young Binthar used all the insults he could remember and some I didn't know the laddie knew, with, I might add, graphic anatomical examples and they didn't even flinch. Except when he made a rude gesture about the female members of their family, in Russian."

"Then how the hell did they manage to get around?"

"Hand gestures, pointing, please and thank you. How did *you* get around Spain last year, you don't speak the lingo?"

"I know how to say, 'Three beers please' and I used a bit of the Latin I used to know, but I get the point."

"So what do we do now?"

"We get hold of Jill up at the tourist board and ask her if she knows anyone who speaks Russian. I'll just have a word with our young expert first though – is he still around?"

"Keeping sightseers away."

Finn turned and went off back down the front path. He returned leading a very young looking police constable with skin the colour of Thornton's toffee and a vaguely scared expression.

"Well, young Devine, what did you make of them?"

"Devine?" Fiona whispered to Heather. "I thought his name was Binthar?"

"It's Devine, but he goes on a lot of cheap breaks, his mum owns a travel agents, so he's *bin thar*, done that, bought the T-shirt."

"Oh, police humour." Fiona nodded sagely. "I thought it was extinct."

"It is," Heather replied.

By now, Devine was looking more and more apprehensive and Fergus was showing signs of climbing the walls.

"Are you seriously trying to tell me that I was nearly shot by three members of the Russian Mafia?" he barked.

"Well …"

"This is Oban, not some drug-crazed inner city overrun with asylum seekers and God knows what else. I mean, what the hell do we have up here that would be of any interest to some two-bit thug from Moscow or wherever it is that the little shit comes from?"

Finn gently intervened by firmly frogmarching Fergus across the accumulated debris into the kitchen and closing the door behind them.

"You need to go home, have a rest, a wash, something to eat and then you can meet the man from the ministry," Finn advised, walking across to the back door and opening it.

"What?"

"We contacted one of the little wizards, he spoke to the chief constable who then spoke to some bigwig in Edinburgh and they then spoke to someone in some secret airless room and now all hell is being let loose."

"And I left the sharpened stakes at home."

There was a tentative knock on the door from the hall. After a slight pause, two heads peered around the corner.

"Heather, will you and Fiona be all right?" Fergus asked, as he was kindly but inexorably pushed outside.

"Aye, we'll be fine, I'll give Mother a ring on the mobile and sort something out while someone ..."

Heather looked hopefully at Finn who grinned sheepishly back.

"Sorts this mess out."

Fergus then left, trailing sawdust, plaster and one very confused large black spider in his wake. Fiona shivered and looked around the darkened rooms as if seeing them for the first time.

"Well," Heather exclaimed, picking up a small headless china dog from the floor. "I've always preferred the minimalist open-plan look."

"Where's the nearest Ikea outlet?" Fiona asked, righting a chair.

"Just think how much fun I can have with the insurance money."

"I shall pretend I dinnae hear that," Finn grunted.

"Come on, let's go home to Mother's, before the heavy mob arrive to inspect the damage. She's probably already waiting with a cup of tea, plate of griddle scones and at least two other foul and midnight hags."

Heather cast a last look at her partly demolished kitchen, picked up her keys, which still hung from their hook on the wall, and admonishing Finn to lock up afterwards in case of burglars, left. They could still hear Finn's chuckles as they wandered towards Heather's Skoda, which, despite squatting amongst a collection of assorted masonry and wood, was completely untouched.

"And I could have done with a new car too," Heather grumbled, turning the key in the ignition, or at least she would have done if Finn's hand hadn't closed on hers at precisely that moment. There was a short silence in which they all looked at one another.

"Not that I think ..."

Finn's voice tailed off.

"Better safe than sorry," Fiona agreed, her face waxen.

"I'll give you a lift," Finn stated.

"Aye, that will be very welcome," Heather agreed.

✳ ✳ ✳

Neville Foolscap crawled gingerly out from the undergrowth shaking in every limb and stopped short. In front of him a pair of black highly polished shoes glared silently back at him.

"And what do we have here, eh?" a voice of deep suspicion asked.

"Er ..."

Another pair of shoes joined the first pair.

"I think it's that journalist, the one who tried gassing himself," a younger voice announced.

"You sure, young Binthar?"

"Yes, Sir, well, I think so."

A face lowered itself to a point just above that of the cowering Neville and asked, "Are you Mr Neville Foolscap?"

Neville nodded and was helped to his feet.

"A journalist you say?" the older policeman asked the younger, ignoring the now quietly cringing Neville. "And you saved him?"

"Well, no not really, he forgot to put any money in the gas meter."

"I can explain ..." Neville squeaked.

"And you honestly think I want to listen?" the older man asked, in tones of incredulity.

"Well, if you put it like that."

"What I do want to know is, while you were in there," the shrubbery was poked at this point, "did you see anything?"

"You mean the three Serbs carrying guns and a large plastic can of something? The ones that poured it through Heather MacDougall's front door and then opened fire when you lot turned up?"

"That's it in the proverbial nutshell."

"No, I didn't."

"What?"

Young PC Devine intervened at this point by standing between them and asking, "How do you know that they were Serbs?"

Neville looked if anything even less trustworthy and shuffled uneasily.

"I was in Serbia a couple of years ago, worked for one of the nationals, spoke Russian you see and the money was good. I realised why when I got out there." He shuddered briefly and then lowered his eyes to the ground. "Look, I'm just a slimy two-faced reporter who nobody really likes, especially that jumped-up DI of yours; I saw no evil, heard no evil and sure as hell ain't going to say nothing."

"Why?"

"I like my testicles where they are, thank you very much."

Both of the policemen gave each other a knowing look

and then carefully steered him towards the road and a waiting car.

"How do you fancy a nice, big cooked breakfast and a pot of tea, no charge?"

"Well …"

"All we need you to do is to translate a few questions the boss would like to ask."

"And if I do?"

"We'll send you on a nice, all expenses paid short holiday to foreign parts."

"Sir?"

"It's all right, PC Devine, I'm sure we can raise enough to buy this brave man a single fare to Edinburgh."

Neville's eyes suddenly lit up and he nodded enthusiastically in agreement.

"Will they have to see me?" he asked.

"No, we'll stick you on our side of a large glass screen with a pair of earphones and a mike. Oh and by the way they appear to be very fond of their mothers so perhaps you could start there."

❋ ❋ ❋

Mr Burke sat and stared unseeingly through the window as Mr Hare stirred another spoonful of sugar into his lightly frothed cappuccino.

"I am not pleased, Mr Hare, not pleased at all."

"I thought not, Mr Burke."

"Guns, explosions, petrol – is there no end to their incompetence?"

"They are, are they not, of foreign extraction and as such not accustomed to the more sophisticated ways of assassination?"

"We will have to go back to our principal and explain that we are unable, due to exceptionally trying circumstances, to complete our task, Mr Hare."

"I don't think that we have ever come across such a problem before, Mr Burke."

"There will, of course, have to be a slight discount, refund even."

They sat in an unhappy silence and drank their respective beverages.

Bill Boots stood on the other side of the street and lounged against a convenient lamp-post. He had no idea who the two men were, but he'd have known the shorter one of the two anywhere. For some reason he had set fire to Quentin Rowse's office and in all probability the Mellrose guesthouse, however, they had not been driving the car that had tried to run Fiona down, but they had been watching from the safety of their own. An innate sense of self-preservation, honed to radar sharpness over the years, told him that the two men were very, very bad news and that they knew far more than anyone he had so far met about the whys and wherefores of young Fiona's uncle's death.

chapter eight

Mrs McKinnon opened the door of her ground-floor flat, still with the chain on, and regarded them with the bright beady eyes of a well-trained mongoose. From the interior came a chorus of shouts and wheezy enquiries. Heather sighed loudly and rolled her eyes.

"Mum, it's me, Heather."

"What do you want? It's not Thursday already is it?" the old lady quavered.

"Will you please let me in?"

"You've got suitcases – I can see them."

"Yes, Mum."

"I'm not taking any of you back. Whatever it is, *you* can fix it, besides which I don't hold with divorce – one harlot in the family is quite enough, quite enough so it is."

"Fergus is not a harlot," Heather muttered between clenched teeth.

"*He* may not have been, but that tart he married was."

"Mother, will you please just let us in!"

"Who's that with you?" the old lady asked suspiciously.

"Fiona, Quentin Rowse's niece and I've got Sergeant Finn with me."

"I'm not harbouring no fornicating runaways."

"Mother!"

"That Finn always had a liking for you, as well you know, young lady, and I think it's disgusting especially with the wee bairns not even grown."

"Mother, I have not left my husband or my children or killed anyone – yet. Nor for that matter have I absconded with the contents of our meagre joint bank account."

"Then why are you here?"

"My home has been soaked in petrol, I have no doors, I have been shot at and there may or may not be a bomb under my car, I'm tired, hungry and ... I need you, Mum."

"Well, why didn't you say so?"

The chain was removed and they were finally welcomed in. On seeing Heather's face in the glaring glow of the overhead striplight, her mother gleefully shooed her cronies, still clutching a selection of playing cards, into the great outdoors with the words: "Family crisis as you can see, so I'll be needing a bit of space."

After seeing her elderly colleagues out by the simple expedient of handing them their coats and blocking the doorway until they had tottered off down the road, she turned and shutting the door with a judicious kick, opened up the batting with the words: "Well, Heather love, I'm going to brew a fresh pot of tea and then you are going to tell me everything."

After enveloping her daughter in a spindly hug and kissing her gently on the cheek, Mrs McKinnon shuffled over to the sink and Heather sank gratefully into one of the hastily vacated and still warm kitchen chairs. Fiona and Finn quietly followed suit.

Heather explained as far as she could, with the occasional intervention by Sergeant Finn. Bill, who had followed them from Heather's by the simple expedient of climbing into the boot with their hastily collected luggage, leaned against the back door looking oddly thoughtful.

They had just finished explaining about the probability of having a family car complete with fully functional ejector seats when the telephone rang.

Mrs McKinnon answered it and after listening for a few minutes snapped, "Aye well, Fergus, I said no good would come of it when you insisted on throwing your life away by coming back here, but you wouldnae listen to me. I've Heather here with young Quentin's niece and I think there's something you ought to know."

There was a pause and then the phone burbled and bleated until Mrs McKinnon dropped her verbal bombshell.

"And if you want to know the name of that poor wee girl burnt alive in young Quentin's apology for a guesthouse you'd better come home now and bring a policeman!" The phone was slammed back down on its cradle.

Heather and Fiona exchanged looks that could roughly be described as poleaxed.

"And will you be catching flies with that expression?" Mrs McKinnon enquired, with a wrinkled scowl.

"Mum, what's going on?" Heather asked.

"You'll find out when your brother drags hiself away from his verra important business. Have you no had any breakfast?"

"No."

"Then I'll get the pan on. Fiona, you can help. Plates are

there, cutlery here and the condiments on that shelf. Finn, you can take those cases and leave them in the spare room before someone falls over them and breaks something."

By the time Fergus had arrived the complete ingredients of the Atkins Diet were being warmed gently on the bottom oven and at least a dozen eggs were awaiting the last rites.

"Wash your hands, son, and show your friends where the basin is. I'll get the eggs on. Fiona lass, set another place for the complete stranger my son has seen fit to invite into my home without so much as a by your leave, mind. Is that tea ready, Heather?"

When Fergus returned with Finn and the grey-suited stranger in tow they all sat at a nod from the family matriarch and ate in chastened silence.

After the meal the stranger was introduced as Ms Aberfeldy, a consultant for the immigration department. She had the clipped androgynous look common to many upwardly mobile female executives. Oddly enough, she reminded Fiona of her old deputy head, a woman of indomitable character who had ruled her old school with hands of iron and a tongue that had most of the school governors metaphorically standing on the stairs, until they were allowed to go home. She had also quite probably been the only member of the female sex who had ever fully terrified Fiona's father apart from Fiona's mother, who still managed to terrify most people. Ms Aberfeldy, however, did not wear purple lisle stockings and a bosom-embracing tweed suit, but she did have a certain bluntness of manner that had even Bill, a staunch sexist, sidling into a shadowy corner just in case he got spotted and had to either explain himself or do lines.

After breakfast, which had been started with a brief prayer and then by the admonishment of not talking while they were eating what a good God had seen fit to provide, they were allowed into a small cluttered lounge. A cheery fire glowed and every surface appeared to be covered in various sized crocheted squares and a motley assortment of garishly coloured china figures.

Fiona gingerly lowered herself into a green, velvet-covered Windsor chair whilst the others settled into and onto a variety of oddly matched furniture. An ancient West Highland terrier yawned from his spreadeagled position on the rag rug in front of the flickering flames and went back to dreams of rabbits and next-door's cat.

After everyone was settled, each with his or her own mug of tea or coffee depending on preference, Mrs McKinnon fixed her son with a gimlet stare and barked, "Who is she then?"

"Who?" Fergus replied.

"Yon stick with legs and an expression to grace the devil himself."

Fiona thought for a horrible minute that the old biddy was talking about Bill until Mrs McKinnon grabbed the long, ebony-coloured walking stick, which had been leaning against her chair, and stabbed it pointedly at Ms Aberfeldy.

"And none of this Ms nonsense mind, she's either with a man or not, and if she's bedded she's wedded as far as I'm concerned."

"Mum!"

"Don't you Mum me, laddie, I've nae time fer your nonsense. Not when there's people out there as should still be swimming around in primordial soup, not letting off shotguns and stuffing petrol down law-abiding citizen's letterboxes!"

"I think I should explain," Ms Aberfeldy remarked in a soft, oddly flat voice with no noticeable regional accent.

"Aye, well that would be a start," Mrs McKinnon barked, settling further into her seat and resting the stick against the side of her chair.

"My department is interested in a small select group of Russian immigrants who appear to be running an illegal and highly lucrative employment agency."

"Russian – aye well that would explain a few things," Mrs McKinnon muttered.

"According to our sources they bring illegal immigrants over from various Scandinavian countries in small boats, land them at a number of remote harbours and slipways in the far north of Scotland and then bring them down to the big cities in ordinary-looking removal vans. The immigrants have paid, or have promised to pay, large sums of money to be brought here and this particular group are extremely good at extracting as much as they can from these people before letting them go, which by the way they often don't. As far as we can tell the younger girls and boys are sold into prostitution or somehow persuaded to appear in some of the nastiest porn videos I've ever had dealings with, and the older ones are forced into doing menial jobs in factories or small hotels and guesthouses. Unfortunately they seem to have flooded the market farther south and are now setting their sights on smaller seaside resorts such as yours. There is something else, but what it is I have been unable to find out, as all the people involved have either met with an unfortunate and fatal accident or they've disappeared."

"That poor wee girl," Mrs McKinnon sighed.

"Yes, that poor girl, which, however, rather begs the question, 'How did you know?'"

"Yes, Mother, how did you know?" Fergus hissed.

"Don't you Mother me, son, and don't you use that tone of voice either, young woman, or I won't tell you!" Mrs McKinnon replied, pursing her lips together in a frown.

"I give up," Fergus groaned.

"Apology accepted. The wee girl's name was Katya and she was here looking for her brother, Stefan. Young Quentin told me that he'd first met her in Edinburgh, I don't know how, but she turned up at that detective agency he ran down near the harbour and asked him to help her do some checking. In return she got a job cleaning at the Mellrose and then the foreign rubbish turned up. They sat here in my kitchen, the cheeky young buggers, and said they could see I needed a bit of help running the place and that they could offer me very reasonable rates and not a penny would I have to pay to the government. Of course when I said I'd have to think about it they tried the heavy-handed approach until I casually dropped your name and occupation into the conversation. Never seen people remove themselves so fast. I told Quentin at that last meeting of the Hoteliers' Association and he said he'd discovered something really nasty was going on and that he wasn't sure how much to tell Katya, as he had reason to believe that her brother was dead or as good as. He wouldnae say any more and the next day he went out fishing with Vernon and never came back. Katya came around to see me afterwards and told me that if anything happened to her, I was to go to the police and get them to look through Quentin's research for his new book."

"Book? What book?" Fiona asked.

"Oh, didn't you know? And you supposedly the closest

thing he'd admit to having as kin. Well apart from that fairy, Vernon."

"Mother!"

"Quentin had a thing for history and he was writing a small piece about a local group of Resurrection Men."

"Burke and Hare?" Fergus queried.

"Nae lad, *they* was murderers – I'm talking about gravediggers," his mother scoffed, obviously pleased at his ignorance.

"But what the hell does that have to do with Katya?"

"I have nae idea."

His mother shrugged.

"These men, can you describe them?" Ms Aberfeldy asked, leaning forward.

"Men?"

"The ones who were running the employment scam."

"Well, only one spoke English and I could have sworn that he was straight from the Glasgow tenements by way of Barlinnie. Wouldnae trusted him even without the matching gorillas. He had the face of the devil's own undertaker and breath to match."

"William Hay," Ms Aberfeldy sighed, looking enormously pleased. "Just the man I'd like to see back sewing mailbags and cleaning toilets with a very small toothbrush for the next fifty years. Acute halitosis and a penchant for black. Hang on, I have some photographs."

For a brief moment she fumbled in the attaché case that had appeared to be glued to her side, before holding out a wad of photographs, some of which were extremely grainy and out of focus, but Mrs McKinnon grabbed at two of them with a sibilant growl.

"That's him, the man on the left in the long coat, and

those two with him were the ones who sat next to him. Didn't say a word all the way through. That thin piece of uselessness kept picking his nose, despite my twice offering him the box of paper tissues. And the other one, the one I called 'auld fox-face' hummed all the time until the cat bit him on the ankle. I told him at the time not to fidget so it was his ain fault. Nasty, shifty pieces of work the lot of them."

"Amber?" Heather said, clearly startled.

"Aye, her as never says boo to the proverbial goose, she went straight up and bit him on the ankle – haven't seen her since though. Verra nervous wee thing she was couldnae understand it at all."

"Look at Finn," a sepulchral voice urgently hissed in Fiona's ear. "He knows something."

Fiona looked from Bill's intent face to that of Finn's shadowed visage and decided to find out what it was that he was anxious not to divulge – afterwards she very much wished she hadn't.

"But you do, don't you, Finn?" Fiona enquired, as gently as she could.

Finn gave her a look that would have frozen steam and an answer she hadn't actually bargained for.

"Amber's dead," he whispered, not meeting the old lady's steady gaze.

"Dead?" Fergus repeated.

"I was going to tell you, but there was all that fuss over the fire and the body, and then the shooting at Heather's ..."

"How?"

"Someone shot her and then put her in a weighted sack. We found it when we were trying to retrieve bits of evidence from the harbour after young Fiona's accident."

"Accident!" Fiona squeaked, glaring at him.

"I reckon poor Amber had been dead a while though and it would have been verra quick."

Mrs McKinnon gave a little shudder and the dog, appearing to sense his mistress's distress, moved from his spot in front of the fire and went to sit at her feet, his cold clammy nose thrust firmly at her shaking, paper thin hands.

Bill surveyed the scene with a thoughtful expression and then, as if receiving some sort of divine communication, sidled back to Fiona and with urgent shooing motions indicated that now would be a good time to talk.

"I think I'd like to use your bathroom if that's OK?" Fiona asked hesitantly, as Bill made even more desperate hand signals from the doorway.

Finally she sat perched on the toilet seat with Bill squashed up against an old wooden towel rail.

"Well, what the hell is more urgent than dead cats and the odd assassination attempt?" she asked.

"I got it."

"What?"

"Cold House."

"What! You mean you finally know what it means?" she squeaked.

"Well, yes and no."

"Well, go on – divulge and educate, or its bells and smells for you, matey."

"Cold House was the name we gave to Gould House."

"Gould House?"

"It was just outside the old town near the water of Leith. It was called 'Cold House' by some of the Resurrection Men, because it had an ice house built into the basement and that was where they took the bodies."

"The bodies?"

"Aye, how else would they be kept fresh until needed?"

"They put them in the ice house and then …"

"The doctor would have them taken out and cleaned up for his anatomy lectures."

"And you remembered this because?"

"Your uncle was writing about the Resurrection Men."

"But that was over two hundred years ago, what the hell does it have to do with Uncle Quentin or Katya, a dead cat and some homicidal Russians?"

"What if …"

"What if what?"

"What if they didn't just get money from prostitution and modern-day slavery, what if they got money from selling bodies?"

"Oh come on, Bill! What on earth would they need bodies for?"

"I don't know, but it's the only reason I have for your uncle writing 'Cold House' on a piece of paper, the same piece of paper that nearly got you killed."

"We may need Fergus."

"Aye, so are you going to let me in or what?" a terse voice whispered through the keyhole.

Fiona opened the door to find Fergus leaning against the opposite wall arms folded and a fairly murderous look on his face.

"I gleaned enough eavesdropping to know that I need to have all the details of what Casper has finally managed to remember," he stated belligerently.

"Don't you need to say goodbye to your friends?" Fiona asked.

"Already done it. And before you ask, the Russians are

being transported somewhere safer, damper, deeper and with no windows, as we speak."

"Your mother?"

"Is going with Heather to stay with Heather's mother-in-law on the Isle of Mull. Finn is sending young Binthar to keep an eye on them and we've asked the Mull Constabulary for their assistance."

"What, *both* of them?"

"Don't get sarcastic with me, young lady: the truth the whole truth and nothing but."

Fiona then relayed all the bits Bill had remembered and added all the odd snatches she had gleaned from her uncle before his death. It didn't make an awful lot of sense so Fergus decided to go and seek a second opinion, which was why twenty minutes later they were firmly ensconced in the local doctor's surgery, awaiting a quick word with one of his old schoolmates, Doctor Edward Knox. An appropriate name in the circumstances and one that had raised both Bill's furry, if non-corporeal, eyebrows.

* * *

Janet Nemesis clutched her small, elegant, brown leather trimmed handbag with the tasteful gold embossed buckle to her chest, and tried not to look as if she was watching the police station across the road.

Robin Bastard sidled up to her and whispered, "Neville's in there and the undertakers are in the white van across the street. Parked next to the yellow Beetle."

"Beetle?"

"A type of car that looks like a beetle."

"It does?"

"Think ladybird and imagine it painted red."

"Well, in the dark I suppose ..."

"I think those two ..."

"The undertakers?"

"Yes."

"Why ..."

"It's a spy thing, like in the movies and Tom Clancy novels, everyone has code names so nobody knows who they really are, although everybody does."

"So what you are trying to tell me is that those two are the paid assassins and you refer to them in code as the undertakers?"

"Yes."

"I see I'm going to have to cut down on your television viewing time."

"But what would I do instead?"

Janet gave him the look.

"Oh, *that*."

"I beg your pardon!"

"Do we have to stand here all day though? I mean to say, Neville is in there helping the police with their enquires."

"Do they still use those interesting little devices that first cut off the blood supply and then ...?"

Janet made a small twisting movement with her hands and grinned up at him. Robin gulped loudly and shook his head.

"Certainly not. They fill in a lot of forms, shout a bit, somebody tapes all the lies and then everyone goes home. It's called 'human rights'."

"What's the point?"

"I have no idea, but it's called progress."

"Sounds a damned silly waste of time to me."

"Can we go back to the hotel now?" Robin asked, tracing a small love heart in the dust at his feet with the point of his shoe.

"Why?"

"I thought we needed to pack before we sort out the undertakers."

"I don't think that vengeance will be fully served by taking those two out."

"Why?"

"I think that they are just subcontractors, paid assassins. What we need is the face behind the mask. The brains and money behind the sword."

"Oh."

"I suspect that the two uglies are as unhappy about the way things are progressing as we are pleased. In fact, I wouldn't be at all surprised if they don't become instruments of divine justice themselves."

Janet gave them a last lingering look and began to saunter back to their hotel.

"Janet."

"Yes, Robin."

"I was watching one of those late night films. It was when you went out to check up on Neville."

"Yes."

"It was called, 'The Postman Always Rings Twice'."

"He does?"

"The thing is we have a desk in the room and I was just thinking that …"

They looked at one another, or at least Robin observed her linen-clad breasts and Janet the growing bulge in his trousers. She linked her arm in his and insisted that he did up his jacket before he was arrested too.

❋ ❋ ❋

Fiona glared at the small urchin in front of her. The child stared back and then loudly coughed again. Fergus looked up from the magazine he was reading and quietly asked him to put his hand over his mouth.

"Why?" the child asked.

"Because we don't want your disgusting germs and you don't want to have to explain to your dad why he's got to come down to the police station to collect you."

"And why would he have to do that?"

"Believe me, laddie, when I say that I will think of something."

The boy looked from one frosty countenance to another and sidled off to the other side of the waiting room where he coughed loudly and wetly over an elderly gentleman with a handlebar moustache. After a matter of seconds the child was back rubbing his thigh.

"He hit me with his walking stick," the child grumbled.

"Good. Saves me the trouble," Fergus replied.

"Aren't you going to arrest him?"

"Any witnesses?"

The boy looked around the silent waiting room. Everybody present was studiously reading, even the receptionist had disappeared from view.

"No."

"Not much I can do then. Sorry."

"No you're not."

"What?"

"Sorry, you're not sorry. I have rights you know. Foreign ones."

At that moment a very pregnant lady opened a far door

and waddled towards them.

"What did you do?" she asked the boy.

He coughed again.

"And will you put your hand over your mouth when you do that? I've told you time and agin that I don't want any of your 'orrid little friends' nasty germs."

They watched as she gave him a cursory flick on the ear and pushed him, still whining, none too gently out into the street.

"Fergus McKinnon," a disembodied voice announced from the wall.

Fergus replaced the magazine on the tottering tatty heap covering a small bowed coffee table and walked towards a far door. Fiona toddled after him closely followed by Bill Boots who was wearing an expression of pained martyr-dom. Waiting rooms may have changed over the years, but neither the patients, ailments nor the doctors had.

Dr Knox was a slightly stooped individual who watched Fergus enter with a certain amount of relief.

"You're not ill, are you?" he asked suspiciously.

"No."

"Good."

"Why?"

"I don't like sick people."

"Isn't that a bit … er … unfortunate considering?"

"Do you like criminals?" Dr Knox replied, reaching for a throat lozenge.

"No."

"Well, there you go then."

Dr Knox rolled the sweet around his mouth and sat back in his chair.

"Right well … er … I'm not sure where to start, but the

thing is ..."

Fergus's voice tailed off. Dr Knox raised a thick black eyebrow and continued to noisily suck his sweet.

"What do you know, if anything, about the Resurrection Men?" Fiona asked.

"And *you* are?" Dr Knox asked.

"Fiona, Quentin Rowse's niece."

"Ah well, I can understand the interest then and I'll tell you what I told Quentin." He paused to crunch the last of the sweet, which he then swallowed. "I do think that the trade in body parts is not now restricted to villages in India and that certain of my illustrious colleagues, especially those in certain private practices, may be turning a blind eye as to the provenance of certain ... er ... organs."

"Oh."

"I can give you copies of the papers I gave your uncle, if that will help?"

"Yes please."

Fergus and Fiona exchanged identical glances. Nothing could be this easy, could it?

"Ah, here they are."

Dr Knox produced a brown folder stuffed with old newspaper cuttings and magazine articles, and handed them over.

"There may be a few that Quentin never got; I continued to collect bits even after his death. I think that on balance he may have been on to something, although ..."

"Yes."

"I suspect that poor Katya's brother is already dead if what Quentin expected to happen, has." He looked from one to the other and then sighed. "You don't have a clue what I'm talking about, do you?"

"No, not really."

"You're not here because you found Quentin's notes?"

"No."

"Where are they then?"

"Burnt, removed by person or persons unknown – who knows? I for one don't," Fergus replied.

"Oh dear, oh dear. I'm not sure where to begin. This is all a bit awkward really. The thing is, Quentin thought that a certain number of young people were involved with a particular high-ranking and influential, privately funded Edinburgh-based medical practice. He believed that young people were smuggled in and that organs were removed in exchange for certain documents."

"Removed?"

"Humans are blessed with two of most things and you can often live with only the one."

"That's – God, that's horrible."

Fiona shuddered.

"That wasn't all. Quentin was also convinced that they were also dealing with organs the removal of which would not in any circumstances be advisable."

"Ah."

"And now we get down to the important bit."

"Money?"

Fergus sighed; the light at the end of the tunnel was brightly shining and he didn't like it at all.

"How much would you pay for your own life or to save that of a loved one?"

"I think I'm beginning to wish that this particular can of worms had remained closed."

"I expect Quentin thinks the same," Dr Knox remarked drily.

"Do you want any of this back?" Fergus asked, waving

the file.

"No. On balance I'd prefer to have no more to do with it."

"I can understand that. Well, if that's all we'd better be off."

Fergus rose to go and then on impulse turned back.

"Was there anything else? Something that isn't in here?"

"Well, it's not much and it may in all probability mean nothing at all, but someone, a friend of mine who works in the mortuary, did give me a name, Anderson and Fiske."

"Anything else?"

"No."

"Ah well, thanks for your help, Ed, and I'd appreciate it if you didn't mention this to anyone else."

"Of course not. I just hope that you have better luck than poor old Quentin."

They left in contemplative silence. Even Bill was subdued enough not to make any derogatory comments about the state of the health service.

Outside, Fergus stood, legs apart and looked upwards.

"I have a really, really bad feeling about this," he muttered.

"By the pricking of my thumbs something wicked this way comes," Fiona recited.

"Aye, and in both hands."

chapter nine

Fergus sat in his car and silently surveyed a scene of quiet and sombre desolation matched perfectly by the darkening expression on Fiona's face. The loch in front of them rippled and blinked in the grey storm-tinged light, as heavy, dark electric blue rimmed clouds poured over the rocky crags above their heads and began to spread upwards and outwards towards the distant horizon.

Somewhere to their right a dog barked briefly and seabirds paddling in amongst the weed at the water's edge stopped and, as a single unit, took flight, only to circle once and then settle a mere matter of yards farther down the beach.

"An ice house was a brick-lined pit twenty-five to thirty feet deep, usually in the shape of a blunt cone with the point downwards. Blocks of ice were cut from rivers or ponds and stacked between layers of straw and could, if properly preserved, last up to three years. Their heyday came during the eighteenth century when no aristocratic estate was without one. Here's a picture of one they found in the basement of what is now a bookshop. Oh, I see it was the town's ice house."

Fergus handed Fiona the sheet of paper from which he had been reading and bit his lips in a ruminative fashion.

"So it is perfectly feasible that someone who had a fair amount of money could and was able to build one of these in the basement of his house during the years when there was a desire for fresh dead bodies?"

"Or maybe someone inherited the house, say during the early part of the eighteenth century, and put it to a different use other than storing ice and chilling dairy products?" Fiona thought before adding, "When was the first one built?"

Fergus consulted the notes he'd been making.

"1619, Greenwich."

"Burke and Hare met in 1827 and Burke was hung in 1829, after confessing to sixteen murders."

"Sixteen times seven – that's about £112. God, that would have been a small fortune in those days, and a damned sight more than you could normally get running a guesthouse or doing the odd delivery or labouring job."

Fiona wondered aloud, thinking of Bill's wife leaving Edinburgh with the princely sum of £7 6s sewn into the hem of her clothes, or at least that's where Bill had seen her put their life savings.

"I wonder how many they really killed," Fergus remarked, scratching the growing stubble on his chin.

"We will never know," Fiona replied, as she read through a brief summary of the life and works of Doctor Robert Knox 1791–1862.

It was actually nine sheets of A4 with no pictures. How could he have denied knowing anything about the way that

Burke and Hare had obtained the bodies he needed for his anatomy lectures? They hadn't, after all, been dug up and so there would have been no clogs of earth clinging to their mortal remains, no putrid smell and no bruised and battered injuries acquired before and during burial. As if reading her thoughts, Bill, who was sprawled across the back seat, began to sing.

"Up the close and down the stair, in the house wi' Burke and Hare. Burke's the butcher, Hare's the thief, Knox the man who buys the beef."

Fiona shivered as the last ghostly notes faded.

"You cold?" Fergus asked solicitously. "I can put the heater on."

"No, I was just thinking."

"Penny for them?"

"Why would Uncle Quentin have been killed for doing a bit of research on local Resurrection Men? As far as I can see, the Anatomy Act of 1832 allowed the legal use of unclaimed bodies and the trade seems to have stopped after that," Fiona pondered aloud.

"Unclaimed?"

"Most people who died in the poorhouse were either there because they had nobody else, or because they were so poor that there was no money for burial anyway. Their bodies would have had to be disposed of by the parish, which would have cost the ratepayers a fair chunk. So all in all, giving them to the hospital for dissection would have made everyone happy."

"Well, I suppose so. This trade seems to have been going on for some considerable time. It says here that in 1742 an angry mob stormed the surgery of a Dr Eccles and discovered the hastily concealed corpse of an Alexander Baxter, lifted from the West Kirk by Resurrection Men the previous night."

"What happened to him?"

"Nothing much, he was cleared of complicity in raising the dead and continued in his respected profession."

"So, no change there then," Fiona muttered.

"Wasn't just Scotland, you know," Bill informed her.

"Where else?" she asked, shushing Fergus who gave her an odd look and began to stretch out a large street map of Edinburgh.

"I remember hearing about the Hope Street Gang in Liverpool. They used to send pickled bodies from Ireland to Liverpool in barrels of brine, only one lot smelled so bad it was discovered by some dockhands. Later on the police followed a lead to a cellar at 11 Hope Street and discovered twenty-two corpses in the process of being further preserved with injections of hot wax."

"Oh, yuk!" Fiona exclaimed, grimacing.

"The worst bit was that it wasn't just people they found, they also discovered a vat of dead babies."

"Babies?"

"Afraid so, I remember because it was in all the papers. It was 1826, a year before Burke and Hare single-headedly took the whole thing into a league of its own, of course I was dead too by then, but even ghosts have feelings. Babies – apparently the foreman of the jury was physically sick when they got to that bit of evidence – didn't feel too good about it myself."

Fiona relayed what Bill had divulged to Fergus who visibly blanched before holding the map up so that Bill could see it from the back.

"Ask him if he can remember anything about the

situation of this Gould House, perhaps it's still there and we can find it."

"Oh, come on," Fiona scoffed, "It's probably a super-market car park by now."

"Not necessarily," Fergus replied. "Those ice houses were expensive."

"Agreed."

"So only the well off could afford one."

"Well, yes."

"So we're talking about a brand new Georgian mansion built in part of the New Town with maybe a separate entrance to the river, and you said that Bill thinks it was owned by a doctor."

"Yes."

"A doctor would have been an educated man of means with possibly a fair amount of inherited cash and property. After all, he could afford to pay for the bodies he wanted, cash on delivery. The balance of which may in part have been made up afterwards by people who paid at the door to see the equivalent of reality television."

Fiona could see what he was getting at now – cash flow.

"Or he could have inherited the house and the large family-sized walk-in fridge and decided to make a bit of extra income by acquiring and storing bodies for other doctors, students, anatomists or whatever. Basically, we are talking about a large, old house in a posh part of the New Town, which will be a listed building and coveted by all those with a burgeoning bank balance, as well as the Scottish National Trust."

"Definitely not the sort of thing you knock down to make way for a municipal car park then?"

"No."

"So it should, all things being equal, still exist complete with ice house?"

"Yes, one would assume so, which makes me very curious as to why that someone doesn't want anyone else to know about it."

"How do you make that out?"

"Have you any idea how many tourists would pay to see a genuine Georgian ice house in good or even bad condition in Edinburgh? I can almost see the grin on the faces of the Edinburgh Tourist Board to say nothing of the Scottish National Trust."

"I suppose it would be on some historical pamphlet," Fiona mused.

"And even if it couldn't be viewed there would be something on the Web. Even if it was just a scrap of information and a line drawing."

"Umm."

"Please tell the big man there that as I was dead and wrapped in a bit of old sacking I have no idea where this house is or was – and it was dark," Bill hissed as an afterthought.

Fiona told Fergus who sniffily remarked about the quality of informers down the ages.

"Shh," she whispered, aware that by now Fergus was really beginning to get up Bill's nose, mainly because the condensation on the inside of the windows began to freeze giving rise to whorls and spiked patterns of indistinct, but scowling, skulls.

"Right, well that's it then," Fergus announced, starting the car and throwing it savagely into reverse.

Bill and Fiona exchanged mutually puzzled looks.

"What?" Fiona quavered.

She clung to the sides of her seat as he did a terrifyingly fast three-point turn in an area smaller than her old flat's kitchen. The kitchen was the kind built in the seventies where if you pulled out the wall table you had to sit on the kitchen units to eat anything.

"How long will it take you to pack?"

"Why," Fiona asked, as a tree that had loomed out of nowhere missed them by mere inches.

"We are going to take a little trip to Edinburgh on the pretext of moving you to a place of safety and in reality so that Casper here can find this bloody house. Even if it means stuffing him in a sack and hiring a cart at midnight!"

"What about your job?"

"Finn can handle the scenes of crime time team and I'm owed at least three weeks' holiday. Besides, I don't fancy going to bed each night wondering if I'm going to be waking up in the morning. More importantly, I have a horrible feeling that a group of thugs who will burn, crush, shoot and or drown their intended victims won't be put off just because you're sleeping with a policeman."

"Sleeping?" Fiona queried a little breathlessly, as by now her stomach was doing a strange cartwheel and her face was the colour of a well-cooked lobster.

"Aye, Edinburgh's damned expensive and it will be cheaper with the one bed," he answered as they erupted onto the main road trailing a variety of the lochside's flora behind them.

✳ ✳ ✳

Neville squinted upwards and growled, "Go away."

The small and sticky child, who was regarding him with

large interested eyes, removed the lolly from its mouth and said:

"No."

The lolly was then inserted back into the orifice and the staring vigil was continued.

Neville closed his eyes and tried to find the inner peace necessary for his third suicide attempt.

"What's he doing?" a shrill-voiced infant asked the first interested onlooker.

"What's it look like, stupid?" came the sneering reply.

"Oh God, there's another one," Neville muttered under his breath.

"Is he going to die?" asked a third disembodied dwarf.

"I reckon his legs will go first," announced the second.

A cold glob of something wet and sticky fell on Neville's upturned face.

"Why?"

"Because they're the bits on the rails."

"Well *doh*."

"I want to see his head squish and all the brains come out and his eyeballs pop."

"Do you think that we could keep some of it in a jar? We could take it to school."

"Mrs Wylie would be sick."

"I've got a lunchbox; I can take the cheese sandwich out first."

"I'm not sure it's big enough. Here, Mister, do you want a sandwich, it's cheese and brown stuff?"

"No I don't."

"How about an apple?"

"Will you clear off and leave me alone," Neville shouted, as the crowd above him grew.

The rails below him were becoming more and more uncomfortable and something sharp was digging into the small of his back. A female voice, strident with impatience and no small degree of annoyance, demanded to know what they were looking at.

"It's a man."

"He's going to die."

"We're waiting for the train to run him over and cut his bits off."

"There will be lots and lots of blood," the imp with the lolly announced gleefully.

"No there won't," the woman barked, rounding up her offspring by the simple expedient of grabbing an ear in each hand. "There's been an accident at Taynuilt and the line will be out for at least twelve hours, so we're catching the bus back."

There was a slowly fading chorus of:

"Aw, Mum!"

"But ..."

"It's not fair."

Neville moaned. The crowd above him thinned until only two shadows remained. A chicken inspecting the platform fluttered down onto the railway track and pecked at the sticky mess congealing against his ear. Neville sat bolt upright and glared at the interested fowl.

"Are you going to be needing the facilities?" asked a blue-uniformed and rotund figure smoking a sagging cigarette.

"Why?" Neville asked.

"Because I'd like to lock up. On the other hand if you was requiring them I can water the petunias first."

Neville slowly stood up rubbing the bits that had lost all feeling and pulled the ticket from his pocket.

"When's the next train due then?" he asked.

"Tomorrow."

"Oh."

"You could always lie in front of the bus."

"Umm."

"It stops over there."

The man pointed to a drunkenly swaying and distant tree.

"Thanks."

"Well, by stopping, I mean it slows down, on account of the bend."

He watched as Neville clambered back onto the deserted platform and slowly and stiffly walked away. On balance, he was pleased that the train had been held up.

"Blood," he advised the chicken, "is the devil itself to get off rails and as for the bits, you're still finding them months later."

The chicken clucked and fluffed the feathers around its throat, making them stand up and thereby, albeit momentarily, turning the dapper rooster into a miniature Elizabethan dandy.

"Although I expect you'd like some of it, eh Albert?"

The rooster put its head on one side and regarded him with temporary intelligence.

The cigarette was dropped from yellow stained fingers and was ground into the dry earth by a scuffed brown leather shoe. The thoughtful fowl gave it a tentative stab with its beak and then ate it. Albert's companion sighed and lit another cigarette before picking up a large, green plastic watering can.

In the distance, Neville had reached the roadside and waited disconsolately for the bus. A sign placed farther up the road announced that ScotRail apologised for the lack of trains due to a derailment of sheep.

Neville groaned and felt in his pocket for the small recently filled bottle still carefully wrapped in a sheet of paper, which he read once more. Third time unlucky. What he needed was to find someone who agreed with assisted suicide and wasn't a mad axe-murderer being temporarily cared for by the community, but he had about as much chance of meeting one of them as winning the Lottery.

Mr Burke rounded the corner and spotted a hunched figure at the side of the road.

It was dancing on the spot and gibbering. He slowed the black Ford Galaxy down and brought it to a smooth stop, inches from Neville's feet.

"Would you like a lift?" Mr Hare enquired, as he wound down the tinted windows.

Neville stopped gyrating and glowered at him.

"I put my hand out and it went for me," he announced. "It damned well sped up and went for me."

Mr Burke exchanged a look of sympathy with Mr Hare.

"Marauding bull, angry farmer?" Mr Hare enquired.

"No, the bloody bus. Went for me, only missed me because I leapt out of the way, quicksilver reflexes see, honed from years of avoiding editors and landladies."

"Perhaps he didn't think you had the right change," Mr Hare said.

"They can be very funny about that sort of thing," Mr Burke agreed, fondly remembering a youthful incident that had since been paid for with interest and the novel use of an old-fashioned ticket punch.

"I don't suppose you could give me a lift?" Neville asked.

"Where are you going?" Mr Hare asked.

"Edinburgh," Neville asserted, his mind made up. "To see a certain publisher about a book. A new book all about, about …"

Mr Hare exchanged a brief but message-laden glance with Mr Burke.

"Edinburgh, the very city to which we are wending our merry way. You could be dropped off right in the very centre and you could regale us with the plot on the way."

Neville nodded and clambered into the back of the car.

Ahead of them Fergus and Fiona bickered about the cost of hotels and behind them Janet and Robin emerged from behind the ScotRail sign and watched the departing ink-black dot until it merged with the shimmering ribbon of tarmac and was gone.

"Do you think he'll be all right?" Robin asked.

"Oh yes," Janet asserted. "As soon as he explains his dream and they realise what it means they'll be only too happy to assist him in his endeavours."

"I hope you're right."

"Of course I am."

"Where to now?"

"Edinburgh, where it all began, and where in precisely sixty-six hours time it will all finally end."

❋ ❋ ❋

Ramsey Snotme Fagends regarded the curtain of vegetation with a certain amount of satisfaction. This was real jungle with proper creepers and assorted deadly fauna. He spat on his hands and then, gripping his trusty machete, began to hack his way through.

The posse of young recruits following his every move

with interest clutched their own sharpened weaponry and prepared to follow.

A snake slithered out of the undergrowth and made a dash for freedom between two muscular young men, one of whom gave a smothered scream and jumped backwards, dislodging a large hairy spider from the drooping shrub beside him. The annoyed arachnid promptly bit him on the back of the neck and dropped to the floor, a dreadful taste of factor thirty sunscreen and bug repellent, jungle strength, clinging to its mandibles.

A large black bird watched the ensuing chaos with a certain amount of interest, as it chomped its way through a large and juicy mango pinned between a wrinkled talon and the thick tree branch upon which it was perched.

"I'm going to die, I'm going to die," whimpered the youth, as he felt the swelling wound growing beneath his clutching fingers.

"You are not going to die," Ramsey Snotme Fagends muttered to him, as he inspected the wound with a detached interest, born of many bites and the experience of years of not standing anywhere near drooping shrubs without wearing a large floppy hat and a tight bandanna around his neck.

"Any idea what sort of spider it was?" Ramsey asked, inspecting the completely inadequate medical kit that a thoughtful expedition administrator had supplied.

"It was big and black and ... er ... hairy," advised a small and spotty youth who had been standing next to the victim before the snake had appeared.

"They are always big and black and hairy," Ramsey snarled. "All right then, show me the tree it came from."

They all pointed to various shrubs. Ramsey sighed and rolled his eyes heavenwards.

"Why don't you just stand where you were standing before the snake?"

They all moved or shuffled to where they thought they had been and looked anxiously at their injured comrade. Ramsey went and looked up at the tree, which nobody was standing anywhere near, and peered into its leafy depths. A small shimmering web glinted in the slight breeze.

"It was a tarantula and I'm going to die," the boy whimpered with a shiver.

"It was not a tarantula," Ramsey snapped authoritatively.

"Wrong sort of habitat for a start and secondly most tarantulas are quite shy and live in burrows. What bit you was probably one of these."

He turned and faced them all, a large, brownish and very hairy spider squatting on one gloved hand.

"This is in fact a good example of the South American spider monkey, also known as a false tarantula and much prized by pet shop owners in the Notting Hill district. Can give you a nasty nip, but not as nasty as the nip from either a black widow or most of the Australian funnel webs and red backs. Mind you, I don't expect you'll be feeling one hundred per cent for a while, but it won't kill you, unfortunately."

There was a short silence as the spider was carefully released back into the wild.

"Now let's see if I've got any antidote for spider venom." Ramsey muttered, setting down his own backpack and carefully rummaging through the contents.

He unearthed a small plastic box and carefully inspected the perspex tubes with which it was carefully packed.

"Scorpion, snake, mamba, water ... Ah, here we are, spider monkey. Now let's see –where in the world did I put the hypo? Ah, here we are, now this may hurt just a bit, but in a couple of days you'll be bouncing off the walls again."

The group parted like the waters of the Red Sea and then closed up as everybody likes watching the inept application of a hypodermic needle on someone incapable of crawling away. There was a short silence broken by a brief scream and a collective intake of breath.

"Right then lads, the show's over, Wayne, get on the ether and request medical assistance, and the rest of you clear a space and set up the shelters."

Ramsey sighed as he'd only taken them about ten miles so far and already they'd been attacked by leeches, terrified by water snakes, seriously traumatised by a large log and had now been stopped by a medium-sized spider.

"And if anyone ever declares war let's just hope this lot are on manoeuvres in the Antarctic," Ramsey muttered to the waiting trees, as he quietly lit another of his large and noxious cigars.

"Aye, silly buggers," squawked Gravel the mynah bird. "Got any gin?" Gravel added hopefully, before dropping the stripped mango stone to the jungle floor.

"No, sorry," Ramsey replied looking upwards. "But I have got a drop of the hard stuff."

"Single malt?"

"Er no, blended."

"Stuff that for a game of soldiers."

Gravel spat at him, before flying off in search of the small discreet and well-stocked treehouse for the more discerning and wealthier tourist that he'd discovered the previous day. He would have liked to have seen the fun they would all have when they discovered they had in fact built their temporary camp, and in particular their cooking area, over a nest of large and irritable ants, but it was nearly Happy Hour and the dry roasted peanuts were about to be dispersed in small and easily pinched plastic bowls.

Ramsey took another long pull on his cigar before turning to the stunned and silent group watching him with horrified interest.

"Nice lot the Uggle Muggle tribe, used to get you at the back of the neck with a well-aimed poisoned dart, wait for you to fall over and then drag you back to their hidden camp for dinner. There they'd have you as the main course after the vegetables."

The injured youth tentatively moved his neck and asked, "Er, they don't still do it do they."

"No, Arthur, not now that they have satellite TV and cold beer."

Ramsey took another long drag on his cigar and regarded the solemn faces that were turned towards him, with a dangerous twinkle in his eye.

"Of course, they could be having one of their heritage weekends where they run around in not much more than a set of blue tattoos and a thong, get roaring drunk and upset all the wildlife for miles around."

"Er …"

"Why do they upset the wildlife? Well now, I guess it's because after all that booze a nice bit of roasted protein is good for settling the stomach."

"They don't still eat people, do they?" Wayne asked, nervously eyeballing a large palm that had started to sway gently in front of him.

"Probably not, but then if you eat someone they'll hardly be in any position to complain afterwards."

Ramsey sat back and observed the shimmering canopy

above his head. It was definitely about to rain. The ants were just beginning to warm up under the hastily lit fire. Some people, who had obviously not read his latest book on how to survive in the rainforest, were going to be in for another wet and cold night with an army of uninvited crawlies armed to the antennae and mad as hell.

He briefly wondered where the bird had gone and then, extracting a small gel pen and notebook from his pocket, added another fun-filled day to his ever increasing diary.

chapter ten

Deep in the bowels of an exclusive and outrageously expensive Edinburgh hotel, its modern bespoke interior heavily disguised by an exterior of uniformly cut slabs of Edinburgh granite, a cacophony of film and television producers mingled with the high and low of their media-related colleagues. Deals were cut and backs were savagely stabbed as the alcohol flowed and artfully arranged bits and pieces were wafted about on large silver trays, their carefully placed paper doilies sticky with mayonnaise and globules of congealed aspic.

Lancelot A. Boyles stabbed a solitary sausage with a long plastic cocktail stick and regarded it balefully. He sighed, and nibbling delicately upon the sticky blackened end pondered the ever-increasing problem of sausages.

There had been a time when you knew exactly what you were getting. If it said sausage on the menu, it was usually pork, fat and inclined to go bang when cooked if not stabbed to death first. Now they were long, thin and curly or even he noticed, flat. There were ones with herbs, leeks, apples, nuts, peppers and – God help him – Cajun flavoured. They even made them out of venison with, if the label was to be believed, a twist of juniper. The world was going to pot and it was all the blame of those damned Europeans. Now, just when he'd found the perfect little sausage made entirely of organically raised wild porker, some nut in the kitchens had covered it in mustard and breakfast marmalade.

"The thing is ..." his companion continued, "unless we bring this particular episode up to his usual high standards ..."

Lancelot choked on the remains of disguised pig and squinted upwards.

"We are still talking about the orange tit?"

"Yes."

"And correct me if the old inner ear has gone, but you said 'high' and then added 'standards' and we are still discussing the orange tit?"

"Yes."

"I knew that if I stayed in television long enough I'd hit the twilight zone."

"Lancelot, sweetie pots, I do wish you'd concentrate as I do need your expertise on this one. I really, *really* do. Because let's face it what the orange tit knows about actual historical fact you could write on the side of a postage stamp and still have room for the holes."

"What about South Bridge?"

"Did it last year; fabulous, absolutely great, got an entire hour of seriously scary stuff and if you believe the tit and his acolytes, a real ghost."

"What about the secret wynd, Mary King's Close? Been down there, only the once though and that was fairly horrible."

"Blue Peter."

"Oh."

"Wasn't there that drummer boy who was lowered into the vaults under the castle and beat his little drum all the way underground to the Tron Kirk?"

"Where it stopped and his emaciated soul still wanders to this day. That crime writer did it last year for some fringe festival production."

"You do realise that 'Auld Reekie' is in danger of being done to death?"

"What about if we present the entire city, or possibly one particular place in it, as a backdrop to real writers and their ghastly, but ghostly, muses?"

"How?"

"An old friend of mine from way back, rang this morning, said he had a really good idea for a ghost story and wondered if I'd be interested."

"What sort of story?"

"He said it involved the Resurrection Men."

"Wasn't that done a year or so ago by that Rankin fellow?"

"The one who cooks or the other one?"

"The other one. Does a lot of arty-farty programmes with intellectual lesbians and has a great line in strangely exotic shirts."

"Not the one who cooks?"

"No."

"Pity," Lancelot muttered, as the remaining sausage was quietly laid to rest in a recumbent ashtray.

A waiter hove into sight bowed down with an elongated tray of sparkling wine and discarded cocktail sticks.

"Hang on, another glass would be wonderful and what

175

are the brown bits in the vole-au-vents? And yes, I did actually say *vole* … Sort of mushrooms? Er … I'll try the prawn one then. Where was I? Oh yes, anyway, he said he had a really good story about a couple of homosexuals, a rogue doctor and a branch of the Russian Mafiosi. Oh, and a ghost or at least he thinks it was a ghost."

"What did it do?"

"Told him this long and involved story and then walked through a wall, with a parrot on its shoulder."

"Sort of Long John Silver?"

"I'm not absolutely sure about that bit, unless of course pirates have breasts."

"Some did, there was that film about it, Anne or Katie something, friend of Blackbeard. Terrible teeth."

"Ah yes, *that* film. Anyway, this friend of mine said that he distinctly remembers breasts and a pair of high-heeled red shoes."

"And then what?"

"He passed out."

"Do you seriously expect me to drum up support for some old pal you haven't seen hide nor hair of for years, who turns up out of the blue with a cock and bull story, which frankly sounds chemical, in the vague hope that there might be a ghost in it?"

"Yes."

"OK, where do we meet him?"

"That organic restaurant at the National Portrait Gallery tomorrow lunchtime. He said he was bringing some friends and that I wasn't to stare too much."

"Why?"

"He didn't say."

"I like the bit about the rogue doctor."

"I thought you might. It's a long time since I kicked some BMA butt."

"Since you were struck off you mean?"

"That was a long time ago and I'm perfectly happy with my new role in life."

"Right." She paused and took a long slug of sparkling wine. "And if there's a truly supernatural element the orange tit will be out of my hair for at least a fortnight. Lancelot, sweetie, I simply *must* meet this friend of yours. I'll even pay for lunch."

❋ ❋ ❋

Fergus looked upwards and then back down at the large metal slab in front of him and rubbed at the growing stubble on his chin.

"This is it, is it?" he asked.

"Aye," Bill replied.

"Yes," Fiona interpreted.

Bill gave her a brief and withering look before disappearing.

"Pretty bleak."

"Aye."

"So where do we start?" Fergus asked, turning around and leaning despondently against the door.

"We find another hotel, one without fleas or whatever it was in those blankets that had teeth," Fiona declared, scratching.

"It was cheap," Fergus whined. "And it had a vacancy sign."

"And we now know why."

"And I agree that you were right about the fact that they

could have removed the red and white tape from the bathroom, especially as Socco had obviously been and gone."

"Do they normally make that much mess?"

"Depends on the amount of blood and other fluids, generally speaking."

"Tonight I am going to sleep in a bed on my own with a duvet that has been regularly cleaned and, more importantly, changed, and where I can eat something, other than out-of-date cereal and cold toast with tinned tomatoes."

"I promise I won't fall asleep that quickly again."

"Or snore?"

"Or snore. By the way, you dribble."

"I do not!"

"Actually, you do," Bill intoned, grinning broadly.

"Oh, you're back are you?"

Fiona glared at him before resuming her tirade against Fergus.

"And you took the entire duvet."

"Only because you had most of it first."

Fiona bared her teeth, took a long, deep and very loud breath and stalked off up the steep slope towards the Mercat Cross and a decent cup of coffee.

"Ah, the first heady flush of true love, I remember it well," Bill sighed, before giving Fergus a comradely shove in the back.

"And you never know next time you might actually manage the deed itself, if that is you don't fall asleep in the middle, and if young Fiona is actually talking to you. Although to be truthful it's often better if they don't; there's nothing more off-putting than a man giving his all and all the object of your desire can think about is whether you're ever going to fix the wet patch on the ceiling."

Fergus shivered and looked around.

"Bill, is that you?"

Bill nodded and draped a ghostly arm across his shoulder.

"Bill, do me a favour; remember where this bloody house is before I do something really stupid."

Bill waited patiently, as he was a good listener.

"Because either I'm going to propose to that southern baggage or I'm going to deposit her in the nearest basement of wet cement I can find."

"You could on the other hand buy her a hot cup of coffee and fork out on a decent hotel room," Bill advised.

"I suppose so."

"Never mind, look on the bright side, at least you won't get any nasty shocks on the honeymoon."

Fergus started and looked around. He could have sworn that somebody was talking to him.

"How do you do that?"

"What?"

"Talk to me. I heard you quite distinctly. How come you haven't done it before?"

"Because I'm home."

"Oh, that makes a difference, does it?"

"Must do, and the physical contact helps."

"Speaking of which, you couldn't just move away a bit, could you?"

"Oh?"

"Not that I'm scared or cold or anything, but I have ice on the inside of my collar."

Bill obligingly changed position and sat on an abandoned oil drum on the opposite side of the cobbled walkway.

"I suppose I ought to go after her."

"That would be a start, especially as we still don't know who is trying to kill her," Bill agreed.

"Oh God, Fiona! I let her walk off. I don't even know where to start looking for her," Fergus moaned, aghast.

"I guess that the cement option is out."

"This is no time to be funny."

"She's by now sitting in that little coffee shop next to the Tron, feeling dead miserable."

"How do you know?"

"Because she drooled when we walked past it and I pinched her purse."

"What?"

"It's in your jacket pocket and I reckon you've got another four minutes to produce a white Americano with cinnamon sprinkles before she goes *bang*."

Fergus gave his pocket a tentative pat and then launched himself up the slope towards the Mercat Cross and a string of excitedly chattering Japanese tourists. They scattered as he approached at a run, and watched, cameras at the ready, in the event that Fergus might do something interesting or even better illegal, as he raced across the stone and cobbled pavement towards the smell of freshly brewed coffee beans.

Fiona looked up as he placed a brimming cup in front of her.

"And before you start, I didn't take your purse, Bill did," he explained, drawing up a seat next to hers.

"Oh," Fiona managed to stammer, her bottom lip quivering.

"I've booked a hotel too, a nice one with a big bath and fluffy towels."

"Oh!"

"And Bill reckons that if I play my cards right, you might

actually smile again before next Christmas."

"He does, does he?"

"You have lovely eyes."

"Oh, Fergus."

"And a really nice …"

"If you say 'bottom' you're a dead man and I cease to converse with you ever," Bill hissed into his ear.

"Smile," Fergus said, looking at her. "And …"

"What?"

"I need to know whether to book two singles or a double?"

Fiona took a long sip of hot creamy liquid and briefly closed her eyes. 'God, why does he have to have eyes like that, and lashes like that and a body like that?' she thought, as she desperately tried to remain cross with him and the rest of the world.

Fergus leaned towards her and smiled, using his eyes, mouth, eyebrows and even managed to waggle his ears engagingly.

Fiona melted.

"How are you going to protect me if we sleep in separate rooms?"

'Bingo!' Fergus thought, sipping his own drink and stroking her hand in a tentative fashion.

"We could go back to the car, find the hotel and get some rest before we start house–hunting," Fergus suggested, a decided twinkle in his eye.

"Or," Fiona whispered, "we can go back to the car, find the hotel, call room service take all our clothes off and send *Bill* out house-hunting."

"Now, that is a much better idea. After all, it would be very wasteful not to use all the facilities."

"And you do like to get your money's worth."

"Have you been talking to my sister?"

"As if."

Bill watched in horrified fascination as they kissed long, lingeringly and, to his mind, far too knowingly.

"Call me when adolescence wears off," he mumbled into Fiona's ear before striding out on to the main street without using the door.

He had an idea where to start and now was as good a time as any.

✳ ✳ ✳

Neville Foolscap shifted in his plastic chair and prodded the green lump in front of him with resigned interest.

"What exactly is it?" he asked.

"Lentil Surprise," came the reply from Mr Burke, who was gently prising open the wholemeal feta pancake in front of him with a fork. Unexploded bombs had been poked less gently.

"The surprise being?" Neville muttered.

"That you can actually get lentils that colour," quipped Mr Hare, who had managed to snare the last piece of wild mushroom quiche.

"Hello, Neville old chap!" a healthily robust voice boomed, as the owner of the voice gave him a comradely slap on the back.

"How's tricks?" he added, before pulling up a chair from a neighbouring table.

A grey-haired elderly lady with dark glasses and a pink knitted hat, glared at him from the corner and with a snort of, 'Well, really,' returned to slagging off the remainder of her family to her silently suffering partner.

"Oh er, hello, Lancelot," Neville gulped.

"Neville, I'd like you to meet a friend of mine. Fenella, Neville. Neville, Fenella."

"Um, hello, Fenella, nice … er … top," Neville gasped, looking up into a bosom that threatened to engulf him.

For a brief moment his world was completely full of sun-ripened, well-moisturised flesh with a cleavage designed by some mad cartoonist with a serious mammary fixation.

Mr Burke and Mr Hare sat in stunned and appreciative silence as the owner of two of Channel Eight's most watched assets sat down.

"Lancelot here tells me that you may have a story that I just might be interested in," Fenella purred.

"Oh, er, yes."

Neville rubbed a bead of sweat from his brow and took a long quick gulp of mineral water.

"Well?" she prompted, daintily dipping a long blue fingernail into a bowl of salad, which had been reverently placed in front of her by a grinning adolescent.

"I didn't think they did waiter service here," Neville observed.

"They *don't*," Fenella replied, blowing the young man a kiss as he went back to the food counter.

"Oh bother!" Fenella exclaimed, dropping her fork.

She leaned from her chair to pick up the silver-coloured implement. A swarthy, casually dressed Italian gentleman of indeterminate age watching in abject fascination failed to spot the stationary, equally fascinated Australian in front of him and collided noisily. Wine, glasses and unidentified boiled vegetables erupted and splattered the surrounding dinners.

After the mess had been cleared and the fawning European had left his hotel room number, Fenella finally managed to extract an interesting tale from an overtly perspiring Neville. For a short while she sat and stared into space, cogs turning slowly in her surprisingly sharp and immensely cynical brain.

"Mind like a steel trap," Lancelot observed, finishing the last of his salad.

"Who?" Neville asked, chasing a recalcitrant lentil onto a ribbon of lettuce.

"Fenella there. Don't be put off by the abundance of womanly virtues, that girl could give Machiavelli tips."

"Oh."

"So," Lancelot asked, lowering his voice to a gentle boom, "who are the goons?"

"Well, I think Peter Sellers was one and Spike –"

"No, not the Goons, the *goons*!"

"Oh, er …"

Mr Burke and Mr Hare went very quiet, so quiet that you could feel the room going on around them.

"They're, um – just – um … friends," Neville gulped.

"Gould House," Fenella muttered to herself.

All eyes turned and stared at her.

"We were only going to film the heady social whirl of a leading surgeon and his attractive yet witty wife and now …"

"Yes?" Lancelot prompted, holding his breath.

"We will film a ghastly exposé of present-day Resurrection Men, complete with acid-washed bones and severed limbs."

"I like it, I like it," Lancelot agreed.

"And so do I. Now, Neville darling, you are sure about

this aren't you? Something will definitely happen?"

"Oh yes."

"Good, because I'd really like to see that snotty, common little cow get her comeuppance."

"Right."

"Lancelot, sweetie pots, we'd better go and brief the crew."

"What *now*?"

"Yes, now."

"But I haven't had any pudding."

"I'll buy you a Mars Bar on the way out. I want as many infrared cameras as we can get and a stack of thermometers. Do you think that Marcus could manage to obtain some of those big black boxes with the glowing dials? I have absolutely no idea what they do, if anything, but they always manage to imbue even the tritest situation with a little extra gravitas. Oh, and then get Abby on the mobile and tell her to sober up the orange tit and get him into something resembling a tuxedo and Lance –"

"Yes, my darling little piranha fish."

"Tell them not to let the cat out of the bag. I want genuine horror and there had better be a real live manifestation or I'll eat someone's liver!"

"I know a little shop just off Prince's Street that does a great Chianti," Mr Burke observed in moribund tones. "Falafel beans are a little more difficult to get," he added, wiping his mouth with a paper napkin.

Together Mr Hare and Mr Burke arose as one and silently left the table.

"Who?" Fenella asked, watching their retreating backs with interest.

"Er friends of mine, eccentric millionaires travelling

incognito," Neville muttered.

"Really?"

"Yes."

"Not members of some Blues Brothers' tribute band?"

"Er, no."

"Or some obscure branch of the Mafioso?"

"No."

"Pity, we could have included them in the programme."

"So how are we going to do this?" Lancelot asked, extracting a small notebook from his commodious brown tweed jacket.

"What we do is this. We set everything up, as per a normal fly-on-the-wall documentary. I go around and interview the great and the good, and we gradually pan in on the entrance to this hidden room, the one that darling Neville here has told us about. Then we get the good doctor to let us in after a certain amount of buttering up."

"And how?" Neville asked.

"If he has a pulse, Fenella can butter with the best of them."

"Oh."

"And then we film whatever we find. Either way we win. Ghastly wannabees socialising with big cat fight at the end, or, even better, a ghostly manifestation with murderous intent and a huge dose of ancient malpractice. Now, Lancelot sweetie, I want all the historical stuff you can find out about this Gould House or 'Cold House' as it was called, while Neville and I discuss the finer aspects of his dream."

Lancelot grinned, and thrusting his notebook back into a handy pocket, stood up to leave. Neville watched him go, a look of horrified desperation on his thin face. After he'd been totally abandoned, Fenella leaned towards him and smiled alarmingly.

"Don't worry, Neville darling, I won't eat you, or at least not just yet."

"Er ... now look here, there's something that ..."

"You're gay, right?"

"Yes."

"Most of my really, really good friends are, I mean look at Lancelot ..."

"Right."

"So tell me, is it true then?"

"What?"

"Well, confidentially of course, our mutual friend told me that you've tried to end it all. Is that right?"

"Yes."

"Why?"

"Because, well, it sounds crazy ..."

"Try me, I've got a master's degree in crazy."

"In my dream ..."

"Yes."

"Well, I can talk to the dead, but well ..."

"Only the dead can do that."

"Yes."

"Crazy."

"Told you so."

"What if you nearly die?"

"What?"

"If you nearly die, you could just float towards the light, but not actually get there."

"Like in the films?"

"Yes."

"Sort of almost kill myself ..."

"Talk to the dead."

"And then come back?"

"Yes."

"How?"

"What if – and it's only a thought, mind – you try to hang yourself, just before we ask the good doctor to open up the door to the room of a hundred sins?"

"Well, I suppose ..."

"We could rig something up, find you just in the nick of time, cut you down and while everyone is having hysterics you can subconsciously bring on the spooks' cabaret. Even if they don't show, our two stooges would be so shaken they might actually say anything, especially if we separate them. That is, if everything you've told me, is actually true?"

"About him having people murdered and ..."

"All the other gory details, like who, when and, most importantly, why?"

"It's true."

"Good, because you see, Neville darling, even if it wasn't we could still make people believe it was."

"Oh."

"That's the wonder of live television, sweetie, it very rarely is."

chapter eleven

Fergus silently prowled the gloom and doom of Edinburgh, a look of such fierce concentrated ferocity on his face that two likely lads out to tickle tourists, in the same way that their predecessors would have tickled trout, hid in a doorway until he'd passed.

He was still fuming. The evening had not gone well. Bill's breakthrough had revealed nothing more than the fact that the law and, in particular, lawyers, were more of an ass than he'd previously believed possible, and that Fiona still hated him.

Well, possibly hate was too strong a word, loathed maybe. He had tried throughout the evening to prove to her that Bill could speak to him. She had not believed him. Bill had reiterated ad nauseam that he'd only managed to communicate on the grounds that they'd been next to the door to the South Bridge Vaults at the time. Fergus remained unconvinced and said so, thus causing their latest and greatest argument, culminating in his morose tramp of the ill-lit streets.

Bill was lying and Fergus knew it. A long history of dealing with witnesses, who were on their day in court about as reliable as a chocolate teapot, had resulted in Fergus's policeman's nose twitching so violently he was in danger of growing a proboscis to rival that of Pinocchio. Bill might be older than the average flotsam that Fergus normally hauled into the cells on a Saturday night, but he was still just as untrustworthy.

If only ... That was it – the only thing Bill really cared about was Fiona, so if ...

Fergus turned on his heel and almost ran back to the hotel ...

He stalked into their hotel room, where Fiona was painstakingly painting her toenails, and slammed the door behind him with such violence that an ornament on a side chest shattered into thousands of glimmering bits as it hit the polished wooden floor. With a growl of menace, rivalling that of Bill Sykes just before he batters poor Nancy to death, Fergus advanced towards Fiona with clenched fists and murderous intent.

Bill turned from the window where he'd been observing an amorous couple in the first throws of pubescent lust, and raced towards him. Bill might have been technically dead, but he could read emotions as well as the next person and Fergus had, in his view, finally flipped.

"*No!*" he screamed, pushing Fergus onto the floor. "You'll really regret it in the morning, believe me, I've experience in that department."

There was a tentative knock on the door.

"And that will be the manager," he added.

Fergus, grinning broadly at them both, turned and with abject apologies began a five-minute explanation involving a gust of wind and not knowing his own strength. A subtle reminder of what he did for a living and the palming of a £20 note into the confused youth's hand also helped.

When the shattered glass and china had been cleared and the hotel settled back down to its usual evening somnolence, Fergus cleared his throat and muttered:

"So, I'll regret it in the morning will I? And by the way what sort of experience have you got, Bill old boy?"

"Bill?" Fiona queried, looking from one flushed face to the other. "Explain how Fergus heard every word and is nowhere near your last haunt?"

"Er …"

"I can't see you like Fiona can, but I can hear you, can't I?" Fergus demanded, flexing his knuckle joints.

"Well, yes, but only when I want you to."

"So can anybody else hear you as well?"

"Yes, but only if I want them to."

"I'm sorry, I didn't quite catch that?"

"*Yes.* Happy now?"

"Very."

"But I still don't see how this is going to help." Fiona sighed in a puzzled fashion and, picking up the bottle of pink nail varnish, began again on her right foot, her toes carefully held apart with yellow foam.

"Don't you?"

"No, I don't."

"Look, we've all searched the New Town until we're seeing absolutely nothing at all. We have no idea where this Cold House is and even less idea about that wretched key. Except for one fact, that as it's a small key it ought to fit a small lock, maybe a padlock of some kind."

"If that strange old man at the locksmith's we visited

this morning is right," Fiona added, and moved position in order to start on her left toes.

"So why don't we go back and talk to the people who might know something?" Fergus continued, pointedly ignoring Fiona's latest interjection.

"Who?" Fiona and Bill asked in unison.

"The members of the pre-Glasnost Russian Tourist Board currently helping Finn and Binthar with my enquiries."

"But what makes you think they'll talk to us?" Fiona queried, fixing him with a puzzled frown.

"Because we have Bill."

Bill looked from one to the other and then backed away, shaking his head vigorously.

"No, no, no and you can't make me."

"Come on, Bill. You can talk to them, but they can't see you. They're a superstitious bunch, according to Binthar, and very fond of their mothers. All we have to do is tell them that their cell is haunted and then we hold a rather unorthodox unofficial interview."

"But what about their rights?" Fiona asked.

"What about *our* rights? Look, Bill, as soon as the thirty-six hours or so that the procurator has agreed we can hold them for has gone they'll be back on the streets and after Fiona here. We can't protect her forever, I have to sleep sometime and how are you going to stop all the bullets from a semi-automatic?"

"Charming," Fiona snorted.

"And all I have to do is persuade them to talk?"

"I'll have an interpreter behind glass. He won't see you, you won't see him, no one else will be present and I hardly think that a bunch of hard nuts will want to admit that they are scared of the dark."

"I blow the lights, produce a few cold spots and generally put the wind up?"

"Yes."

"I've never in two hundred-odd years ever helped the police out, you do realise this!"

"Look if it makes you any happier I'll forget the interpreter, get Binthar to fix up a few cameras and a mike and I'll watch the whole thing off duty. Then we have no evidence and you can't be accused of helping anybody, least of all the local constabulary."

"And what, pray, would be the point?"

"Because we, I mean *you*, just might be able to scare them enough for them to name names and quite frankly any name at all is better than the large sheet of blank paper that we currently have."

Bill wandered around the room, rearranging various objects en route.

He stopped abruptly and muttered, "I suppose if you put it like that, it could be quite a lot of fun."

"Yes."

"All right then, I'll do it."

Bill chuckled as he began to repack their scant wardrobe into two black plastic holdalls.

"Hang on, what about my comfortable bed?" Fiona cried out, smudging pink polish across the towel she'd laid under her feet.

"You can sleep in the car," Fergus advised, checking his pockets for keys. "Bill, you finish packing and then bring the bags and baggage down to the front desk while I go down and settle up."

"OK," Bill agreed, gaily clearing drawers by simply

tipping the contents straight out and into the waiting holdalls.

When Fergus had finally gone Fiona glared furiously at Bill.

"Why didn't you tell me that Fergus could hear you? Why on earth did you have to lie about it?"

Bill shrugged and wafted into the bathroom.

"And what did he mean about the bags and baggage – what baggage?"

"Aye well, I rather think he was referring to you. Got everything? Good, let's go."

Bill threw the holdalls to Fiona and then vanished.

Fiona stood for a moment and gently fumed.

"Bloody men – they're all the bloody same. First they spend all their energy getting you into bed and then when they do, they won't let you stay there."

❋ ❋ ❋

Rebecca Denzel-Oakes regarded her large and handsome husband with a frown.

"I beg your pardon?" she said, in tones of ice.

"I said 'Yes', dear," her husband replied, spreading thick orange marmalade on his toast.

He took a bite and then frowned down at his plate.

"This toast is cold," he observed plaintively.

"Bugger the toast," his wife growled. "How stupid can you get?"

"What?"

"Have you any idea what you have done?"

"But ..."

"No, of course you haven't!"

"All I did ..."

"All you have done ..." she growled at him and took a deep and pointed breath. "All you have done, is to invite some second-rate ham actor and his attendant sycophants into our home, during one of my parties, to make some sort of ghastly reality television programme. A television programme watched by the sort of people who can't afford a decent bottle of wine, let alone your fees."

"But I thought it would help publicity-wise, after all you're always saying that not enough people know about us. I thought you'd be pleased."

"Well, you were wrong."

"Obviously."

There was a short pause, broken by the drumming of Rebecca's fingers against the polished surface of the long and overtly ornate table at which they were sitting. Beyond the open French windows birds sang and twittered, and beyond them the sounds of a busy road filtered through the drooping leaves of the beeches, which gallantly sheltered their home from the surrounding city.

"I don't want them anywhere other than the rooms I'll be using for the party," Rebecca demanded.

"Yes dear."

"And I don't want them to trample all over my new Japanese rock garden."

"No dear."

"I'll have to let the caterers know, of course. Do you have a contact number?"

"Well, no, not really, but Daphne said she'd sort it out."

"Daphne would."

"I don't know why you don't like her; she's a jolly good secretary."

"Oh yes, salt of the earth," Rebecca sneered derisively.

"There is nothing wrong with that," her husband snapped back.

Rebecca gave him a brief poisonous look and then smiled.

"I'm sorry, darling. You know how I get just before one of my little parties."

"Oh yes."

"It's just that I do so want to have everything just right. It's so important for your image, my love."

"I know and don't think that I'm not grateful it's just that ..."

"Yes Charles?"

"Well, does it have to be so damned expensive? I'm not made of money you know and ..."

"Tell you what, darling, how about if I have a word with Daphne and arrange a short holiday immediately after this party? A lovely vacation just made for the two of us, somewhere quiet and peaceful. After all, darling, you've been working so hard recently."

"Well ..."

"We could use the money the television people are paying you ..."

"Er ..."

"They *are* paying you, aren't they?"

"Oh yes, of course, wouldn't have allowed it at all if they weren't."

"Good. Well, you finish your breakfast and I'll go and have a word with Phipps about the pots in the entrance hall."

She arose elegantly and, after kissing her husband gently on the forehead, quietly left the room via the open French windows.

Charles watched her go with a certain amount of pride and no little degree of fear. Just recently she had not been quite so eager to entertain Mr Winky and he rather missed their bathtime romps. Perhaps it was the money? He would talk to Daphne and see if he couldn't fit in a few extra patients before the end of the week and he would cancel his round of golf with the chief constable. Yes, that's what he'd do.

Charles licked the last of the marmalade from his fingers and sighed. Today he would give Mr Argambi a new kidney and with any luck he could bank the cheque by Thursday. Stroke of luck that kidney turning up like that, the right blood type and tissue match. He must remember to congratulate young Phipps when he saw him. Honestly, it was bloody marvellous what you could get on the Internet nowadays.

❋ ❋ ❋

Rebecca scowled down at the gravel beneath her feet and then looked up and into the sharp black eyes of Phipps senior.

"How many do we have left?"

"One."

"We have to get rid of everything before tonight."

"Where do you want it stored?"

Rebecca ground the gravel beneath an expensive metal-tipped heel.

"About here," she answered, pointing to the ground with her toe.

"I'll clear the decks, and then if anyone goes snooping, all they'll find is an empty cellar and a spotlessly clean historical monument."

"Good."

"Charles is beginning to ask questions."

"Oh."

"Yes, he's queried the way we get the organs. Paul doesn't reckon he can palm him off much longer with the Internet story."

"Pity."

"So?"

"I've promised him a few days off fishing, that should do it."

"Somewhere quiet and out of the way. A tragic accident and a great loss to the medical profession."

"Exactly."

"And then?"

"I retire to mourn in private at my country retreat."

"Which just happens to be next door to the recently divorced honourable member?"

"We can console each other."

"Be careful, you're not …"

"As young as I was?"

"I was going to say 'unknown'."

"Ah."

"He's a politician and you'll be vetted. You do realise that?"

"They won't find anything."

"They had better not."

Phipps moved closer and whispered, "For *your* sake."

Rebecca gave a small shudder as Phipps moved away.

"I'll see to those pots now Mrs, before the sun gets too hot," he said loudly, and pulling the peaked gardening cap over his eyes, moved away towards the side of the house.

Rebecca watched him go, her eyes narrowed against the morning light.

"Damn him to hell," she muttered. "But the bastard's right."

She turned on her heel and stalked off in the opposite direction, her mind rapidly listing available and susceptible men with the required amounts of cash and social standing.

chapter twelve

Binthar stretched and yawned.

Finn scratched his nose with his pen, and the dumpy bespectacled advocate from Edinburgh scowled at the gently humming tape recorder as if it were an unexploded bomb. His clients sat in various attitudes of overt boredom and collectively picked, scratched or inspected various orifices. The translator sat on the sidelines and hummed a stanza or two from 'Tosca', but nobody actually said anything.

A fly buzzed drearily at a small window made of glass bricks and then suddenly stopped. All eyes turned to the cessation of noise and, as one, they watched its furry, blue-black body fall with a soft scrunch onto the concrete floor.

Finn looked first at Binthar and then at his watch.

"Christ!" he exclaimed. "It's almost seven o'clock."

Binthar stared at him and then hurriedly turned to the tape.

"Interview terminated at 1900 hours, Constable Devine and Sergeant Finn leaving the room."

Mr Tortascue, the advocate, stared at them in disbelief. "What are you doing?" he asked.

"Leaving," Binthar muttered, switching off the tape and extracting the cassette.

"I'll escort Tweedledum, Tweedledumber and The Mad Hatter to the cells and we'll start again in the morning," Finn explained, hurriedly looking around.

Mr Tortascue glared at them both and then, drawing himself up to his full height, looked Finn in the stomach and hissed, "This is intolerable; I've only just managed to get here and now you want to leave?"

"Yes," Binthar and Finn asserted.

The translator, who had now realised that something was actually happening, started translating madly and the three accused sat back in their respective chairs and watched avidly.

"Why?" Mr Tortascue demanded.

"Er ..." Finn began, and then as if startled, turned and glared at the wall behind him.

"Look, it will sound a bit stupid," Finn replied, edging uneasily towards the door.

"Try me – I'm a lawyer and I'm experienced in stupid, brainless, lumpish, witless, asinine and downright barmy."

"Well, all right, but off the record and this is *strictly* off the record ..."

"Yes, cross my heart and hope to expire horribly."

"Well ..."

"Please just tell him, Sir, my Mum gets nervous if I'm down here at night and it's five past already," Binthar squeaked.

"All right, all right, it just sounds you know ..."

"Sir!"

"This police station has a ghost."

"And nobody likes being down in the custody suite at night on account of it," Binthar finished hurriedly.

"You're pulling my wig!" Tortascue laughed.

Behind him his clients looked for the first time as if they would like to be somewhere else.

"Go on, tell me what sort of ghost? A headless horseman, Rob Roy or some other kilted madman clutching a set of wailing pipes?" Tortascue scoffed.

"Well, no, to be frank it would be better if it was," Finn mumbled.

"So, go on – scare me, what exactly does this entity do?"

"Well, he doesn't do much more than frighten the bejabers out of you really ..." Binthar explained nervously.

"How?"

"Cold spots, moving stuff around ..."

"You wouldn't believe the sets of keys we mislay down here."

"And he pinches you unawares."

"Old McBride said he once finished his crossword in Gaelic, so he refused to do night shifts after that. In the end the boss had to transfer him to Lothian and Borders."

"Poor old McBride. Do you remember how his hair turned snow white and he couldn't drink a cup of tea afterwards?"

"Why, what was so frightening about the tea?" Tortascue asked, intrigued despite his obvious cynicism.

"He said he put his mug down to answer a call of nature and when he came back it was full of flies – dead ones."

As one, every eye turned towards the blowfly that was still lying on the floor with its black hairy legs pointing heavenwards.

"What about my clients?" Tortascue demanded.

"What about them?" Finn replied, opening the door and beckoning someone they couldn't see towards him.

"Will they be all right?"

"Of course they will. After all, as you have yourself endlessly pontificated, they were in the wrong place at the wrong time, and were merely searching for the railway station," Binthar stated, as a tall morose policeman joined them.

"So this ghost won't manifest itself?"

"Shouldn't think so, he only goes for criminals who have actually done something, murderers mostly. But as we don't get any of them, or at least only domestics, we haven't had an incident for ages."

"Incident?"

"About five years ago we had some nut here on holiday from Brighton. He got into an argument with one of the fisherman down at the Laughing Lobster and stabbed the man to death, took five of us to get him into the wagon and then down to the cells. Anyway, we left him to cool off and sober up; next thing we know the custody sergeant is white as a sheet and the poor sod is stretched out on his mattress dead as the proverbial dormouse with an expression on his face that could freeze a man's blood."

"What did he die of?"

"The coroner and the police doctor both agreed that he'd died of coronary failure. What they failed to agree on was how, although, as old Dr Gaspin said at the inquest, he looked like he'd seen the devil himself just before the old ticker gave out."

"Oh!"

There was a flurry of guttural noises from the translator

and Mr Tortascue's clients, culminating in the translator asking, "And you say he only inflicts the guilty person?"

"Well, yes, apart from the odd bit of ... well I suppose you'd call it, ghostly horseplay."

"Oh, and do you know the name of this ... er ... ghost?" the translator asked.

"No, we had the vicar down a couple of times and a Catholic priest who was over from Ireland on holiday, and things did slow down a bit for a while."

"I see." Mr Tortascue looked from one to the other. "And you have no actual proof of these manifestations?"

"Not anything that would stand up in court, it's all circumstantial really, just like your clients."

"I see."

Mr Tortascue might have been a lawyer, but he wasn't immune to tales of the supernatural, his favourite nightly viewing consisting of supernatural reality shows and back episodes of 'Charmed'. Purely, as he told himself, for the clothing – or rather lack of it – worn by a variety of American magical totty. As far as he was concerned his clients were in all likelihood as guilty as hell or why else had they contacted him, and if they had to spend a night in a haunted cell it would probably do them the world of good. Apart from which, their continual sniping in some obscure Russian dialect was driving him very slightly mad, especially as he was convinced that they could understand and speak a certain amount of English, even if it had been picked up on the lower level of the Glaswegian criminal strata.

"Well, in that case I shall return in the morning. I believe that the Fish Café is very good?"

"Bloody marvellous actually and if the scallops are on, you must try them," Finn agreed, standing aside to let him pass.

The three prisoners looked anxiously to left and right before being escorted out and shivered as they passed the door. The translator picked up her handbag and left hastily, rubbing her right buttock in a pensive fashion, and Mr Tortascue, following in her wake, was suddenly aware that not only was he in for a good dinner, but that he had walked through his first really authentic cold spot.

Fergus sat behind the mirrored wall and chuckled.

"Let the games commence," he murmured happily, as he rubbed his hands together in happy anticipation. "Let the games commence."

Binthar and Finn watched from the doorway and Finn sighed and shook his head.

"You know, young Binthar, I've finally realised what we can get the boss for a leaving present."

"What's that, Sarge?"

"A big white fluffy cat."

"And an eye patch, Sarge, they all have an eye patch."

"Aye, you're right, lad, all the best despots heading for world domination need one of them."

"And the cat, Sarge, that goes without saying."

Fergus eyed them for a moment and then beckoned them towards him.

"This is it, Binthar, time to unleash the laser beams or whatever fiendish device he's installed in the cells, which will probably result in all of us looking for alternative employment."

"I've already written the letter, Sarge."

"Good laddie, ye may well need it."

"Finn, Binthar, shut up."

"Yes Boss."

Finn and Binthar both stood to attention and saluted, clicking their heels in unison.

Fergus eyed them with a certain amount of genuine amusement before producing a large bottle of Oban malt and three plastic mugs.

"Did you put them in the same cell?" he asked, pouring out three generous portions and consulting his watch.

"Yes, and they seemed very happy to be together," Finn remarked, picking up one of the mugs.

"And did you stick the ... er ... devices in the right place?" Fergus enquired, casually handing a mug to Binthar, who pulled up a chair and gratefully loosened his tie.

"Yes, Sir, I did it just like you said and I wired them up, just like the booklet showed on page five."

"Good. Three, two, one, go – we are now officially off duty and can switch on the machine and watch the latest thing in reality television, 'Big Brother Meets Cell Block H'."

Fergus switched on the television screen in front of him and then connected it to a small black box. A green light glowed momentarily and then the cell in which the three prisoners were incarcerated was eerily visible. All three inmates were sprawled over their mattresses and were arguing earnestly.

"This is nae legal is it?" Finn asked, taking a sip of whisky.

"Not entirely," Fergus agreed, playing with the volume control.

"Run it by me again, boss, but exactly which bit is not going to have us wending our merry way to the situations vacant page?"

"Er ..."

"I thought so. Well, this had better be good, whatever it is, although I still can't see what you can possibly get them to say by sticking them in a supposedly haunted cell for the night," Finn muttered.

"I mean to say it's not as if we had a *real* ghost," Binthar agreed sagely, before taking a gulp of orange liquid.

Fergus rummaged around in the carrier bag at his feet and, careful to avoid eye contact, produced a large packet of mini sausage rolls and a selection of pre-wrapped sandwiches.

"There you go, lads; tuck in. It could be a long night."

"Fergus?"

"Yes, Finn."

"We've known each other a long time, haven't we?"

"Yes, why?"

"And you wouldn't hide something really important from one of your oldest friends would you?"

"Er …"

Binthar paused in the unwrapping of a chicken salad sandwich with lemon mayonnaise on wholegrain bread, and looked from one to the other.

There was an uneasy silence and then the television screamed at them. All three inmates were standing on their mattresses and one was pointing at the wall. A cup lay at the foot of the whitewashed wall of bricks, now stained a dark brown. As all six men watched in growing disbelief, letters appeared.

"It says, 'Get Out'," Binthar whispered in amazement.

"That's OK, they can't read English," Finn explained, taking a bite out of an egg and crispy bacon.

"Oh, can't they," Fergus chuckled.

Below them in the cells, Danovitz crawled under his

blanket and whimpered piteously.

"Pull yourself together, Danno," the oldest of the three admonished. "It's just a trick. Nothing can frighten us remember, ve are after all ex-KGB. Ve frighten others not the other vay around. Besides vich ve vill be out in the morning. All ve have to do is not say a single vord about you know who and you know vot."

"Have you ever, you know, met them?"

"Who?"

"You know, Mr Anderson and Mr Fiske?"

"No Tirnip, nobody ever meets them, that's the whole point."

"Oh."

"I feel cold," Danovitz cried.

"They have probably turned off the heating to save on money."

"Tirnip is right, Danno, there is nothing to be scared of, it is just their Scottish humour."

The third member of the gang felt the radiator beside him and hastily stuck his hand in the sink and turned on the tap. As he watched, the tap turned itself off and someone pinched both his ample buttocks. At any other time he would have been quite happy with the attention, but deep in a Scottish cell it was not his idea of romance.

"Who did that?" he asked, turning with ferocity bordering on madness upon his two companions, both of whom were now staring at the wall behind him.

A pair of boots had appeared and were walking purposely towards him. Then a pair of ice cold hands lifted him by the neck until he was dangling a few inches from the floor and a deep bass voice demanded:

"Who are Anderson and Fiske?"

"If it's a trick," Tirnip muttered, "it's a bloody good one."

"Tell him, tell him," Danovitz mumbled from the safety of his blanket.

"I don't know, I don't know, ye ken."

"Spoken like the true McDonald ye undoubtedly are," whispered the boots, which then vanished.

"How?"

"Do I know who ye are? Ye smell like a McDonald and I have nere been able to forget the smell of a McDonald, ye ken?"

"Aye."

"So, tell me again, laddie, who exactly are Anderson and Fiske?"

McDonald eyed Tirnip warily and then crawled into the farthest corner away from him.

"Are you still there?" he whispered.

"Aye, and where else would I be, I have nae place else tae go and have nae done for many a long year," a ghostly voice whispered back, and a cold hand clapped itself upon McDonald's shoulder like a vice.

"I don't know who they are, but ..."

"Go on, laddie, go on, because believe me when I say that I hate ruining a good heart by squeezing it to a stand-still."

McDonald shivered, each layer of fat wobbling violently.

"My employer knows who they are."

"Oh."

"He wasnae happy with leaving them in the sole charge of a certain job so he sent us doon to keep an eye on things and to silence any additional witnesses."

He made a cutting motion against his own throat as he said this and the hand gripping him slackened a little.

"Go on," the air whispered.

"There is a phone number we are to ring, it's how he stays in contact."

"With you or them?"

"With them. We leave a message and it gets passed on down the line."

"And that's all you know?"

"Yes."

"Are you sure?"

"Ye –"

The remainder of the word was cut off as he felt something grip him again around the throat and he was hurled onto his bed where a size ten boot kneed him viciously in the groin.

Then the voice laughed. A laugh that would be described on any script as maniacal, the sort of laugh that would have had both Stephen King and Dean Koontz reaching for the nearest laptop and a bottle of Schnapps.

Above, in the interview room, Finn sat and stared at the screen in mounting horror.

"How did you do that?" he asked

"Yes, Sir, how did you do that?" Binthar reiterated, as Fergus switched the television off and carefully disconnected the black box.

"Am I to believe that you have been dabbling in the world of the seriously twisted and supernatural?" Finn urged.

"I might have, but then again would anybody believe me if I said yes?" Fergus replied.

"Er ..."

"Well, that's about it lads, show's over. The fat man has definitely sung and Elvis has probably left the building."

"Do you think we ought to see if they're all right?" Finn

asked.

"Oh, they'll be all right, besides which we aren't here, are we?"

"Well, no."

"So we didn't see anything?"

"Well, no."

"Good."

"Where are you off to now?" Finn asked, watching him put the box in his pocket.

"To tell the custody sergeant to let them go and then after I've removed a certain device, which by rights should be sitting inside the smoke alarm above the rugby club bar, I'm going to see a man about a telephone number and I may be some time. So don't wait up."

With that, Fergus blew them both an airy kiss and quietly left the room. Finn and Binthar regarded each other in mute bemusement.

"You don't think?" Binthar asked.

"No, no, I don't. Come on, laddie, you and I both know that there are no such things as ghosts."

"Right."

"Although saying that, Fergus has met a lot of funny people and I'm not convinced that all of them had a pulse."

"Sarge!"

✻ ✻ ✻

Fergus lurked under an overhanging bush at the water's edge and checked again that nobody was around.

After a minute or two he took the mobile from his pocket. It was brand new and still in its plastic wrapper. He peered at the shiny pay as you go card containing ten pounds worth of credit and carefully punched in the numbers above the barcode. He waited for a few minutes as he tried to identify all the buttons and then, with some difficulty as he was wearing a pair of gloves he'd pinched from Forensics, he eventually tapped out the numbers that McDonald had furtively whispered to Bill, and that Bill had gleefully whispered to him half an hour previously.

"Anderson and Fiske, purveyors of bespoke assassinations at reasonable rates are currently unavailable but if you wish to leave your name and number one of our members of staff will get back to you as soon as possible. Please leave a message after the dirge, thank you," the phone intoned mournfully, before playing the first few notes of the Funeral March.

Fergus shivered, moistened his lips and then, speaking slowly through a large cotton handkerchief, lisped the words:

"Tell Mr Anderson and Mr Fiske that the Oban police are on to them, the Russian connection has joined the choir and that they might want to share information about their mutual employer, who by the way doesn't appear to trust their judgement much. I will be at the Waverley tomorrow at three. Take the taxicab with the number 666 on the plate."

Fergus hung up and then tossed the mobile phone into the nearby water, where it landed with a soft liquid splash and then sank.

"Do you think they'll be there?" Bill asked from the darkening shadows.

"Oh yes, they'll be there. The main advantage that they have, according to a mate at St Leonards, is that they have been operating for years and still nobody knows who the hell they are. Unofficially, they call them 'the cleaners';

someone makes a mess and they step in, for a certain fiscal consideration, clean up and get out. Only this time someone was daft enough to not entirely trust them and I'd lay odds on that it's pretty mutual. Anyway, I'll be there driving the cab and you, my spectral friend, will be right beside me."

"And after all no one expects the Spanish Inquisition."

"Bill?"

"Aye."

"Just exactly how much did you watch on the small screen at your last scaring place?"

"Oh lots, the security guard had a passion bordering on total obsession for all the latest video releases, however awful. I think he worked part-time in one of those big video hire places and he used to write up his own reviews to pass the time. He wasn't that bad either."

"Right, and I guess that explains the odd Americanisation too."

"Pardon?"

"You told hat spotty git outside the Waverley railway station, the one who threatened to throw up over the bonnet of the cab, 'not' – and I quote – 'to hurl on the shell' as you'd only just waxed it."

"'Finding Nemo'; I liked the shark the best."

"Everyone liked the shark."

"The spotty git – was that the idiot with the personal stereo and eyebrow pierced with the tincey-wincey skull and crossbones on a chain?"

"That was him."

"The one who didn't manage to get to the bathroom in time."

"Despite your offers of help, yes."

"Ah. Didn't think you'd seen that one. You didn't, did you?"

"No, but I've played enough games of very bad cricket to know the delightful sound of leather smacking plump buttock when I hear it."

"Ah."

"The thing is, are you going to stop scaring around and play nice or do I have to add this piece of silver to my growing collection of marine mobiles?"

Fergus held Bill's silver tooth between finger and thumb, where it briefly glinted in the ebbing light.

"I'll be good."

"Sweet."

Fergus turned and humming softly to himself, extracted his ample frame from the small copse in which he'd been hiding. Bill glared after him and then abruptly vanished.

✳ ✳ ✳

Mr Burke sat and contemplated the froth on his pint of 'Old Socks' and mused upon the rival merits of the garrotte as opposed to the usual length of nylon washing line and a slip knot, both of which he decided, upon reflection, had their merits.

Mr Hare sidled into the seat opposite him and quietly opened a packet of pork scratchings, which he sucked methodically.

"I have had, Mr Hare, what I would call an odd phone call."

"Odder than usual, Mr Burke?"

"And threatening."

"Oh."

"Apparently our latest employer is not to be trusted."

"But we knew that from the outset, Mr Burke."

"Ah, but we didn't know *how* untrustworthy."

"What exactly has he done now?"

"He has employed a bunch of lower caste morons with the cranial equivalent of wet sand and they have talked, Mr Hare. They have opened their mouths and as one have joined in a chorus worthy of Gilbert and indeed Sullivan. They have named names and divested themselves of our private number and not only have they done this of their own free will, but they have co-operated with the police."

"Surely not!"

"I have had a call from a certain detective inspector who has no better idea of disguising his vocal proclivities than by putting a handkerchief over his mouth."

"What did he want?"

"He doesn't want, he *demands* that we meet him at the Waverley in a cab with the delightful number of 666."

"Not a good omen, 666."

"No."

"So, what do we do?"

"We meet him of course – after all what other option do we have?"

"We could …"

"I've thought of that, but something is protecting both him and the girl. No, I think that on balance we shall meet him as he has so charmingly requested, give him certain items of information and drop our client neatly in the legal equivalent of quick drying cement. After all, we do have our other ladies and gentlemen to consider."

"Indeed we do, Mr Hare."

They sat in a convivial silence broken by the pop of the

gas fire and the muted noises caused by a fight breaking out next to the dartboard. There was the sound of hastily moving bodies followed by the unmistakable crack of wood on bone, as someone did a tolerably good impersonation of a lion tamer with a chair.

"I see that Clarence has not lost his technique since leaving the ring."

"I must say it's a pleasure to watch him work."

"And he never fails to please the crowd when he resorts to the pickled egg jar."

The soft tinkle of breaking glass followed by the unmistakable odour of malt vinegar wafted towards them.

There was a brief cheer and mild round of applause before Clarence returned to his side of the bar for the dustpan and broom. Mr Burke finished the last of his drink and stood up, slowly stretching and flexing each toned and darkly hidden muscle.

"Is the car outside?"

"Parked around the corner next to the fish wholesaler."

"And where precisely is our friendly hack?"

"Discussing the final details of 'Operation Hokum'."

"Good, good. Then we have nothing to lose and everything to gain, and more importantly no reason at all for not helping the police with their enquiries."

"Exactly, a sting par excellence and with no cash outlay to speak of."

"Apart from the cost of the rope?"

"As I said, nothing to speak of."

Mr Hare carefully folded his empty foil packet into a very small square and tucked it into the ashtray provided, before following his partner out into the wet and glistening streets of a newly washed and gently steaming Edinburgh.

chapter thirteen

Mr Burke casually folded his copy of *The Scotsman* and sauntered towards the waiting taxi, the numbers 666 clearly visible on the number plate. Mr Hare, who had been keeping a watchful eye on the vehicle from the opposite side of the bridge, crossed over and joined him.

Between them they had watched the driver for nearly an hour. He had done nothing more, in that time, than drink two cups of coffee from a plaid-covered flask beside him and read both *The Spectator* and the previous week's *Private Eye*. No one had phoned him, no one had approached the taxi, and a handwritten sign saying 'Private hire, waiting for client' was still taped to the passenger side front window.

As Mr Burke and Mr Hare casually sauntered towards the back door it opened of its own accord, whilst the driver remained hunched up and chuckling over the scurrilous tale he was still evidently enjoying.

"I don't like this, Mr Burke."

"Neither do I, Mr Hare."

"Couldn't we just walk by, shoot him gently in the back of the head and keep on going? Our lemon trees are growing very well this year and we could do with a bit of time off?"

"Unfortunately if we did that we would never find out how the gentleman in the driving seat appears to know what we look like, when even our own mothers would have great difficulty in recognising us."

"I see that we could indeed have a problem."

"For all we know, he may have sent all his information about us to various colleagues already."

"So we talk and then shoot him?"

"Did you bring a spare silencer?"

"Seam pocket, left arm."

"Then I suggest we get into the car."

Mr Burke and Mr Hare clambered into the black cab, the sign was removed from the window by the driver and the back door shut with a metallic clunk. They sat in prim silence as the engine was started and the taxi pulled out and into the stream of impatient vehicles surging towards the traffic lights. The driver weaved a path between waiting buses and delivery vans, until finally it parked in a small side street at the back of Blackfriars Church. The driver stretched and then, without saying a word, got out and sauntered towards a flight of dark and grimy steps.

Mr Burke and Mr Hare waited until the back door was flung open and a slightly peeved voice shouted, "For God's sake get out, we haven't got all day!"

Mr Burke and Mr Hare shot out like champagne corks from a shaken bottle and then hastily slid after the driver who had rounded the top of the steps and disappeared from view. They found him a few minutes later, sitting on a bench under a spreading tree admiring the grey and lichen-clad tombstones surrounding him. He was capless and apparently totally at ease.

Mr Burke sat himself down on one side and Mr Hare on the other. Normally their joint proximity would have caused immediate unease and a loss of control in certain bodily functions. Mr Burke briefly wondered as to their companion's provenance before finally addressing him in a soft menacing whisper.

"We meet at last, Detective Inspector McKinnon."

"Actually I'd prefer being addressed as plain Mr McKinnon, if it's all the same to you."

"You are not here in an official capacity then?" Mr Hare intoned, fingering the small firearm in his right pocket.

"No."

"I see. Why not?" Mr Burke asked, mildly surprised at the turn events were beginning to take.

"Because I have been a little bit unorthodox."

"You haven't gone by the book?"

"Tore it up and threw it through the window. I may even leave the force after this is all over."

"Ah."

"Why did you murder Quentin Rowse and Vernon Flint?"

"For the money," Mr Burke explained, taking a packet of sugar-free gum from his pocket. He extracted a long, thin white stick and after peeling off the wrapper, which he carefully folded, popped it into his mouth.

"It's what we do. Nothing personal," Mr Hare added, crushing a beetle with the toe of his highly polished, black patent leather shoes.

"What I meant was ..."

"I know what you meant," Mr Burke snapped. "What I don't understand is why you want to know and why you are here without the rest of the Oban heavy mob?"

"That's a bit harsh, Finn's not that big or at least not since his wife put him on the Slimfast, and you could stand Binthar against stripy wallpaper and lose him entirely."

"Mr McKinnon, what do you want?"

"I want you to leave Fiona alone."

"The young lady?"

"Yes."

"Done."

"Nothing is this easy," Fergus remarked, looking from one face to the other.

Mr Hare and Mr Burke both wore very black sunglasses and had short, neatly trimmed hair. Both wore the same blank expressions and he knew both would kill him without the proverbial backwards or indeed forwards glance.

"Apart from setting fire to the Mellrose Guesthouse and the optimistically named detective agency we have not even tried to injure your ... er ... friend."

"Then ..."

"Our brief was to remove the threat of a certain book being published and that included the poor girl who started it all. We have completed that brief, unfortunately not to the satisfaction of our client who of his own volition has employed what we can only describe as a bunch of poorly trained amateurs."

"The three stooges."

"Exactly."

"So you won't harm Fiona?"

"No, not now. After all what would be the point?"

"That's what I hoped."

"Of course we may have to silence you, purely in the interests of good business practice, you understand," Mr Burke muttered in a low voice, studying the surrounding area before extracting a long, thin metallic tube from an inside pocket.

"Oh, I understand perfectly, which is why I took precautions."

Mr Burke stopped in the act of screwing a small American-made revolver onto the end of the tube.

"Precautions?"

"Good grief, Fergus lad, if you had a pair of shades like them you could add Blues Brothers impersonations to your ever growing and truly horrible repertoire. Come on you three, make room for a little one."

Mr Hare was unceremoniously pushed farther down the bench and found himself sitting next to a block of invisible ice. Slowly the blood drained from his face and he shivered violently. Mr Burke looked at the space between Mr Hare and Mr McKinnon, and sorrowfully unscrewed the silencer from the gun and then stowed them both back into various carefully concealed pockets.

"Now, that would explain a lot," he observed thoughtfully. "May I ask for an introduction?"

"Mr er ... Which one are you by the way? Anderson or Fiske?"

"Neither, I am Mr Burke and my companion is Mr Hare."

Fergus, temporarily lost for words, stared at them both in astonishment.

"You are kidding?"

"I never joke," Mr Burke advised in sepulchral tones. "It wouldn't fit the corporate image."

"And our clients do expect certain standards," Mr Hare

added.

"Right, silly me."

"Yes, silly you," muttered his invisible companion.

"Mr Burke meet William Reginald Winkie aka Bill Boots, Bill meet Mr Burke and Mr Hare."

Mr Burke stretched out his hand, which was duly gripped and wrung by cold, transparent and bony fingers. He was unnerved not by the handshake, which he'd expected, but by the fact that the hand was calloused and one of the fingers appeared to be missing.

"You ought to be Irish with names like that," Mr Boots complained, taking a finger out of his pocket and sticking it back on.

"Please accept our firm's sincere apologies," Mr Hare snorted.

"Bill," Fergus rumbled, fingering the silver tooth nestling in his trouser pocket.

"They are that close to …"

"You are not helping. Look, Mr Burke, I'll lay my cards on the table. I'm not interested in you, well not much, but I want the man or woman behind you because your client appears to be almost if not entirely mad."

"The lights are on, but nobody's in, lift not going to the top floor, one sandwich short of a …"

"Bill, shut up."

"And you won't upgrade or amend any files?"

"Haven't made any and I hate unnecessary paperwork, plays hell with my current handicap."

"Well, in that case, we may assist you, purely in the interests of our other clients you understand."

Mr Burke nodded and glanced briefly at Mr Hare.

"We don't have a name."

"We prefer not to use names," Mr Hare advised.

"What we do have is a phone number and because of our client's rapidly growing dementia, an address, which I will now write down for you."

"Does it have an ice house?" Bill asked.

"I have no idea, does it matter?"

Fergus looked at the address and whistled.

"How the hell are we going to get into *that* place?" he asked, showing the slip of paper to Bill.

"Ah, well now, we may be able to help you out a bit there," Mr Burke advised, and actually smiled. "Although it would be a trifle unorthodox."

"Trust me I can do unorthodox standing on my head with both hands tied behind me."

"And we would need the help of your associate; in fact his help would be essential to carrying out our plan, which, by the way, is already being set in motion. To be honest it was at first conceived purely as a warning shot across the bows, but with your friend here, I believe that we could turn up the pressure several notches and prepare to ram."

"I like it, I like it," Bill chuckled merrily, the icy air thawing.

"So do I," Fergus agreed.

"Then I think that a large coffee is in order, Mr Hare."

"On expenses?"

"Of course, Mr Hare, after all if our client can employ subcontractors I can see no reason why *we* can't."

* * *

Neville looked up at the wall and turned imploringly to his grey-clad companion.

"Are you absolutely sure about this?"

"Yes."

"Oh."

"Got the rope?"

"Yes."

"And you put the knot in it just like I showed you?"

"Yes."

"Good. Right, well, up you go then."

Neville was pushed and prodded upwards, until finally he managed to clutch the top stones and haul himself over. He fell with a thud onto the dry earth and leaves on the other side and lay in a faintly moaning heap as he tried to get his breath back.

Somewhere within the depths of the darkened house in front of him a red light flashed silently.

Picking himself up, he lumbered off towards the largest of the stately beeches lining a gravelled drive and finding one with a reassuringly thick lower branch, threw the end of the rope over the moonlit limb. He was just about to test the knot when the drive blazed with light and a voice calmly asked him what the hell he thought he was up to.

"I want to die," he muttered, blinking at the figures he could barely see behind the glaring searchlights.

"Why?" asked another voice.

"What the hell difference does it make to you?" Neville stuttered, realising that one of the figures was holding the leash of a large and silent dog.

The dog resembled his imagination's lurid depiction of the Hound of the Baskervilles, right down to the gently dripping jaws and reddened eyes.

"Want me to let the dogs loose, Mr Phipps?" a voice at the back asked.

Neville gulped. 'Dogs?' he thought desperately, 'As in more than one?'

"Not just yet, Harry lad, let the man speak. I asked you why?"

"Because the bastards won't publish my book," Neville spat. "But this way, found dead in socialite's garden, well that will make them sit up and take notice. 'Not a name' they told me! After this I'll be a name all right."

"I see."

"Now, why don't you switch the lights off and bugger off so I can get this bloody knot done? I won't be long and then you can cut me down and ring the press."

"You don't want the police first?"

"No, the press – and photos, I want photos."

"Right."

"Lots of photos."

"Sure."

"In colour."

"Of course."

"So you're not going to stop me?"

"Well, no, not as you appear so set on it, but wouldn't you like to discuss a more lucrative means of revenge?"

"Such as?"

"How about publishing this book of yours yourself?"

"Money."

"Money?"

"Lack of."

"Oh."

"Now, if you all don't mind, I'd like to get on with it before the alcohol wears off."

"You mean you are a little drunk?"

"Absolutely nissed as a pewt."

"I see."

"How else do you think I'm going to go through with this?"

"What if I offered you an alternative?"

"What sort of an alternative?"

"A lot of money and a chance to actually wreak your revenge, and from the comfort of a small island in the sun."

"You're just saying that."

"Oh no, I never joke about things like death and money, especially not money."

"I suppose we could discuss it."

"Good man."

Mr Phipps moved closer and, placing a gentle hand on Neville's shoulder, steered him towards the back of the house.

In the gloom, made darker by the sudden cessation of light, Janet and Robin gently removed the still swinging rope from the tree.

"Well, that went well," Robin muttered.

"Yes it did, didn't it?"

"Reminded me of that time with the horse."

"Horse?"

"You know, big wooden one, room for a man and a small boy with a large screwdriver and a sharpened set of chisels."

"Ah, *that* horse."

"You don't suppose they actually will ... you know ..."

Robin made a cutting motion against his throat with a pallid index finger.

"Oh no, not until he sobers up and the alcohol in his system finally dissipates."

"With our Neville they could be in for a long wait."

"I expect that even now they will be boiling up the kettle and grinding the coffee beans."

"Which gives us a certain amount of time to set the scene and prime the props."

Janet rubbed her hands and then abruptly vanished, closely followed by Robin.

Harry tentatively banged the screen in front of him; the grey shadows that had floated into view were just as suddenly absent. He briefly thought about reporting it and then just as quickly changed his mind. It was probably just some sort of optical illusion and the laugh, well, that must have been an echo or something. Maybe someone was laughing behind the wall and somehow the laugh had... Sheesh, but he needed a holiday and somewhere miles away from Gould House, which was steadily and inexorably giving him the willies.

Neville lay on the spotlessly clean bed and looked around the room. There wasn't a speck of dirt anywhere. A set of papers lay in front of him together with a neatly written cheque for a sum that could have kept him and Gravel in gin for a year.

He signed the bottom of the form with the pen thoughtfully provided for that purpose by Mr Phipps, and turning on his side, took another sip of coffee. The operating gown hung from a hook on the wall and gently moved in a nonexistent breeze. He closed his eyes against the sterile room and then upon hearing a faint rustle, opened them again.

A woman dressed in a long flowing robe sat on the end of his bed and smiled at him.

"Ah, Neville," she said. "We meet again."

"Again?"

"And in similar circumstances," she added, depositing a

coil of rope on his bed.

Neville gulped.

"You're not a dream then?"

"No."

"Not even a nightmare?"

"Well, possibly to some people, but not for you."

Janet patted him gently on the knee and then leaned conspiratorially towards him.

"The thing is, Neville, that I have a proposition to put to you; one that will guarantee you a place in media history and lots and lots of lovely money and, unlike your current contract, one that will allow you to live to enjoy it."

"But …"

"Do you know what will happen to you after the removal of certain … er … assets?"

"What?"

"Absolutely nothing."

"You mean?"

"Why pay someone who unfortunately doesn't wake up?"

"Ah."

"So do we have a deal?"

"Do I have a choice?"

"Oh yes, you always have a choice."

"Just not much of one," Robin interrupted. "Look can we please get on with it; I can't cover this camera lens for ever."

"Well, Neville?"

"Why not? Just one thing."

"What?"

"I do actually get to talk to dead people, like in my dream?"

"Oh yes."

"Good."

"After all, Robin and I aren't exactly alive."

"Ah."

"Robin, bring the rope and, Neville, try and stay alert and be very, very, quiet."

chapter fourteen

Fergus looked up at the still imposing Georgian edifice and groaned. Mr Burke adjusted something in one of his many pockets and gave Fergus an enquiring look, which involved the raising of his left eyebrow above the frames of his designer sunglasses.

Bill leaned against the wall adjoining the newly washed steps and said with the intonation of Victor Meldrew, the day that he'd received a demand for ten years' back taxes, "I don't believe it."

An immaculately dressed and coiffured lady, built most definitely for comfort and not for speed, eyed them all with a certain amount of barely concealed disdain as she stepped delicately from a large sleek Mercedes. She sniffed in a pointed fashion before purposefully climbing the steps towards the glossy white door at the top. Beside it hung a highly polished brass plate advising the interested that the offices of Anderson and Fiske, Advocates and Solicitors at Law, were open and touting for business.

"This is it?" Fergus asked.

"Yes."

"This is where your client, the slime ball who has tried to shoot, maim and flatten my girl resides?"

"Yes."

"But this is the first place we looked."

"Oh."

"And correct me if I'm wrong, but aren't you two Anderson and Fiske?"

"Ah."

"Because I distinctly remember ringing up Anderson and Fiske and *you* answered."

"Same name, different branch."

"The point of it being?"

"Who would suspect a respected legal office to be the base for a pair of highly paid and discreet assassins?"

"You mean apart from other lawyers?"

"Naughty naughty, Mr McKinnon."

"Don't you ever get a wrong number, you know – someone ringing up because next door's leylandii are cutting out the light to the attic?"

"Sometimes, and to be perfectly frank our methods are usually far more effective than the average writ."

"And a good deal cheaper."

"What do you ...? Never mind, I really don't want to know."

"For heaven's sake get on with it," Mr Boots growled at them.

"Sorry, Bill. Now where was I?"

"You were complaining of déjà vu."

"Right, well, as I was saying, this was the first place we looked, after consulting the phone book and a pal at Fettes, and nobody knew anything."

"But did you ask the right questions?"

"What?"

"Follow me and don't under any circumstances say anything. Do you have a pair of dark glasses?"

"Yes."

"Then put them on. Remove the cap and the jacket. Mr Hare, do you have a spare tie?"

A thin black tie was produced from an inner pocket and expertly applied to the neck of Fergus's, thankfully, plain collar.

"I feel like a thug," Fergus complained. "And I look like an extra from 'Men in Black'," he added, spotting his reflection in the window of a parked car.

"Welcome to my world," intoned Mr Hare, purposely walking ahead of him up the flight of steps to where Mr Burke already stood.

They entered an imposing hall, complete with an ornate gilded chandelier glittering with teardrop crystals the size of golf balls and found themselves being scrutinised by a tall, immaculately dressed blonde, in a Chanel-style suit and large pearl earrings.

"Can I help you?" she enquired with icy politeness and the clipped tones of one of the better public schools.

"We wish to see Mr Tortascue," Mr Burke said.

Fergus gave a slight start and resolutely stared at a large grandfather clock poised next to a long sweeping staircase.

"Do you have an appointment?" she asked, consulting a large leather-backed book that lay open on her desk.

"No, but he always makes time for me. Tell him that Mr Burke would like a word about his life insurance policy."

"His life insurance?"

"Yes, it's coming up for renewal, although he might find that the cost of the premiums have become more than he can afford."

She looked from one to the other and then picked up a white telephone and punched two numbers into it.

"Mr Tortascue, I'm sorry to bother you, but there is a Mr Burke here who wishes to see you about your life insurance. He says that the premiums have gone up."

They all waited as the telephone sat silently in her hand, but at last a faint noise emanated from its plastic depths and she muttered 'three' into it. There was another pause and then a burst of noise, after which she replaced the phone and with a wave of one perfectly manicured hand motioned them towards the staircase. Mr Burke thanked her with a small bow and stalked towards the stairs.

They climbed upwards past a disapproving bunch of darkly glowering portraits, turned left and then right, wandered down a heavily carpeted corridor and finally arrived at a large panelled door. Mr Burke gave a brief tap on the wood and then, pushing the door open, entered a dark and oddly dismal room.

The walls were lined with bookcases and filing cabinets, none of which matched. There were no windows, although a blue velvet curtain hung the length of the opposite wall where a window should have been, and the only light came from the fireplace where a small gas fire coughed and spluttered despondently.

"Mr Burke, how nice of you to pop in," Mr Tortascue muttered insincerely, as he arose from a high-backed chair next to the fireplace and moved towards them.

"Can I offer you some tea or perhaps coffee?"

"No thank you, Mr Tortascue, this isn't a social visit."

"No, I didn't think it was."

"My partner and I have been put in an unfortunate

position," Mr Burke remarked, moving a step towards the gently perspiring lawyer, who nervously backed away and then sat back down in his chair.

Mr Hare went and stood against the door and quietly motioned Fergus to stay with him. Bill wandered around the room and enthusiastically read anything and everything that was lying around unattended.

"Oh indeed, I'm sorry to hear that," Mr Tortascue muttered, wiping a bead of sweat from his brow with a deep burgundy-red silk handkerchief.

"Unfortunately we operate in relative secrecy, the circumstances of our employment deeming it of the utmost importance that we remain in the shadows so to speak."

"Quite."

"However, because of a certain client who has now added impatience to his or her previous list of crimes, our existence has come to the notice of the police."

"Ah."

"In which case, my partner and I will unfortunately feel compelled to tidy away a few loose ends, to secure the continued safety and indeed future security of our other clients."

"Oh dear."

"Unfortunately one of those loose ends is your good self."

"Couldn't we negotiate?"

"I'm afraid that that window of opportunity is now firmly and irrevocably closed."

"Oh dear, oh my."

"We can of course promise a quick and painless passing, in accordance with our own strict code of professional conduct."

"What, here?"

"There is, I believe, no time like the present."

"But what about Mrs Scrope-Tattersall?"

"Who?"

"My receptionist."

"Another loose end."

Mr Tortascue swallowed loudly then threw himself on the floor and grovelled earnestly. Mr Burke gazed down at him and gave a deep and heartfelt sigh, whilst at the same time screwing a small silencer onto the end of a black and businesslike gun.

"It wasn't *me*," Mr Tortascue whimpered.

"Then who was it?" Mr Burke asked.

"I … Oh damn it, the idiot deserves all he gets and so does she, for that matter, supercilious bitch."

Mr Burke eyed the stricken lawyer for a brief moment and then unscrewed the silencer and slipped both metal objects back into their various pockets.

"The man you want is a consultant by the name of Charles Denzel-Oakes; he's a doctor of sorts. Started off by doing dodgy abortions and then majored in plastic surgery for people who would rather not look like themselves for a while. He runs a posh consultancy and private nursing home with his wife, Rebecca. You must have seen her – she's in all the glossy magazines hosting this or that gala, the body of a goddess and the morals and mind of a Borgia."

"Tall blonde, legs up to her navel, eyes like blue ice picks?"

"That's her."

"Mr Hare, do you remember young Betty Walker?"

"Wasn't she that sixteen-year-old with the face of an angel and the body of a Greek statue? I believe that she topped her entire family by cutting the brakeline of the family saloon and then she shagged the investigating officer into early retirement?"

"You do remember."

"How could one forget? Didn't she marry the prosecuting council?"

"That's the one, bled him dry. He committed suicide in chambers I believe."

"Left a note and everything, pity the spelling wasn't quite up to its usual standard."

"Although I believe that the firm forked out on a dictionary and a thesaurus afterwards."

"I wondered what had happened to her. She was a brunette then –"

"Very dainty little black widow and just as dangerous," Mr Tortascue interrupted, reaching for a file from a stack on the floor.

"She and her husband have been dabbling in the lucrative world of spare part surgery, only the parts used have not necessarily been willingly given. To be honest, I was so horrified when I stumbled across one of their … er … donors, he was of course dying at the time, that I broke all my legal oaths and promises and sent an anonymous note to the BMA. Not that they have done anything. Then that private eye from Oban turns up demanding the whereabouts of some Serbian bartender. Last seen entering the portals of Gould House Sanatorium, before that is, he was found washed up on a beach just outside Aberdeen with all his internal organs missing and some of his external ones as well."

"And that was when …"

"I called your firm up to do a bit of highland clearing."

"Unfortunately your clients also employed their own

amateur team."

"A circumstance I was unaware of until a few days ago, yes."

"And now?"

"I wash my hands of them."

"A wise decision."

"Is there anything else you need to know?"

"This Gould House, does it have what I believe is known as an ice house?"

"I really couldn't say, I don't believe it can have, otherwise someone would have said something. They are, I believe, quite rare?"

"Oh yes, quite."

"Although considering the times it is highly likely that one was included as I believe that they were the 'must have' of the eighteenth century. There is one other thing that might be of some interest."

"Yes?"

"Gould House was originally built to be one of the embassies bought by foreign powers wishing to improve the trade relations between Scotland and themselves. I did know which one, but ... no matter. The point I'm trying to make is that the ambassador then in residence was fond of a livelier life than was allowed by his faith and his upright and I believe incredibly plain and straight-laced wife. He, therefore, built a tunnel or corridor that went from the basement of Gould House to this building, which in those far-off days housed an establishment offering more licentious entertainment than was readily available at home."

"Ah, I believe I understand your drift."

"Indeed, unfortunately I have no means of showing you this ... er ... rather unorthodox access to our mutual client's place of residence, but I can show you the entrance."

In mutual silence, they filed out of the small cluttered room, down the corridor, descended the staircase and left the building. Carefully looking to right and left Mr Tortascue escorted them to a side entrance that backed on to the adjoining road and then showed them a small dingy door let into the wall, under the flight of steps leading to the main door. The door was old and scuffed, and very firmly padlocked with a length of rusting chain and a steel bar.

Fergus started and felt in his pocket for the small silver key Quentin had left in the puzzled care of his niece, Fiona. He would cheerfully have betted his entire year's salary on the fact that it would fit the lock on the padlock.

Mr Tortascue palmed a small piece of paper to Mr Burke as they shook hands and then he fled back to his office.

Fergus looked up at the building and noticed that one of the end windows had been bricked up from the inside. He briefly wondered why, until he remembered that small curtained room and shivered.

"I presume," Mr Burke intoned, lighting a long slim panatella, "that you have the key?"

"Yes."

"I thought so."

"How?"

"What else did you think our client was so very anxious to have back?"

"Ah."

"I think that tonight may be a very good opportunity to find out what is really going on and to humiliate and expose to the entire world, especially the rancid press, our two meddling murderers."

"And how exactly are we going to do that?"

"Well, firstly we need to set up an unforgettable episode of 'Totally Terrified' with our mutual friendly ghost and then we need to involve a few of your Edinburgh colleagues, for which I believe we may need the key to that lock."

"And you think it will work?"

"Oh yes."

"But what if it doesn't?"

"Then you go back to Oban where you may find next month's obituaries really interesting."

"Either way Fiona is safe?"

"Either way, although you may find my first idea far more satisfying."

They regarded each other for a brief moment and then solemnly shook hands. Fergus knew that deep down he'd crossed a line from a place to which he would not be able to return, but he also knew that as long as Fiona and his family were safe he really no longer cared.

chapter fifteen

Bill screamed in Fergus's ear and with a flurry of cold dank air, disappeared in disgust. He reappeared beside Fiona scowling horribly and muttering a string of traditional obscenities under his breath, the anatomical content of which had been banned in several countries since the dispersal of the Spanish Inquisition.

"Well?" Fiona asked, licking the pate de foie gras from a small, round, savoury biscuit.

"He's a dyed-in-the-wool, born-again plonker and a fraud. Psychic! He's about as psychic as your left testicle."

"Sorry to have to break it to you, Bill, but Fiona is a girl."

"Ah, you've finally noticed."

Fiona grinned before taking a sip of white wine. The grin stopped short as the wine hit several tastebuds, which collectively packed their own bags and moved out immediately.

"God, that's awful!" Fiona gasped, setting the glass down on a nearby shelf.

"I know, I tried everything I could think of, blowing down the back of his neck, screaming in his ear ..."

"I meant the wine," Fiona explained. "Well, no one need worry about an oil shortage, you could run tanks on that."

"Are you even listening to me?" Bill asked.

"Yes," Fiona replied.

"So what do we do now?" Fergus demanded, running a hand through his hair. "We have to get them to investigate the ice house before it's too late and we can't do that without them."

He pointed despairingly to the television crew trailing behind the good and the great, including Edinburgh society's answer to Cruella de Ville and Dr Frankenstein.

"Well, how about adding a little spice to the mix?" Bill chortled, his voice suddenly sly.

"What exactly do you mean?" Fergus whispered, his voice dripping with suspicion.

"Well, if you don't trust me ..." Bill muttered.

"No, go on, at the moment anything's worth a try."

"Do Bonnie and Clyde know what Fiona looks like?"

"Hang on a minute, I'll ask," Fergus replied, before skirting the crowd until he found Fenella and Mr Burke deep in conversation.

He interrupted just as Mr Burke was explaining the difference between a set of gallows with and without a trapdoor drop. He was just giving a lively demonstration with the aid of several cocktail sticks, a length of dental floss, a Ritz cracker and a pickled onion when Fergus made cutting motions to his own throat with a plastic swizzle stick. Mr Burke hurriedly thrust the contraption into Fenella's hands and with a gentle admonishment to find a small sausage for the body, turned to the impatiently waiting Fergus

241

with what looked suspiciously like a grin.

"I like it, death by cocktail cherry, although I'm not sure that the mangled lemon segment will catch on," Mr Burke chuckled mischievously.

"Do the evil twins know what Fiona looks like?"

"No."

"Are you sure?"

"Positive. They don't even know what *we* look like, let alone the little people they decide to eliminate. Why should they? After all, it's not as if they have any use for them other than that they die, quickly, cleanly and nowhere near their backyard."

"Oh."

"What about the Russians?"

"They only saw her from the back after dark and the last thing I'd heard was that they were on the first available boat to anywhere other than here."

"You are really sure about this?"

"Positive. Look, they asked us for one a few days ago, by which time we weren't even on payment terms."

"You didn't send anything?"

"No."

"Right."

"Why?"

"It was something Bill wanted to know."

"Bill."

"You know, Mr Boots."

"Ah, *that* Mr Boots."

Mr Burke looked momentarily pensive and then, threading his arm through Fergus's, pushed him gently towards Fiona, who was cautiously sipping a new glass of red wine.

"Don't touch the white," Mr Burke advised. "No known

antidote except a large dose of cascara and or a stomach pump."

"Too much information way too late," Fiona replied, taking another tentative sip.

"Bill?" Fergus whispered.

"Behind you," Bill replied, giving Mr Burke a gentle prod in the left buttock.

"Will you stop messing about and do whatever it is you have to do, as they are about to start?"

"All right, all right. Fiona love, can I just borrow you for a minute?"

"What?" Fiona asked, turning towards Fergus with a frown.

Bill shimmered briefly towards her, merged and then with a tiny shudder Fiona closed her eyes and then gently folded up and collapsed onto the floor.

"Fiona – are you all right?" Fergus urged, picking her up and hauling her into a nearby chair.

"Doctor – we need a doctor!" Mr Burke shouted.

The room suddenly became silent as all eyes turned towards the group clustered around Fiona's inert figure.

"What just happened?" Mr Burke hissed to Fergus.

"I have no bloody idea," Fergus whispered back.

"Hang on, here comes mine host with the entire crew of 'Totally Terrified' and the orange tit himself," Mr Burke snorted sotto voce.

Voices began asking mundane questions.

"Is she all right?"

"What happened?"

"She's not pregnant, is she?"

The assembled company were just about to call for an ambulance when Fiona stirred and then, opening her eyes with a tremulous shudder worthy of Lady Macbeth finding Duncan's blood on her hands, leapt from her chair and screamed. After that she gibbered in Gaelic and with another blood-curdling scream hissed in a deep male voice, whilst pointing a trembling finger at mine host.

"Murderer!"

"I'm sure I don't know what you mean, my dear, you must be under some ..."

Cameras whirred and clicked, the director making frantic motions for his crew to gag the normal presenters and not under any circumstances to lose the girl.

Fiona stood to her full height and then levitated a good foot off the ground. A white mist shimmered around her and the surrounding air froze.

"Murderer of souls, mutilator of children, killer of an unborn child," Fiona continued, pointing at him and then turning she moved with a soft glide and swish of unseen skirts towards the far wall and a painting of the Madonna and Child.

"Here is the lair of the beast and here the vault of the devil," she shouted, banging the wall with her fist.

"Now steady on," Dr Denzel-Oakes shouted, sweat beading on his forehead now puckered with lines of pure terror.

"Open the door, spawn of Beelzebub, open the door and let the darkness of centuries unleash the furies and the immortal souls of those condemned to wander the outer walls."

"What door? There is no door!" Rebecca shouted, rushing towards Fiona. "You stupid cow, how dare you come here and accuse my husband ..."

"Foul and midnight hag, how you prattle! Husband killer, poisoner ..."

Livid with rage, Rebecca turned on the assembled company like a cobra with fangs poised.

"Get out all of you! Security remove this mad woman immediately, and smash those fucking cameras now!"

"What door?" asked the director, now absolutely fascinated.

"The door to hell, the door to …"

Here Fiona stopped, and with all ears listening and all eyes watching her every move, including at least three cameras set on zoom, pointed to a small crack in the wall barely perceptible until now. The crack grew with alarming speed until it traversed the wall from floor to ceiling. Three further cracks appeared and joined it at right angles forming the shape of a door. Plaster split and fell in dusty plates to the ground, leaving a hole in which the glaring shape of a keyhole could be seen rimmed with rust.

There was complete silence as the last particle of dust met gravity and gave up. Rebecca groaned and leant against a waiter. Her husband picked himself up off the floor and his face turning the ghastly colour of B&Q putty stared helplessly at the assembled company.

"I have no idea what she …"

Fiona lowered her finger and suddenly lunged at him, her fingers outstretched like an eagle's talons.

"The door to Cold House," Fiona spat at him, her voice unnaturally low.

"You have the key, the key to the house, built under this one. The house that Lucifer built upon the bones of the dead."

"She's barking, absolutely nuts, anyone can see that, can't you?"

Warily, people moved away from him as he grovelled.

"The key – you have the key around your neck so use it," Fiona snarled.

"I don't have a key to that door!" he shouted back. "I didn't even know that we had a door there."

"The key is truth and truth is now the key," Fiona intoned, and then gently folded and collapsed at his feet.

Fergus looked at Mr Burke and then at Fiona. Bill prodded him gently in the stomach and hissed:

"Use the bloody key now."

"What?"

"The key – the one yon cowering bitch has on a chain around her throat."

"Er …"

"I canna hold the wee idiot up any longer!" Bill spat.

Fergus grabbed the violently swearing Rebecca, tore the key from the chain hanging loosely from around her neck and hurled himself at the newly visible keyhole. Almost in a daze he pushed the key into the lock, twiddled it until the catch caught and then gave the wall a hefty kick. The door creaked open revealing amongst the floating dust motes, caught glittering in the lights of the cameras, a torso swinging to and fro on a rope.

A woman screamed and then fainted. Several burly waiters pushed to the front of the crowd and one armed with a cleaver launched himself at the swinging body. The cadaver swung towards the now silent crowd and opened its eyes.

"She did it," Neville hissed, raising a shaking finger and pointing it straight at Rebecca.

"Blood hath been shed ere now," Neville continued, finding words he never knew that he had learned. "Ay, and since too, murders have been performed too terrible for the ear. The time has been that, when the brains were out, the man would die, and there an end."

Neville swallowed and blinked at the silently staring crowd.

"But now they rise again with twenty mortal murders on their crowns and push us from our stools."

He lowered his hand slowly, all eyes following the bony digits now indicating the fallen chair below his feet. Hearing the sharp intake of collective breath Neville glared and again raised a grimy finger, which he stabbed in Rebecca's direction.

"She kills them and then she and her lover pocket the cash he's paid the so-called donor before he operates. Not that he doesn't suspect, I mean you can live without one kidney, lung, whatever, but two?"

Neville swallowed. The rope around his neck was now far too tight and he was seeing stars. Suddenly and with an awful clarity he knew what he didn't now want.

"I don't want to die," he whispered, and then passed out.

Rebecca shuddered and then taking a deep breath fumbled in her evening bag for the small gilt handgun she had taken the liberty of stealing from her husband's gun cabinet. It wasn't there!

Neville now lay on the floor ominously still, his face blue and his neck a livid red.

Desperately she looked around her until she spotted her husband flanked on either side by waiters and a grim-faced Fergus. Then Rebecca did what any self-preserving black widow would do – she metaphorically ate her husband.

"It was his fault, he made me keep quiet. *He* did it, he butchered them. Oh God, I was so scared, so scared, you just have to believe me."

She looked piteously at them, her beautiful lips trembling

and her great violet eyes rimmed with tears.

Fergus walked towards her, a faint smile on his lips.

"You're good," he said admiringly. "But you're not *that* good."

A dusky waiter detached himself from a small group at the door and stalked towards them.

"Constable Binthar, Sergeant Smallett, take the wicked witch of the west aside and read her her rights."

"Yes, Sir."

"And you, doctor, you can open the door to the old ice house under the stairs and prove that either your wife's a liar or you are."

chapter sixteen

They stood outside the main gates, in a small bedraggled huddle, as the last of the ambulances, police cars and fire engines finally drove off.

"Well," said Bill, "that was fun!"

"I just wonder why on earth she did it," Fiona remarked, rubbing smoke smuts off her face with her own saliva and a paper tissue.

"What?" Fergus asked.

"Set fire to her own house."

"Spite?"

"Possibly."

"At least she did it after you got to see the inside of the infamous ice house."

"Much good it did us."

"I just can't believe that there was nothing in there," Bill moaned.

"Neither could I, which is why I rang forensics and got them out of bed and on their way down here with every little bag of tricks they could lay their grimy little paws on."

"I suppose that they might have found something the

cleaners had missed."

"Probably, they normally manage to."

"Anyway, we will never know now, what with the fire and the gallons of water the firefighters used."

"Who would have thought that a couple of bottles of vodka and voile curtains could have done that much damage, that quickly?"

"That guy from the television company was almost in tears. He said that the heat and smoke had damaged most of the videotape or whatever it is that they use now."

"Spoilt your television debut eh, Fiona?" Bill smirked.

"Shut up."

"The thing is ..." Fergus growled.

"Yes?"

"Where the hell did they put the bodies? I mean, they must have stashed them somewhere."

"God knows."

Mr Burke detached himself from a looming shadow and tapped Fergus on the shoulder. Fergus jumped and Fiona, startled, eyed him with a certain amount of trepidation.

"What do you want?" Fergus asked, fingering the long length of lead pipe in his trouser pocket.

"I just wanted you to know that the slate is now cleared and that we are delighted with the outcome of our joint venture."

"Oh."

"Oh yes indeed, delighted, absolutely delighted. Of course if you ever have any future use for our services, purely on a business footing you understand, you can of course contact us on the usual number."

Mr Burke allowed himself a smile before taking a small piece of cardboard from a top pocket.

"My card."

Fergus looked down at it without the vestige of a smile and kept his hands firmly in his pockets. Bill gave him a quiet nudge and then with a sigh picked the card up and after looking at it intently stuffed it into one of Fergus's pockets.

"Oi!" Fergus grunted. "Do you mind?"

"Not much, as the actress said to the bishop. Anyway, you may need to call in the professionals at some point and having the best on tap may be the decider."

"Of what?"

"Whether you remain in this world or mine," Bill answered.

"I see that your friend is still around," Mr Burke observed, after he'd watched the floating card deposit itself within the folds of Fergus's jacket.

"Yes," Fergus replied.

"I don't suppose he could be persuaded to indulge in a little freelance activity, the odd sub-contract for, let us say, an unusual assignment?"

"No."

"Oh well, never mind, can't blame me for asking."

"No."

"Mr Hare and I will be off then. If you see Mr Foolscap please send him our best wishes and let him know that we will look forward to reading his exposé in due course."

Mr Burke gave a slight bow, which was little more than a nod of the head, and then silently merged with a shadow cast by a man walking his St Bernard in front of a nearby lamp-post, and vanished.

The man, pausing to light a large fat cigar, walked up to Fergus and Fiona who were still watching the last wisp of steam rise heavenwards.

"Bit of a fire, what?"

"Yes."

"That's that private place run by that doctor and his wife. The one with the enormous ..."

"Yes."

"It was on the news."

"Oh."

"I expect it will make the front page of *The Scotsman* tomorrow."

"Probably."

"I saw an excerpt of the show, sort of trailer. The missus reckons it's all done with wires and things."

"Right."

"Couldn't believe it myself. I mean, we had dinner with them only a week ago and they didn't look much like murdering thugs to me. Mind you, you never seem to be able to tell nowadays, but you'd think him being a doctor and all ..."

"Dare I mention, Crippen, Shipman and Christie to name but a few?" Fergus muttered.

"And Knox, don't forget him," Bill hissed.

"That was never proved," Fergus countered.

Bill snorted derisively.

"What wasn't?" the man with the cigar asked.

"Er ... nothing."

"Anyway, when I heard what had been going on, well ..."

"You had to come and take a look," Fiona stated, shivering despite the warmth of the evening.

The man looked up and then scratched the stubble on the side of his chin.

"What we need is a jolly good storm, clear all this mugginess up, get rid of the smell."

"Smell?" Fergus asked, sniffing the air.

There was, laced in between the odour of dampened walls, charred furniture and hot steam, an increasing odour of roasting drains.

"Smelled something like that during foot and mouth, before I retired had to organise some of the disposals. Of course, by the time the ostrich twins at the top sorted out the paperwork and actually admitted that we might have a problem, some of the animals had been hanging around for a while."

"Fergus?"

Fiona sniffed again. There was very definitely a distinct smell and it was coming from beyond the wall separating the garden, such as it was, from the road.

"Unmistakable really, once you've smelled one burnt corpse you can smell 'em all."

The man with the cigar grinned at them in a knowing fashion. Fiona had a sudden and extremely strong urge to make him eat the remainder of his smouldering cigar, but was restrained by Bill who grabbed a shoulder in each hand and pinned her to the wall.

Fergus rummaged in his pocket and after dumping a quantity of loose change, several keys and a wad of chewing gum, finally found his mobile phone.

"Bill," he whispered. "Go and have a look."

The man and his dog watched with interest as Fergus punched in a few numbers and then waited for someone human to answer.

"DI McKinnon here, get me Corduroy Jenks – and hurry."

At the sound of the words DI the man and his dog hurried away, or rather the dog started to sniff the base of the wall and the man, now sweating profusely, dragged him slowly off down the smoke-rimmed street.

After he'd gone, Bill materialised by the simple expedient of walking back through the wall and then slumped down, his back to the crumbling stone.

"Well?" Fergus asked impatiently.

"I think that you may have found all the evidence you may ever want," Bill declared, looking down at the ground.

"Ah."

"And if it wasn't for the fact that I don't actually have any, I would at this very moment be spewing my guts up," Bill managed to croak.

"Why?" Fiona asked, attempting to find a foothold at the base of the wall.

"No, don't!" Bill shouted.

Fergus pulled her back.

"What exactly did you find?" Fiona asked.

"The ground's opening up and there are bodies floating around in the mud. Some have been there some time, some haven't had quite so long and still look like well, bodies, others are just bits. Torsos with big holes cut into them, arms, legs, a child's hand."

"Oh God," Fergus mumbled.

"I really don't think that God had an awful lot to do with what went on in there," Bill retorted.

"No wonder we didn't find anything. They must have buried the evidence in shallow graves, covered the lot in gravel and hoped no one would look too hard at the reason why you would want a Japanese rock garden in the centre of Edinburgh."

"The water from the hoses must have dislodged the covering stones," Fiona murmured.

"How many do you reckon?" Fergus asked.

"Think alphabet soup and then substitute human remains for the pasta and the vegetables," Bill murmured.

"That's ..."

Fiona stopped and then slumped down beside him.

"I was hoping that there weren't that many," she mumbled.

"Yeah, well it's been going on some time," Fergus replied, his eyes brightening as a police car slewed to a halt beside them and Jenks emerged.

"So what have we got?" Jenks asked, sniffing the air.

Fergus pointed to the wall behind them.

"Seems like the earth may be giving up its secrets."

Jenks removed a small folding aluminium ladder from the boot of his car and proceeded to climb up. He stopped when he reached the top and then, after surveying what lay beyond, hurriedly came back down.

"Tom, Joe and you with the nose, find a back way in. Adele, get on to HQ and arrange for a major forensics team. Get hold of Dr Fergey-Woods and get her down here pronto, tell her to bring large wellies and a strong empty stomach, and then find me an earth mover and something to remove part of this damned wall."

Fergus and Fiona watched the sudden flurry of activity in a detached manner and Bill, who had said nothing more, went and sat on a wooden bench farther down the pavement.

Jenks gave Fergus an enquiring glance that asked all sorts of silent questions to which he received a blank stare.

"Will you be needing me?" Fergus asked.

"Not for now, but I'd like to see you in my office at some point tomorrow, or rather today."

"Fair enough."

"Fergus."

"Yes."

"Don't leave town."

"Right."

Jenks nodded a brief dismissal to them both and then moved away to two yellow-jacketed shapes, carefully setting up a set of powerful searchlights. A fire engine stormed towards them, blue lights flashing and sirens blaring.

"Fancy a drink?" Fergus asked, drawing one of Fiona's hands into one of his.

"Oh yes. A long, hot frothy coffee and ..."

"An inch of malt," Fergus finished, smiling down at her.

"If nothing better is on offer?" she quipped.

"That's what I like about you, lass, you are completely without morals."

"What about Bill?" Fiona asked, turning to watch the huddled shadow.

"He'll come back, after all, I still have the tooth."

✳ ✳ ✳

Bill Boots leaned against the street-lamp and glared at the pavement without in any way seeing it at all.

"Excuse me?" enquired a nasal voice of transatlantic tones.

"Bloody Americans," Mr Boots muttered without looking up.

"Actually, I'm Canadian and agree with you entirely," the voice stated.

Mr Boots slowly raised his eyes and regarded the speaker with a jaundiced eye.

"Good costume," the young man in front of him stated. "Very authentic, especially the boots."

"Ah yes." Bill looked down and then back up. "So you can see me?"

"Of course. The moment I caught sight of you I thought to myself, now there's a man who knows his history. I suppose ..."

"What?"

"You don't happen to know if the Vault is still open?"

"Sorry, son, the last tour went in about ten minutes ago."

"Oh"

"They'll start again tomorrow morning. If you nip up to the Mercat Cross bright and early I'm sure they'll have a space left."

Bill watched the young face fall in dismay and thought, for a fleeting moment, of his own son, Charlie.

"I suppose I should have come before, but I got the times all wrong and it took longer to get a taxi and ..."

"And?"

"I go back home to Quebec tomorrow."

"Right. Still it's not all it's cracked up to be down there and not half as scary, at least not now," Mr Boots added in an undertone.

"Mother will kill me."

"I'm sorry, but ..."

Bill watched the young man with a puzzled frown, the lad was actually looking downright terrified and he hadn't even said 'boo' yet.

"Not that it would have done much," the young man muttered, kicking a stray can with his foot.

"You have now lost me completely," Bill remarked,

scratching his chin absentmindedly before adding as the thought hit him, "Have you been drinking?"

"A bit," the youth admitted. "And you would too if you'd been asked to recite a bloody awful poem in the dark to a wall."

"Perhaps you haven't drunk enough," Bill quipped.

"I hate that pillock, Burns."

"It's because you have nae got the rhythm in the voice. You need to find the musical undertones before you can get the hang of the actual words."

"Spelling them correctly in the first place would have helped."

"Now, now. Anyway, it can't be that bad. Which one is it, 'The Wee Mousie' or 'Air to an Upstanding Haggis'?"

"Neither. It's this."

The youth produced a crumpled piece of paper from his jacket pocket and after smoothing out the worst of the creases handed it over. Bill held it under the light and began to read aloud.

"Ae fond kiss, and then we sever;
Ae fareweel, and then for ever!
Deep in heart wrung tears I'll pledge thee,
Warring sighs and groans I'll wage thee,
Who shall say that fortune grieves him,
While the star of hope she leaves him?
Me, nae cheerful twinkle lights me;
Dark despair around benights me.
Fare-thee-weel, thou first and fairest!
Fare-thee-weel, thou best and dearest!
Thine be ilka joy and treasure,
Peace, enjoyment, love and pleasure!
Ae fond kiss and then we sever!

Ae fareweel, alas, for ever!"

Bill stopped, his voice breaking, and stared at the young man in front of him.

"That was beautiful, truly beautiful. I never really understood it before," the Canadian muttered, staring at him in awe.

"It was the wife's favourite."

"And my great-great-great-grandmother's. I'm David, by the way."

"Bill."

"It's why I'm here really, to recite that, apart from a job interview for a job I may or may not get."

"Oh."

"Oil – I'm a geologist or I will be if they employ me. Just out of college and the firm paid for me to come over and there's this tradition that whichever member of the family gets to come to Edinburgh has to recite that down there, before the old whisky still, if it still exists."

"And that will do what?"

"I have no idea, but great-grandma left this request in her will, together with my great-grandfather's gold watch and tobacco pouch."

"And now you've read the poem you can collect the watch and pouch?"

"I suppose so, although I didn't go down."

"But I think you could have been said to have succeeded in the spirit of the thing," Bill observed kindly, and held the crumpled page out towards him.

"No, you keep it," David urged, moving back out of the light. "I'm supposed to leave it behind."

"I'll take it down when the guards have locked up for the night," Bill promised, and then, at the puzzled look on

David's face, added, "I have to wait for the last tour to come out, greet them with a spooky witticism and a bit of a scare, and then everyone goes home happy."

"Oh, you work for the tour company?"

"Something like that."

"Great. Right, well, I'll leave it in your capable hands then."

"You do that, lad, and I hope you get the job."

"Oh, I hope so too."

"By the way, your great, great, etc., grandma, what happened to her?"

"Died of old age after years of running one of the best taverns in Quebec, brought up five children single-handed after her husband died and they emigrated from Scotland. Saw her thirty-two grandchildren scatter and marry. I guess she had a good life."

"But ..."

"My grandmother said that she never got over the death of her William and that every June twenty-fifth she'd lock herself in the kitchen and get drunk making the worst toffee west of the St Lawrence."

"Why?"

"No one ever found out. Perhaps she was a little mad?"

"Perhaps."

"Anyway, I'd better get back to the hotel. Haven't packed yet and there's this girl I met ..."

"There's always a girl." Bill grinned at him and then laughed outright. "So best not to keep her waiting, they go off the boil and ring down for room service."

David smiled and reddened before turning and walking back up the cobbled street. Halfway up he turned.

"I'm sorry, but I didn't catch your name," he called out, but the man in the boots had vanished.

chapter seventeen

Clive nodded in agreement and thrust in his two penn'orth. After all, he thought to himself, I've actually been there at the sharp end when it had all happened. He'd been right there behind the camera panning in on the gently gyrating body and then, when it suddenly and horribly opened its eyes, he'd carried on regardless, despite the damp feeling in his nether regions.

"He's got a good face, all angles and folds, like a very sad bloodhound with maybe a bit of stoat in the nasal department."

"And he's good with words, I mean to say, that quote was almost word perfect," Nigel the soundman echoed in agreement.

"Besides which the orange tit fainted," Lancelot added as an afterthought, and tried again to light a fat and smelly cigar.

"I know he did, I was there, wasn't I?" Boris the director spat, scratching his backside in a thoughtful fashion.

"Well, you were this time," a voice at the back mutinously muttered.

There was a cautious murmur of agreement.

"All right already, so sometimes I have other things to do, apart from holding your hands," Boris snapped back.

"You mean like giving our Barbie a standing ovation as soon as the lights go out?" Clive replied, polishing a lens cap with his sleeve.

"That's enough," Boris grumbled. "Look, does anybody know where he is?"

"Half an hour ago he was being seen to by a doctor and after that he was helping the police with their enquiries," the senior gaffer replied from the depths of a Jackie Collins novel.

"It's a pity we can't use all that stuff with the girl and Mrs Macbeth, although God alone knows why it all went black and wobbly," Nigel observed, trying to find a warmer bit of wall to lean against and yawning loudly.

Then everybody else yawned.

"Well, we couldn't have used it anyway or at least not until after the court case," a spotty youth with a Game Boy remarked.

"Well, thank you for that, young Rumpole."

Boris glared at the youth in a thought-filled fashion. Give some spotty oik a university education and a law degree, and he was still totally useless at everything they attempted to teach him. Unfortunately he knew that they knew it and had every precedent and legal case pertaining to unfair dismissal, scrawled illegibly in a small notebook with a picture of Winnie the Pooh and Piglet on the front cover.

"Shh, something's happening!" Gloria squeaked from the edge of the huddled group.

A door opened in the building they had been jealously watching, light spilled out and a small, stooped black shadow scuttled forth. The door shut with a clunk and as a body they ran and enveloped their prey, before it had even the slimmest chance of escape.

"Neville Foolscap?" Boris asked, eyes gleaming.

"Why?" Neville queried, sinking further into his own flesh whilst his eyes vainly searched for some avenue of escape.

"Neville, we were wondering if we could ask you a few questions?"

"What about?"

"Well, about tonight."

"Oh."

"How did you get behind that door for instance?"

"Er, what door?"

"Don't even think of messing me about, my son. You know perfectly well which door."

"I don't know."

"And survive hanging without any possible means of support?"

"Er I was drugged, I'm sorry ..."

Neville attempted to push himself away, but stopped abruptly when Boris whispered:

"So how long have you been talking to dead people?"

"Er ..."

"The thing is, Neville old son, Boris here thinks you may have a really bright future," Lancelot announced soothingly, taking him by the arm and shoving some of the crew aside by the simple expedient of thrusting a bony elbow into any soft and vulnerable part he could reach.

"Oh," Neville gulped.

"In television."

"The thing is, Lancelot old pal," Neville whimpered

plaintively. "I'd rather set my heart on getting my book published."

"And now you can," Lancelot agreed. "But Boris here and indeed the network, believe that you also have a great future in presenting programmes for them."

"What sort of programmes?"

"'Totally Terrified'," Boris replied.

"What! Not that daft reality television thingy with the red-haired git and the blonde with the high pitched squeal and the very tight jumpers?"

"Yes."

"Total crap for the gullible from start to finish and the historical correctness of a year nine project, written with the aid of a heritage website."

"Er ..."

"I love that programme."

"Oh ... er ... good, so how would you like to present it?"

"But what about the ..."

"Orange tit?"

"Yes."

"Fenella just altered his programme schedule; from now on he's doing 'Historical Gardens' and 'Homes from Hell'."

Boris sniggered, placing the mobile in which he'd been animatedly conversing, back into the snug confines of his left front jeans pocket. He found on balance that if kept there the ensuing vibration, as it tried to ring, was oddly erotic.

Neville looked from one to the other and mentally held his breath.

"Will I get paid?" he asked.

"Of course and quite a nice round sum it is too, to say nothing of international coverage and the very high probability of becoming a national treasure," Boris advised him with a broad wink.

"Book sales will go sky high."

Lancelot grinned and patted his shoulder.

"Oh."

Neville basked in his sudden and unexpected good luck.

"All you have to do is a little local research and look as if you can see ghosts and other nocturnal apparitions."

"That's all I have to do?"

"Yes."

"But what if I don't see anything?"

"That's never been a problem, all you do is look really scared or even better, *totally terrified* and then we add something in afterwards – the punters never know."

"But I thought it was live?"

"Neville my son, in our business – your business – there is no such thing as live television. Why else do you think we have one of the best mobile editing suites money can buy?"

"Oh."

"Well?"

"Don't you want someone better looking?"

"No. What we want is someone who can look haunted and you, Neville my son, can do that standing on your head."

"And when necessary with a rope around your neck," Clive added.

"I don't know what to say." Neville stuttered.

"How about 'Yes'?" Boris barked. "And then we can all go back to the hotel and open a bottle before we discuss our next location."

"Which is where exactly?"

"Well, actually I think you'll really like it. It's an old converted manor house complete with headless corpses, hooded monks and a singing nun."

"It's also next to a gin factory," Lancelot smirked.

"I'll do it!" Neville announced with alacrity.

"Good man."

Boris chuckled and with a gentle prod began to steer him towards his waiting hotel room and recently and hastily drawn-up contract.

Janet and Robin stood in the shadows of a weeping cherry and watched as Neville was escorted off towards a long and pampered career in media lying.

"Do you think he'll be all right?" Robin asked.

"What, *Neville*? He's an ex–journalist, of course he'll be all right," Janet scoffed.

"It's just that it's a bit of a jump."

"What from being paid a pittance for writing up obituaries and the local court reports, some of which I should remind you, he made up. Not that anybody noticed at the time."

"Well, yes, but ..."

"Neville will have a nicer flat with a cleaner and he'll never have to cook or race around trying to find a clean shirt. He'll be waited on hand and foot, be fed gin through a straw, and he'll get to see as many young men in tight jeans as his eyes will allow without temporary blindness setting in."

"Oh."

"Not everybody is a boob man, Robin."

"Oh."

"Anyway, we've got what we came for – revenge and

retribution."

"Do we have to go back?"

"Yes, I'm afraid so."

"Oh."

"By the way are you doing anything Thursday afternoon, all afternoon?"

"Er, no. Why?"

"Apparently I have to attend some sort of reunion in Rio, according to head office, and I may need assistance."

"Oh."

"Especially as the festivities don't start until it gets dark."

"Ah."

"It's all done with infrared automatic sights now, I believe."

"I see."

"You could wear those new jeans and the white T-shirt with the picture of Jack Nicholson and a large ..."

"Oh, *that* T-shirt." Robin grinned. "Well, it just so happens that Thursday is my day off."

He turned and after giving her bottom a proprietorial pat disappeared with a lewd and encouraging wink.

Janet allowed herself a momentary preen after he'd gone before announcing to the tree beside her, "You can come out now."

Bill Boots sidled around the trunk and warily watched her from a safe distance of several feet.

"You do realise that you are free to go?" Janet advised.

"Right."

"The light will take you straight there."

"I can see Morag and the bairns?"

"Oh yes."

"No questions asked."

"None."

"And all I have to do is step into the light?"

"Correct in all boxes."

Bill stood undecided and regarded the gently approaching glow with a thoughtful frown.

"Anyway, it's up to you," Janet advised and then with a shimmer, vanished.

"That's right," Bill muttered to himself, as the glow deepened and grew. "It's entirely up to me."

✳ ✳ ✳

She arose from the waves in a graceful swoop that had every scrap of white bikini straining as it valiantly tried to hold on to the golden globes of flesh it was attempting to keep together.

Mr Burke sipped his dry martini in a ruminative fashion and flexed his toes one by one.

"Darling," she purred, climbing the ladder that hung from the back of the boat. "The water is simply divine and so exhilarating."

Slowly she advanced, sinuously stretching, the bikini flexing with every step.

Mr Burke closed his eyes and took another sip. She is, he thought, just like that bird whose name I can never remember, rising from the depths in the first James Bond film. It had something to do with taking your clothes off and money laundering, Usury Undress, or something very like it.

"I'm wet," she announced, eyes flashing. "Want to dry me off?"

Mr Burke opened his eyes and let them take in the

expanse of remarkably, considering the age, athletic skin.

"All I have is a small napkin," he murmured. "A very, very small napkin."

"That will do," she whispered, kneeling at his feet and removing the olive from the depths of his glass with her tongue.

He was just beginning to rise to the occasion when there was the sharp insistent whine of a mobile phone. He picked it up from the table at his side and pressed a small green button.

"It's for you," he advised, handing it to her and pouring himself another drink from a tall silver cocktail shaker.

"Yes," she barked, sitting abruptly at Mr Burke's feet. "Offer him what you think he'll accept and then sack someone, either that or tell the network we need more money for locations ... Because as soon as they see his ascetic features scowling across a badly lit room they'll be queuing up to purchase prime-time space."

There was a brief pause filled by Mr Burke handing her a balloon glass rimmed with sugar and containing a brownish liquid with what looked like a small bonsai tree drowning in it.

"Just sort it, Lancelot old bean, that's what I pay you for. You can tell our mutual pain in the ass from me that if he doesn't like it, I still have the photographs from the last Christmas party, the one with the actress, the bishop and the indecent salami."

Carefully she disconnected the mobile and then threw it over the side of the boat.

"Now, where were we?"

"I think that we were going to finish our drinks and then I was going to dry you off with very little difficulty, Fenella sweetheart."

They smiled at each other, two sharks from very different seas, but with remarkably similar grins.

❋ ❋ ❋

Fergus sat in front of the computer screen and rubbed tired eyes with the back of his hand. 'How hard is it to find someone?' he asked himself.

Fiona leaned over him and placed a steaming cup of coffee on the mouse mat.

"So how's it going?" she murmured.

"Better than expected, but not fast enough to actually make a living," he replied, clicking the mouse to tick a box on the screen.

"'Totally Terrified' is on in five minutes and your mother rang."

"What did the evil old hag want this time?"

"Something to do with fixing the bathroom light."

"Oh goodie."

"Finn's downstairs with Binthar and a small chap with troll-like tendencies and a squint."

"That will be Hamish, he's a traffic warden."

"He brought a box of beer and a crate of wine, and asked if we do interesting things on sticks."

"I'll be down in a minute, I just have to switch this off or put an axe through the screen."

"We don't have an axe."

"Pity."

Five minutes later he sat wedged on the sofa between Binthar and Mr Hare, who was almost unrecognisable without the glasses and the black overcoat.

It had been almost six months since the ground had opened up and divulged its bony and semi-decomposed, unsanctified, secrets, some of which were still awaiting names.

Neville Foolscap smiled across at them from the comfy and capacious studio sofa, from which he pontificated weekly.

"Glad to see old Neville doing well," Binthar announced, loudly opening a packet of mini poppadoms with his teeth. "You know we never did find that wretched bird of his."

"I expect it will turn up. Things usually do," Finn remarked, slapping a large piece of smoked ham onto a very small cracker.

"Like bodies," Mr Hare agreed, prodding a plate of sausages with a thoughtful fork.

None of them moved so he ate three.

"I heard from Mr … er … our mutual friend today," he whispered to Fergus who was in the act of pouring froth into a tall glass.

"Oh."

"Yes, he and his companion are enjoying a slow cruise in the Med; they should be back next month."

"Right."

"I must say that as a brief sabbatical, rearranging traffic has been most restful and at times, downright entertaining."

"I did hear about the original way you had with a Post-it note and an ordinary car jack," Finn smirked.

"So how are you getting on with opening up your newest venture?" Mr Hare asked.

"The detective agency?"

"Yes."

"Well, it's a bit slow, but since the insurance came through we've at least got the place painted and the desk in. All I need now is my final pay cheque and it's chocks away."

"Shh, he's about to open the haunted barn door," Fiona admonished.

"After the haunted horse, has of course, bolted."

"Binthar."

"Yes, boss?"

"Shut up."

"Yes, Mrs Boss."

✳ ✳ ✳

Fiona pinned the final poster to the wall and stood back to admire her handiwork.

Fergus, entering with a collection of papers and assorted envelopes gave her bottom a brief squeeze and handed her a packet of sugar.

"I'll do the post, you make the coffee."

"Yes, *Sir*."

Fergus chuckled and opened the first envelope.

"Do we need exterior painting?"

"We can't afford *interior* paint."

"Right, bin that one. 'Tracing your Ancestors' and 'Internet Browsing' need to go back to the library."

"Where is it?"

"In the pending box."

"Do we need a loan?"

Fiona looked over his shoulder and whistled.

"I'd rather ask Mr Burke and Mr Hare, at least they only cut off your limbs."

"Bin. Hey, look at this: *Dear Sirs, in answer to your recent advertisement I would like your opinion on …*"

"What?"

"Strange noises and what sounds like fraudulent use, or in this case misuse, of petty cash."

"Petty cash?"

"Well, I guess it's not that petty, it would pay the rent on this place for a couple of years and still leave enough over for a new car."

"Car?"

"Soft top, chrome wheels, leather seats, walnut dash and nought to sixty in under three seconds."

"Oh, *that* sort of car."

"Where is it?"

"Some sleepy, five-star hotel, in the depths of hobbit country."

"I don't think we can do strange noises, I mean that sounds, well, occult in origin."

"Probably some guy in a sheet with a tape recorder and a piece of string."

"But …"

"I guess you're right – bin?"

"Anything else?"

"Only a bill for the electricity with several noughts and a desire to see us in court at some unspecified time."

Fergus and Fiona looked around their small and uncluttered office, and sighed in unison. Things were not looking up.

The letter Fergus had tossed towards the bin, unfolded slowly and then floated gently to the floor.

"What you need is an expert in the field of the paranormal and occult, with the emphasis on ectoplasmic manifestations and … er … infestations."

"Bill?" Fiona squeaked. "Is that really you?"

"At your service and I might add, not a moment too soon by the looks of things. Tut-tut, young Fergus, fancy turning away good lucrative detective work like that."

The letter was blown across the room and settled with a soft flutter in the in-tray. Bill Boots slowly materialised amongst the dancing dust motes and grinned at them both.

"Er, I cannot only now hear the old bastard, but I can see him too." Fergus groaned and Bill smiled toothily.

"McKinnon, Harris and Winkie, sounds like a good solid name for a detective agency," Bill announced, producing one of their small blue-edged address cards with Winkie added on in fluorescent pink gel pen.

"Winkie?" Fergus queried, taking hold of the card.

"All right then, Boots it is."

Fergus watched as the card rewrote itself, the word Winkie disappearing before his startled gaze to be replaced moments later by the word Boots in black gothic script.

"How?"

"I've seen the light and decided not to bother, so I've been on a course instead."

"A course for ghosts?"

"Well, not officially, it's actually one of those research projects for paranormal activity, but jolly useful all the same. It really is amazing what they can do with a bit of wire, a bottle cap and a glass tube."

"Right."

"Anyway, I saw your advert and here I am – Elvis has left the building and Mr Boots is back in town."

Fiona and Fergus exchanged a wry smile and then, as one, turned to shake hands with their newest and oldest partner.

The firm of McKinnon, Harris and Boots was officially open.

The end ... For now!

And now that you've read the last daft page why not visit the place where it all started and take a Mercat Tour under the South Bridge – after all, you don't really know who else might be down there ...